Volume 7
Robert Bloch
and others

Edited and Compiled by
Gregory Luce

I0541397

ARMCHAIR FICTION
PO Box 4369, Medford, Oregon 97504

The original text of these stories first appeared in Fantastic Adventures, Astounding Stories of Super-Science, Weird Tales, Beyond Fantasy Fiction, and Orbit Science Fiction

Compiled and edited by Gregory Luce
Assistant Editor, Leanne Wray
Scan Manager, Kathy Stephens

For more information about Armchair Books and products, visit our website at…

www.armchairfiction.com

Or email us at…

armchairfiction@yahoo.com

ALARMING APPARITIONS AND GRISLY GIMMICKS...

It is said that possession is nine-tenths of the law. In "A Crystal and the Spell" and "The Devil Bat," you may find ownership to be more than you bargained for.

In "House...Wife" and "The Fiddler's Fee," concessions are made—and paid for—in order to gain the love of another.

And just what miracles, or monstrosities, is modern medicine capable of? "The Corpse on the Grating," "Schizoid Creator," and "Resurrection from Hell" are sure to keep you wondering, "Who are these medical geniuses anyway?"

Haunts and taunts abound in yet another truly frightening, occasionally humorous, but wonderfully entertaining compilation of Armchair Fiction's Horror Gems! Let the madness begin...

TABLE OF CONTENTS

THE FIDDLER'S FEE

By Robert Bloch

Genius for sale—at a price that could not be repaid in all Eternity.

THE door of the inn swung open and the Devil entered. He was as thin as a corpse, and whiter than the shroud a corpse lies in. His eyes were deep and dark as graves. His mouth was redder than the gate of Hell; his hair was blacker than the pits below. He dressed like a dandy, and he came from a fine coach, but it was assuredly he: Satan, Father of Lies.

The innkeeper cringed. He had no fancy to play host to this emissary from Darkness. The innkeeper trembled under Satan's smile, while his eyes searched Satan's person for signs of a tail, of cloven hoofs. Then he noticed that Satan carried a violin-case.

It was not Satan, then. The innkeeper breathed a silent prayer of relief. It was only momentary. A minute later he was trembling with augmented fear. If this was not Satan, this man who looked like the Devil and carried a violin-case—then it must be—

"Signor Paganini," whispered mine host. The stranger inclined his dark head with a slow smile.

"Welcome," quavered the innkeeper, but there was no smile on his face. It was almost as though he preferred confirmation of his first fear rather than this. Satan one could deal with, perhaps—but the child of Satan?

Everyone knew that Paganini was the son of the Devil himself. He looked like the Devil, and many were the diabolical legends concerning his unholy life. He was said to drink, gamble, and love like the Prince of Darkness, and to entertain an equal hatred of all men. Certainly he played like Lucifer—in that case under his arm he carried an instrument of hellish power; a violin whose sublime singing drove all Europe mad.

5

Yes, even here in this tiny village men knew and feared the strange and terrible legend that had grown up about the destiny of the world's most famed violinist. New and fantastic stories were continually pouring in from Milan, from Florence, from Rome—and half the capitals of the Continent as well. "Paganini murdered his wife and sold her body to Satan." "Paganini has formed a Society against all God-loving men." "Paganini's mistresses are offered in the Black Mass." "Paganini's music is written by the very fiends of Hell." "Paganini is the son of the Devil."

Legends these might be, but the atrocious conduct attributed to the *maestro*—that was fact. His scandalous amours, his disgraceful attitude toward the great and the nobility had been confirmed time and time again. Gossip, slander, malice these things were in part. But one shining truth remained.

No one had ever played the violin like Nicolo Paganini.

Therefore the innkeeper bowed despite his fear. He sent a lad to change horses and serve the driver of the coach, ushered Signor to the best room, and awaited his presence in the parlor of the inn with a carefully prepared table.

Another awaited his presence as well—the innkeeper's son, also called Nicolo.

Young Nicolo knew even more about the great man than his father. The lad knew more about the violin than anyone in the village, with the exception of Carlo, the wine merchant's son. Both boys had studied at the local conservatory since early childhood, and there was keen rivalry between them; between their families, each of whom fostered the budding genius of their heirs.

Now Nicolo awaited his glimpse of the great man. What a triumph over Carlo! What a thing to talk about in weeks to come! Perhaps he, Nicolo, might even speak to the illustrious musician—might, if the saints were kind, receive a word in return. But that was almost too much to hope for. Paganini was not interested in boys. Still, Nicolo was determined to see him; he did not fear the legends. So the lad waited, working on the preparations for the meal in the kitchen with his sensitive ears attuned to the sound of footsteps on the stairs above.

They came.

PAGANINI sat in solitary splendor at the great table of the inn. No other customers were present to stare at the great man, and he seemed oddly content to be alone—he who loved applause, adulation, obeisance. His thin, hawk-like face— singularly Satanic in the lamplight it was—cast a black blurred shadow on the wall behind. His carefully curled hair rose in two horn-like projections against that shadow, so that the innkeeper noticed it as he entered, and nearly spilled the wine.

Paganini ate and drank sparingly—as fiends do. He said never a word, nor did he exhibit the humanity of smile or scowl. When he had finished, he sat back and seemed to stare into the candle flame.

It was as though his eyes turned homeward to Hell.

The innkeeper left the room, crossing himself. This silent guest *was indeed* a son of Satan. In the passage he came upon Nicolo, staring at the pale violinist.

"No, no—come away," the father whispered. "You must not."

But Nicolo, moving as one entranced, entered the parlor. A voice that was unlike any his father had heard came almost mechanically from his throat.

"Good evening, *Signor Paganini.*"

The eyes left the flame, after partaking of their glare. A long, deliberate glance pierced Nicolo's face like a dark lance.

"The whelp knows my name. Well…"

"I have heard much of you, *Signor.* Who in Italy does not know the name of Paganini?"

"And—fear it," said the violinist, gravely.

"I do not fear you," answered the boy, slowly. His eyes did not fall when the *maestro* smiled his wolfish smile.

"Yes?" The voice purred. "Yes that is right. You do not fear me. I feel that. And—why?"

"Because I love Music."

"Because he loves Music," parroted Paganini, cruelly mimicking the intonations until the statement stood naked in its triteness. Then, slowly, as the stare came again: "But you do love Music, boy. I feel it—strange."

A hand reached out, a pale ghost of a hand with great sinews that hinted at delicate strength, however paradoxical that might seem. The hand gestured Nicolo to a seat. The hand poured wine into a glass. The hand drummed on the table slowly.

"Do you play?"

"Y-yes, *maestro.*"

"Play for me, then."

Nicolo raced to his room. The beloved violin rested against his heart as he ran back.

"It is such a poor thing, *maestro*. It does not sing."

"Play."

Nicolo played. He never remembered what he played that night; he only knew that it came to him, and he played as he never had played before.

And the face of Satan smiled through the music.

Nicolo stopped. Paganini asked his name. He answered. Paganini asked of his teacher, his practice, his plans. Nicolo answered all questions. And then Paganini laughed. The innkeeper, listening in his turn in the passageway, shuddered when he heard that laugh.

It was a laugh that cracked through the earth and came up from Hell. It was the laugh of a sobbing violin played by a fallen angel in the Pit.

"Fools," shouted the *maestro*.

Then he stared at Nicolo. Something inside the lad begged him to turn away. But as he had before, the boy returned the stare, until the master musician spoke.

"What can I say? Should I advise you to go to a good teacher, buy a better violin? Should I even give you money for that purpose? Yes, but to what end? You have the gift, but you will never use it."

Paganini sneered.

"You may be competent. You may even win small fame, a certain amount of success. But true greatness you cannot achieve through teacher or instrument or training. You must be inspired—as I was."

Nicolo stood trembling, he knew not why. There was a horrible conviction in the words he heard. It frightened him that hint of certain authority, of final knowledge.

"A man must compose his own work, play his own work," the voice went on. "And no human teacher can give you that gift."

Suddenly Paganini stood up.

"My pardon, I forgot. I came to this place because I have an—appointment nearby. I cannot keep my—the one I must see—waiting. I shall go now. But thank you for your playing."

Nicolo's face fell. He was convinced that in a moment or so more the *maestro* would have revealed something to him that he very much wanted to know. For Nicolo felt as Paganini did about his work. He knew that within him lay great talent; knew that any ordinary training would subdue that talent in channels of mere mechanical perfection. There was a bond between his humble self and the greatness of the master before him. And if only Paganini had spoken… Now it was too late.

The black cloak swirled as the violinist went to the door. Then in a rush of ebony Paganini swept back the garment as he turned.

"Wait."

He stared, and Nicolo felt his soul lifted and examined and torn and probed by the red-hot pincers of Paganini's eyes.

"Come with me. We shall keep our appointment together."

An almost audible gasp issued from the passageway at the end of the room. Nicolo knew it came from his father, listening. But he did not care. As the door swung against darkness, he moved to the musician's side. They left together.

"I will apprentice you this night to a true Master," Paganini whispered.

CHAPTER TWO

IT WAS a long walk up the mountainside to the Cave of Fools. The road was lonely in the midnight, but then it was always lonely, for men hereabouts feared the Cave. The Devil was said to dwell in its mists, and the Cave itself was unexplored by those who deemed its depths led down to Tartarus itself.

It was a long and lonely walk, and the way was strange amidst winding paths and twisting passages of rock; yet Paganini never faltered. He had walked this way before.

Now, the bony hand gripped Nicolo's brown fingers in an icy clasp so filled with cold, inhuman strength that the lad shuddered. But he followed through the steam and mist and fog that hid the clean light of the stars; followed to the mouth of the Cave as though impelled by the magic of Paganini's voice.

For the *maestro* spoke all that way, and spoke without reticence. Sensing a kindred soul, he revealed.

"They say I am a spawn of the Devil, and that is a lie. All my life they told me so—even my father, cursed fool. In the academies my fellow students made the sign of the horns at me and the girls fled screaming.

"They screamed at me, who lived for Music and Beauty. But at first I did not care. I lived for my work, and I worked hard. Always I felt within me that spark, glowing to a flame.

"And then when I made my first appearances, I came again into the world of men. My music was acclaimed, but I was hated. 'Child of the Devil' they called me, because I was ugly, and my temper bad. I tried again to drown myself in work, but this time it no longer sufficed, because I knew my playing was not good enough. I had genius, but I could not express it.

"After a while one begins to reason. My work was not enough. The world hated me. 'Child of the Devil?' Why not?

"I knew the way. I studied. I read the old forbidden books I found in the great libraries of Florence. And I came here. There is a legend of Faust, you know.

"There are ways of meeting Powers that grant things to men in return for an exchange."

They entered the Cave now, and when Nicolo's hands trembled at the words the musician's grip tightened.

"Do not fear, lad. It is worth the cost. Thirteen years ago tonight I was just such a lad as you; perhaps a bit older. I came this way alone, and with the same fears. And it was well.

"When I came forth I had within me the gift I craved. Since that time, you know, all the world knows, my story. Fame, wealth, beautiful women—all earthly success is mine to command. But more than that, greater than that, is my Music. I learned to compose, and to play. They say His songs moved the angels and the stars. I have that gift. And you, who know, love, and have born within you, Music—you shall this night partake of the same gift."

NICOLO wanted to run, to get out of this deep cavern where the steam swirled in fantastic shapes. He wanted to make the sign of the cross as he heard the bubbling and the booming from the depths ahead. And then a curious picture came to his mind—the vision of Carlo Zuttio, the wine-merchant's son. Carlo went to the conservatory, and he was a fool. But he had a better violin, and private lessons, so that he played more masterfully than Nicolo. And his parents were wealthy, and they boasted to Nicolo's father of their son and his music. The whole town knew that Carlo would go on to the big school in Milan. He, Nicolo, would not go on—he would remain and take over the inn, and sometime when he was old and fat he might play at country weddings for drinks. Carlo would be rich and famous, and wear silk when he returned to visit. Nicolo would no longer be a rival, then—merely a country innkeeper.

It was this vision, and no love of Music that came to Nicolo in the bowels of the earth. It was this vision that made him smile and follow Paganini as they advanced into the heart of the hot smoke and knelt upon the stones in the darkness.

Then Paganini called a Secret Name and the earth thundered. He made a sign not of the cross, and he prayed in a voice that was black and crawling.

Then the mists grew red and the thundering swelled, and Nicolo was formally introduced to his Teacher.

CHAPTER THREE

PAGANINI had been crafty. It was a bargain. Three years for him, and no more, where Paganini had gained thirteen. But the other ten years went to the *maestro* as payment for leading the way. It was a fair arrangement, a business arrangement.

That was what shocked Nicolo more than anything else when he returned home. It had all been so business-like. There was behind it a terrible hint of purpose, the Power knew what it was doing—there was no aimlessness, no blind evil. It was all so *arranged.*

Three years.

But there was singing in Nicolo's heart, singing that over-rode the sound of his father's quavering prayers, singing that rose to triumphant heights when he played at the conservatory the next afternoon.

"Paganini taught me," is all that Nicolo would say when the faculty exclaimed. "Paganini taught me," Nicolo told Carlo with a smile.

The singing rose higher as the weeks passed.

Nicolo, who read notes poorly, composed.

Nicolo improvised.

The faculty bought him a new violin, and on the festival day it was Nicolo who appeared as soloist with the orchestra from Venice; though Carlo was second in competition for the post.

Nicolo won the scholarship and went to Milan.

His father prayed but said nothing. Paganini did not write, but word came of his triumphs in France.

In Milan, Nicolo was a sensation at the school. Carlo came too, his parents paying his tuition; and Carlo was successful. He studied hard, worked diligently, played expertly.

But Nicolo's soaring tones were born of inspiration within. He was mastering a technique against which mere practice could not compete.

Through the year it was a constant competition between the two country boys—Nicolo and Carlo. The whole school knew it. Nicolo had the talent. Carlo had the ambition. The battle for perfection was deadly.

Nicolo was aging. His face was already maturing in set lines, and the color had left it set and harsh. It was whispered that his nights were spent in study that left him wasted.

The truth was that Nicolo's nights were spent in fear. He was remembering the tryst in the Cave of Fools, and he was anticipating the days to come. Only two years now—and so much to do!

He had been a fool. But Paganini's personality had overshadowed his own, dominated it. He had been led. He knew that now. Paganini had wanted a dupe, so that he might make such a bargain and extend his own life at the expense of another's. That is why he had taken Nicolo. Nicolo often wondered just what might have happened had Paganini gone alone to his accounting. He wondered, because in two years he must go—and there would be no dupe for him.

Two years... Nicolo would toss on his pillow and shudder at the thought. He could not hope to do what Paganini had done in thirteen. He could not win much but initial acclaim; none of the fame and the riches would be his in so short a time. But one thing he could do—beat his rival, Carlo.

Nicolo hated Carlo now. He hadn't used to hate him. They had been rivals, but friendly enough. Ever since that night in the Cave of Fools Nicolo had hated.

Carlo was keeping up. Nicolo found that his work came to him almost effortlessly. His hands moved without thought along the bow, and his fingering seemed undirected. There was no triumphant thrill for him in his music, no sense of mastery in his easy playing.

Carlo had this, because Carlo had to work and sweat to compete, and when he did so he felt satisfied. Moreover, aided by no supernatural gift, Carlo was competing too closely for comfort.

And the school liked Carlo. The teachers knew his work and praised him for it. They did not praise Nicolo because they could not understand his methods. He puzzled them.

The other pupils liked Carlo. He had money, and he was generous. He bought sweets for his friends, laughed with them at their parties. Nicolo had no money for sweets, no fine clothes for parties. The pupils were in awe of him, and they distrusted his face.

Carlo was handsome, too. The girls liked Carlo. Even Elissa liked him. And that added to the agony of Nicolo's nights.

CHAPTER FOUR

ELISSA'S hair was yellow flame on a pillow. Elissa's eyes were the jewels on the breast of Passion. Elissa's mouth was a red gateway to delight. Elissa's arms were—

It was no use. Nicolo couldn't think of anything more poetic. All he knew was that Elissa burned within him at all times. Her beauty was like a lash across his naked heart.

Actually, Elissa Robbia was a very pretty blond student, but Nicolo was in love and Youth knows only a goddess.

Elissa walked with Carlo, and she went to parties with him, and they danced at the festival together. Throughout the second year they were together always.

Always Nicolo watched from the corner. Once or twice he spoke to the object of his worship, but she did not seem to notice him, despite his efforts to be ingratiating. She preferred the handsome Carlo.

So Nicolo worked. He outplayed Carlo, though it was not easy now. Despite Nicolo's secret power, Carlo seemed inspired by love. Carlo followed his most difficult trills, mastered every detail of the well-nigh flawless technique that Nicolo mastered.

Still, Nicolo triumphed always in the end. The better teachers were now confounded by the spectacle of their two notable students. Often outsiders witnessed performances. The Opera sent conductors down to listen, and notables from all over the South attended the salons in local aristocratic homes when the star pupils played.

Nothing was said officially, but it was understood that one or the other of the boys would be groomed for concert debut within the year.

Both of them knew it, though they no longer spoke to each other. Both of them worked frantically. The final concert of the season would decide; they suspected that. Both had been asked for a performance of some solo composition.

Nicolo went to work a month in advance. What took place in his dark room will never be known, but he emerged with what he felt was a true masterpiece. He had worked as never before. He would win, he would shame Carlo before them all; shame him before Elissa.

He could hardly wait for the night.

The stage of the school was lighted and the house was filled with those of a station to allow their jewels to reflect that light. Rumor had passed, and in the audience were musical notables from all Italy. And the Master was there, too—yes, the great Paganini himself. Come to watch Nicolo, his former pupil, they said.

What a triumph! Nicolo shivered with ecstasy, fondling his violin as he waited in the wings for the solos to end. Tonight he would appear before Paganini himself when he took victory over his rival. Nothing could make his happiness more complete.

Where was Carlo, by the way? He had not appeared in the wings as yet.

But—there he was—*in the audience! With Elissa.*

What did this mean?

A number ended. The director was announcing his name.

"Unfortunately the soloist who was to compete with Signor Nicolo this evening, Carlo Zuttio…"

What was that?

"Resigned from the school…"

Yes?

"Marriage to…"

Married? To Elissa?

He had done that, knowing he would lose tonight he'd given up music, retired to his father's business, and married Elissa. And now he had arranged for it to be announced, to rob Nicolo of his victory. Bitter despair rose in Nicolo's heart, and black anger.

But when his name was called he stepped forth and played.

He played his number, but it was not the original he had planned. For now he improvised, or rather, hate improvised for him. Hate tore at the strings, plucked frenetically at a flayed violin.

And waves of horror crept through the house.

Through red mists, the black eyes of Paganini blazed, the smile dropped from Carlo's face, the lips of Elissa grew pale. Nicolo saw her eyes grow blank, and poured his music into them. She had never noticed him before, eh? Well, she would not forget him now—not this, and *this*.

Swooping to Hell, spiraling to Heaven, shrieking and whispering of damnation and glory, the violin sang accompaniment to dark voices that yammered in Nicolo's brain.

Nicolo had no arms, no fingers. He was all violin. His body was part of the instrument, his brain a part of the song. Both were being played by *Another*.

He finished.

Silence.

Then the thunder.

And while he bowed and smiled and the sound tore at his eardrums, his eyes blazed into Elissa's empty face through the standing crowd.

Nicolo had won and lost tonight. But he would win again.

CHAPTER FIVE

THEY came to him after the concert. They offered him money, for private study.

In a year, they said, he would come back and perform in a solo concert at the school.

Nicolo accepted the money gravely. It was supposed that he would use that money to spend his year in Rome, working under the great *maestro* as a private pupil.

But Nicolo had other plans. He knew that Carlo and Elissa would return to the village, and he meant to follow them there. He thanked the directors of the school and prepared to depart.

In the hallway stood a cloaked figure. It was Paganini.

Without a word the pale genius took Nicolo's hand, just as he had that night two years before. Together they walked the dark streets.

"You played well tonight, my son. They said your music was like Paganini's." He smiled. "And well it might be, since we study under the same Master."

Nicolo shuddered.

"Do not fear. In a year's time you shall have had all the fame and glory you desire. The world will bow before your power. That is as you desired, no?"

"No." Nicolo shook his head. "I shall not study and I shall not go to Rome. My desire lies elsewhere." He told Paganini of Carlo and Elissa. The *maestro* listened.

"So you return to the village, eh? Well, if it is that what you seek, I am sure you will be aided in your quest. Do not despair."

Nicolo sighed.

"I am afraid of that aid. This music—this playing—it is not a part of me. It comes from other sources, and I feel no satisfaction in stirring my listeners. Carlo and Elissa were stirred tonight; but it was the music that did it, not myself. Don't you understand?"

A cold whisper bit through the darkness as Paganini spoke.

"Yes, I understand, perfectly, but you do not. Tonight you played through hate, and there was hate in the hall. *But when you go to Elissa, you will play through love.* She will be stirred. For our Master is eminently successful in amours. Let your violin speak and she shall become yours."

"But what of him? What of Carlo?"

"Again, let your violin speak. It has a voice that drives men mad. Let him hear that voice."

A slow laugh crawled out of Paganini's lips.

"I know how it will be. Ah, I know... Years ago I discovered that secret, and well have I used it. Madden the cuckold and woo the mistress, and rejoice in the gift of the Teacher. I envy you your year, my friend. It will be a great triumph for you."

Nicolo's heart was pounding.

"You really believe I can do it?" he asked.

"Certainly. You were given the power; let it guide you to your purpose." Paganini's voice grew grave. "But it was not of that which I proposed to speak when I awaited you this evening. There is another thing.

"I want to remind you that a year from tonight you have an appointment in the Cave of Fools."

"I am afraid."

"It was a bargain, and you must go."

"What if I do not go?"

"That I cannot speak of. *He* will come for you then, I know it. *He* will revenge himself horribly."

"I wish," and Nicolo's voice was low with hatred, "I wish that I had never met you. You led me to this—tricked me into this infernal bargain. I was a fool, and I should kill you for it."

Paganini stopped and faced the youth. His eyes were ice.

"Perhaps. But think—think of the coming year. You shall win Elissa, and drive Carlo mad. Win Elissa and drive Carlo mad. Win Elissa and drive Carlo mad—"

His voice was like his violin, playing and replaying the same damnable, wheedling trill until it surged through Nicolo's brain.

"Think not of revenge. Go to the Cave of Fools a year from tonight; but first, win Elissa and drive Carlo mad—"

Still whispering the words, Paganini turned in the darkness and disappeared. And Nicolo walked the streets, muttering to himself:

"I shall win Elissa and drive Carlo mad."

CHAPTER SIX

NICOLO did not stay at his father's inn when he returned. He had money now, and he procured rooms in townrooms below the apartment of the newlywed couple he had followed.

He did not see them for a month. He was in his dark room with the violin. He played in darkness now, for he needed no notes in this composition. He developed only two themes. One was soft and sweet and tender, thrilling was passionate beauty. As Nicolo played, his face would glow in ecstasy and warmth flooded his being.

The second theme slithered out of the darkness. Then it padded. Then it began to run, and leap, and dance. At first it squeaked like a rat, then it howled like a dog, finally it bayed like a black wolf. It was a fiendish howling of terrific power, and when Nicolo played it his hands trembled and he closed his eyes.

For a month Nicolo played the two themes over and over in his tiny room—alone. Not quite alone, for there was a whispering in his brain that prompted each tone, and an unseen hand that guided the bow over the strings. Nicolo played and played, and he grew thin and gaunt. After a month the music was a part of him, and he was ready.

It took him a week to become friendly with his neighbors again. In another week he had learned their habits; knew when Carlo worked at the wine-press and left Elissa alone.

Then, one afternoon, Nicolo visited Elissa. She sat regal in her blond beauty while they talked, and after a while Nicolo suggested that he play something for her. He took out his violin and drew the bow across the strings, eyes on her face.

His eyes never left her face while he played. His eyes feasted on her face as the music feasted on her soul.

The tune came forth, reiterated; in endless variations it rose in soaring rhapsody. And Elissa rose in soaring rhapsody and came toward him, her eyes empty save for the soul-filling majesty of the music.

Then Nicolo put down the violin and took her in his arms.

He came the next day, and the next. Always he brought his violin. Always he played and always she surrendered to the music.

For months Nicolo was happy. For many months he played each day, and his nights were peaceful at last. Carlo suspected nothing.

Nicolo began to plan. In a little while he would return to Milan for the solo concert. After that he would be famous—go on tour. He had, under the inspiration of his love, written enough to insure his success at the debut. He would take Elissa with him, and together they would scale the heights.

Then he remembered.

He could not go to Milan, or the concert. That night he had an appointment in the Cave of Fools.

Nicolo didn't want to die. He didn't want to give his soul. That cursed bargain!

But there was no way out.

Every day he saw Elissa he longed for life with greater fervor. Knowing the end was near, he came oftener, took greater and greater chances. He was counting the hours now, the minutes.

Three days before the time appointed he went there in the evening. Carlo would be late at the winepress, so Nicolo played. Elissa sat there, her face blank as it always was when he played. Sometimes Nicolo would find himself wishing that he had no music to do his wooing—that he himself would inspire such adoration in the woman he loved. But that was too much to hope for. Elissa loved Carlo, and only the music gave her to Nicolo. It sufficed. The spell was strong. Nicolo played tonight as he had never played before, and as the music rose it drowned out the sound of footsteps on the stairs.

Carlo was in the room.

NICOLO stopped playing. Elissa's eyes opened as though she was wakening from profound depths of sleep.

And Carlo faced them both. He was a big man, Carlo, with strong hands that now opened and closed convulsively at his sides. Carlo's heavy body was lunging across the room and the hands moved for Nicolo's throat.

They never reached it.

Nicolo's delicate hands were on the violin. He began to play.

It was not the love-strain that he played this time. It was the other—the song of madness.

At the sound of the rat-like squeaking Carlo stopped. Nicolo watched him as the shrieking mounted. Carlo's eyes grew wide. The shrieking became a moan. Carlo's wide eyes were growing red. The moaning was a rising bark, a yelp of agony. Carlo's hands went to his head. He stepped back, sank to his knees. Then Nicolo played. The violin screamed, the bow moved up and down upon it like a red-hot poker descending on human flesh. Nicolo played until Carlo lay rolling on the floor, baying in rhythm as the foam poured from his lips. Nicolo played until the room pulsed with horrid sound, until the glass shivered with the vibration and the candlelight wavered and the flame danced in agony. Nicolo played, and then he stopped.

Carlo lay there moaning, and he rose to his knees and looked at Nicolo. Then he looked at Elissa.

Nicolo followed his glance.

Elissa—he had forgotten Elissa! He had played the music of madness and forgotten she was in the room. Elissa lay where she had fallen and her face was white with the unmistakable whiteness of death. Carlo looked at her and began to laugh.

Nicolo sobbed. Tears rolled down his cheeks.

Husband and lover laughed and sobbed together.

It was all over. She was dead, and he was mad. And two nights from now Nicolo must go to that rendezvous in the Cave of Fools.

So this was Satan's gift? This awful mockery was what it had brought him.

The dead woman lay on the floor as the madman crawled toward her, cackling.

Nicolo rose to go. His bow accidentally scraped the strings. The mad Carlo rose, laughing, and seized the violin. He broke it across the bridge and hurled it from the window.

Still laughing, he turned, but there was no sane hatred in his eyes.

And then the thought came to Nicolo.

"Carlo," he whispered. "Carlo."

The idiot husband laughed.

"Carlo, your wife is dead. But I did not kill her. I swear it. It was the Devil, Carlo. The Devil who dwells in the Cave of Fools. You want to avenge your wife's death, don't you, Carlo? Then seek out the Devil two nights from tonight in the Cave of Fools. Remember, Carlo—two nights from tonight in the Cave of Fools. I will stay with you until then and tell you where to go."

The madman laughed.

Softly, Nicolo repeated his suggestion. He whispered it all that night as the deranged Carlo slept. He whispered it the next day as they sat beside the body of the dead woman. At last, when Nicolo rose to leave on the coach for Milan, he felt that Carlo understood and would go. Smiling, the violinist withdrew, leaving the chuckling lunatic and his dead wife in the dark room.

CHAPTER SEVEN

IN THE night of travel Nicolo smiled bitterly but often. It had worked out after all. He would trick Satan then; sending Carlo in his stead. Thus he could play the concert and go on to fame. Poor Elissa was dead, of course, but there were other women to hear the song of love. It was good.

It was good to hear the praise in Milan. His old teachers spoke, his friends gathered around him and whispered of the celebrities who would attend the concert tonight.

Nicolo was so busy that day that he forgot a very important item. Indeed, he had just finished a meal in his dressing room when he remembered.

Carlo had broken his violin!

Confused by tragedy, by lack of sleep and overmuch planning, it had slipped Nicolo's thoughts. His violin—not a precious instrument to him, for Nicolo knew that he could produce his music on any violin. Still, it was necessary.

He rose to summon the director, when the door opened. Carlo entered.

Carlo was mad. His eyes glittered and his teeth were bared, but he walked erect. He was able to control himself sufficiently to pass unnoticed, it seemed.

Nicolo, beholding him, nearly froze on the spot. A wave of fear rose chokingly in his throat.

"Carlo—why are you here? Don't you remember—the Cave of Fools and your appointment?"

Carlo grinned.

"I went last night, Nicolo," he whispered. "I went last night. Tonight I am here to see you play. You will be playing soon, Nicolo."

Nicolo stammered wildly. "But—but what did you find in the Cave? I mean—there was One who waited, and he wanted something from you—?"

Carlo grinned wider.

"Do not trouble yourself. I gave Him what He wanted. It was all arranged last night."

"You mean that?" Nicolo whispered. *"You gave your soul?"*

"I gave my soul. We made a bargain," Carlo chuckled.

"Then why are you here?"

"To bring you this. I broke your violin, and tonight you must play."

Carlo thrust a bundle into Nicolo's hands. At that moment the prompter entered.

"Maestro. The concert is starting. You are wanted on stage. Oh, what a crowd is here for your debut! Ah, there has never been such a tribute—you played but once, a year ago, but they remember and have returned. It is wonderful. But hurry, hurry!"

Nicolo left, and the grinning Carlo followed, standing in the wings as the violinist stepped on the stage. In his confusion, Nicolo unwrapped the parcel and tossed the paper to the wings as he took the violin and bow in his hands and faced the applauding audience.

Nicolo's eyes sparkled. This was triumph!

His heart was light within him. Fame was here, and poor Carlo had settled matters with the Master. He had made a bargain, and that did not concern Nicolo. What concerned him was that he was free, and this was the greatest evening of his life, and he would play as he had never played before.

"Automatically he gripped the violin and raised it to his chin. It felt heavy; an ordinary instrument. But it would suffice. Poor Carlo was mad; bringing a violin to the man who had killed his wife...

But—*play.*

Yes, play with the Devil's gift, play the Devil's love-song that won Elissa. Let it win the audience tonight. What matter the violin, or Carlo chuckling in the wings? Play...

NICOLO played. His bow stroked the opening strains of the melody. But a droning arose.

What was wrong?

Nicolo tried to correct his stroke. But his fingers moved automatically. He tried to stop.

But his fingers, his wrist, his arm moved on. He could not stop. The power within him would not swerve. And the droning increased.

This was the song of madness!

Nicolo's fingers flew, his arm flailed. He fought, trying to hold back. But the sounds increased. Rats scurried and chittered and then the Hounds of Hell began to bark. Fiends brayed in his brain.

Yes—in *his* brain.

The audience, he dimly realized, was hooting and jeering. They were not being driven mad by the music. He was.

Nicolo closed his eyes, clenched his jaw to make the violin slip; and still it played. He wanted to think of something else, anything but the music that now shrieked in his skull. A vision of Paganini's satanic face, of Elissa's dead features, of Carlo's mad red eyes, of the black Cave of Fools where he should be tonight—these things swept on wings of horror through his brain. And then the music broke through and Nicolo fiddled madly.

Eyes jerked open and stared down at the violin—at the coarse wood, the peculiar strings, the ghastly bridge glistening with pearly brilliance.

And then the voice of the music screamed the truth to him. Mad Carlo had gone to the Cave of Fools last night, to make a bargain. He had said that, and Nicolo had believed that it meant he was free. But what had that bargain been?

Carlo had sold his soul for vengeance. What could that vengeance be?

That One had told him to make this violin!

And now Nicolo stared at the violin—the violin he was helplessly playing, but which made a music that drove him mad.

Nicolo stared at the coarse wood. He had seen such wood before. Where? *Why did it remind him of Elissa?*

The wood was stained red; ghastly red. *Why did the red stain remind him of Elissa?*

Music thundered in Nicolo's ears, and still he played and stared.

The glistening bridge of the violin was pearly. *Why did that bridge remind him of Elissa?*

The bridge grinned up at Nicolo, grinned insanely as Elissa had grinned when she was driven mad by music. The violin tones rose to a shattering crescendo, and Nicolo staggered. His blurring eyes glanced at the golden strings of the violin that were singing his doom. In a burst of ghastly fear he seemed to recognize them.

Why did those strings remind him of Elissa?

And then he understood.

The music he was playing was the music that had driven her to madness, to death. In some way this violin now held her soul.

He was not playing a violin, he was playing her soul, and its madness was pouring out to drive him mad.

He looked down again as the shrieking music rose in his ears, and he saw.

He did not hold a violin in his arms, but the dead body of a woman—the body of Elissa. He was playing on her body, playing on the gray ghost of her body, drawing the bow across long golden strands that he recognized in a final burst of fear that tore his brain to shreds.

Nicolo played her body like a violin and drew the madness out into his own being, and then he recognized the wood, the stain, the bridge, and the horribly familiar strings.

That was why Elissa's soul was in the violin.

Nicolo suddenly began to laugh, insanely, and the music rose to drown out his laughter as he held the horrible thing playing in his arms. Then with a lurch Nicolo fell, face black with agony.

The curtains dropped, the hysterical manager ran to the dead body of the violinist.

Then the madman that was Carlo crept slyly from the wings and crouched over the body, tittering in a shrill voice. He took the violin from the dead Nicolo's breast and laughed.

His fingers lovingly caressed the wood he had carved from Elissa's coffin, the stain of blood he had drawn from Elissa's body, the pearly teeth on the bridge he had taken from Elissa's throat. And finally, his fingers fell to stroking the long, smooth golden strings on which the music of madness had been played—the long, golden strands of dead Elissa's hair.

THE END

THE DEVIL BAT

By Gregory Luce
Copyright 2014 by Gregory Luce

Spring Training, Phoenix, March 15th.

If you're a veteran ballplayer, it's hell playing for an expansion team; but if you're a 23-year old rookie like me, it doesn't matter. All that matters is the show, the bigs, the majors—just getting there. Who the hell cares what team you play for. The Portland Grizzlies picked me up over the winter in the expansion draft, a cast-off from the Baltimore farm system.

I met Gus Cantrill the first day of spring training, one month ago today.

The guy is practically a legend: two MVPs, four home run championships, a batting title, and a couple of World Series rings to go along with it. He's also the kind of long-time player who can't stomach being on anything but a winner, which is why coming to the Grizzlies is probably going to be a nightmare for him.

His attitude was apparent with the first words he spoke to me. He was leaning against the batting cage, talking with a couple of reporters when I introduced myself. I extended my hand and smiled.

"Hey, Gus. Nice to meet you. Name's Brady...Brady Jackson."

"Another damn rookie, huh?"

Gus is like that with most people. Shoot from the hip and to hell with diplomacy. As it's turned out, we've become pretty good friends during the first few weeks of spring training, so good in fact that we've been paired up as roomies on road trips after the season starts, which is something a player with his credentials doesn't have to do unless he wants to.

"I hate roomin' by myself," he told me the other day. "You'll do."

Time has not been good to Gus, and it's been evident from the first day of camp. Those once mighty legs that were so fleet on the base paths and covered so much territory in the outfield are now a detriment to his overall play.

"Can't run much anymore, kid," Gus told me after being gunned down at the plate during an intra-squad game. "Too many darn surgeries."

His once mighty bat has quieted, too. Just six years ago, Gus nearly won the Triple Crown. He helped San Francisco win the World Series that season, leading the league with 55 homers and 152 RBI. He barely missed the batting title, finishing third, a mere four percentage points behind the league leader. However, the years of overeating and refusing to stay in condition (Gus detests weight training) have taken their toll. Gus doesn't have a problem with booze; it's the solid stuff he can't say no to. He's ballooned up to 255, and he just hates working it off in the weight room. As his overall strength and stamina have decreased over the years, his vulnerability to injuries has skyrocketed, resulting in three surgeries over the past five seasons. By the time he got to camp, his slip was more than noticeable. Last year's stats: a .247 batting average, 23 homers, and 71 RBI—a far cry from the glory years of the past. San Francisco made him available in the expansion draft over the winter.

Yet in spite of his many problems, Gus still has a kid's love for the game. Never married, he is a fanatical baseball memorabilia collector, spending thousands of dollars to acquire anything from rare baseball cards to authentic pieces of historical memorabilia such as uniforms, gloves, bats, photos, trophies—you name it.

He loves kids, too. A couple of days ago after an early exhibition game against Anaheim, he grabbed me as I was leaving the locker room.

"Grab your cleats and come with me kid. I'll show ya some real baseball."

We drove around in a limo until we found a local ballpark on the north side of Tempe where some little league kids were having a practice game. You should have seen their faces when we climbed out of the limo. Nobody knew me, but every kid on the field recognized Gus. He offered our "services," and we ended up playing the whole game, one inning for one team, the next inning for the other. The kids loved it; Gus and I had a great time.

Spring Training, Phoenix, April 4th.

The spring is finishing up better than I could have hoped for. Our manager, Ed Garber, practically came out and told me I was going to be his starting left fielder. Garber, who managed Philadelphia's triple A farm club in Norfolk for the past three seasons, was previously a long-time hitting instructor for San Francisco. He knows Gus well and has decided to use him as his primary designated hitter with an occasional start at first base. Gus' outfield days are over and he knows it.

"Seven guys'll have to get injured before I see the outfield again," he commented from the bench one afternoon.

Management has been looking hard at a lot of rookies, but there are plenty of vets trying to make the club, too. The only "name" other than Gus is Bob Reed, who came over from Chicago. At one time Reed was a brilliant lefthander with an assortment of screwy pitches and a former rookie-of-the-year. He was also runner-up for the Cy Young Award a few years back. However, he's also known as a temperamental problem child who has a serious problem with women and too much booze. At 29, his career is already on the skids. When he was let go for the expansion draft, the Grizzlies decided to take a chance and offered him a "meager" one million-dollar contract for one season. Reed has behaved himself this spring, though, and has all but locked up the lead spot in the starting rotation.

By April first the team was pretty much in place except for a few bench and bullpen cuts. Eleven rookies, including myself, have made the club's final 25-man roster.

We're heading north soon for the season opener in Portland.

Portland, May 20th.

Wes Cowley got released before the game this evening. He was picked up on waivers from Detroit right after the start of the season. Cowley had been a solid infielder a few years back and Garber thought he could help us at third, but after 14 games his average was down around the .150 mark—the lowest on the team. On top of that he's been a total butcher in the infield, committing seven errors. It's been pitiful. Cowley stormed out of Garber's office when he got the news. He heaved a ball at the water cooler on the way out, but true to his fielding of late, he missed by a couple of feet.

Gus and I were sitting in front of our lockers when it happened. Gus gave out a low whistle. "I wonder who's next?"

It was a fair question because the Grizzlies have been stinking up the whole league. I guess I've been doing okay for a rookie, but most everyone else on the team is having a rough time of it. The pitching is the worst; our team ERA is well over six. Bob Reed, who looked so promising in spring training, is 2-5 and drinking heavily again. Matt Sturges, a rookie from Omaha, was the worst on the staff, though. After six starts he was 0-5 with an ERA over ten. He got sent down to double-A ball at Savannah.

The hitting hasn't been much better. Only one player is hitting over .300 and that's our centerfielder, Tim Castleberry. Gus is struggling terribly and Garber isn't happy about it. He's already missed a number of games because of nagging injuries and is only hitting .241 with three homers. His strikeouts are way up, too.

When we got into the dugout tonight, Gus noticed a piece of paper taped on the part of the bench where he usually sits. Scrawled across it were the words, "wasted space."

"Some punk's idea of a joke," I told him.

Gus shrugged it off. "Let's warm up."

Anaheim clubbed us 7-3. I had a pair of singles, but Gus went hitless, striking out twice and stranding five runners. They booed him a lot his last time up. The Grizzlies' record has fallen to 14-27.

After the game Gus and I went out for a beer. We drove over to an offbeat tavern in Beaverton that Gus stumbled onto not long after the season opened. The place is called "The Pig's Trough." Its big claim to fame is that they have the fattest barmaids in town. In fact, they don't even call them barmaids, they're called "weightresses." We sat inside drinking beer out of pig-shaped mugs.

"Too bad about Cowley," Gus said staring into his beer.

"Yeah."

"Same thing's comin' my way."

"Relax, Gus. Management's not gonna let you go. You're the only guy on the team who brings fans into the ballpark." I lifted my glass and took another drink. "You'll come around. Wait and see."

Gus got a philosophical look on his face. "Ain't got many bat-screamers left in me, kid."

"What's a bat-screamer?"

"That's my name for an uncatchable ball…a ball hit so hard it doesn't matter whether there's somebody waiting to catch it or not. Bad fielders can't possibly catch 'em and good fielders don't want to…that's a bat-screamer."

Portland, May 24th.

We got to the ballpark early today. In the locker room Gus asked me to go with him to a sports memorabilia auction after the game.

"Ya gotta see this place," he said with a kid's look of excitement, "they got more baseball crap than anyplace I've ever been to in my life. You can find really, *really* rare stuff on just about any hall 'a famer you can think of...Mays, Hubbell, Gehrig, Koufax, Williams, Hornsby, Mantle...you name 'em. Last time I was there they had Babe Ruth's last home run bat up for auction...the one he hit three homers with for the Braves."

"Ruth played for the Braves?" I asked.

"His last season...1935. This place has everything, kid...you'll love it. We'll drive over after the game."

It was a Saturday afternoon interleague contest against Atlanta. The Atlanta pitcher was a guy named Joey Laker whom Gus particularly dislikes, but loves hitting against. Laker has beaned Gus several times over the years, mainly because Gus has amassed a .473 lifetime batting average against him. Laker, who is probably the skinniest player in the league, has an amazing slider that nobody can figure out—nobody except Gus. Just last year he nailed Gus in the ribs after Gus launched a couple of pitches into the left field bleachers. A bench-clearing brawl had ensued with Laker getting the worst of it from Gus. Both of them got tossed by the home plate umpire. Laker had the last laugh today, though. Gus went 0-4 and looked bad doing it. His average has now sunk to a paltry .229. He sat in front of his locker after the game, staring at the floor and shaking his head.

"You'll be getting a new roommate if this doesn't get any better."

"Quit worrying about it so much," I said. "You're just in a slump. You'll come out of it."

We showered and dressed. A little later we peeled out of the parking lot in Gus' blue Ferrari and headed for the auction house. It was a tiny little place south of Portland in Lake Oswego called Smitty's Memorabilia. Smitty is one of those guys who have no life except for sports. He's only open a couple of weeks a month, the rest of the time he travels around the country digging up the rarest sports memorabilia imaginable.

His store is crammed with the kind of stuff collectors go ga-ga over. Sometimes he has auctions on weekends for the pricier stuff.

When we got to Smitty's the auction was about to start. We made our way through the main shop area—which was inundated with an enormous amount of memorabilia—toward the rear of the store. There were probably 25 people crammed into a tiny, smoke-filled back room, standing along the walls or sitting on foldout chairs. Gus has already become a regular at Smitty's and is considered royalty by the other patrons who range from couch-hounds in tee shirts and cutoffs to businessmen in suits and ties. Most of them called out greetings to Gus as we walked into the room; two or three even applauded.

Smitty is a short, skinny guy with a squeaky voice and glasses. An old Seattle Pilots baseball cap sat on top of his curly white hair. He stood behind a little podium at the far end of the room holding a little kids baseball bat in one hand. Presently he banged it down a few times on the podium.

"All right, Gentlemen…let's begin."

There were about 20 items up for bid—all ultra rare stuff. Gus picked up a Harmon Killebrew jersey, but was outbid on a pair of Ralph Kiner home run balls—both autographed. However, the highlight of the auction, for Gus at least, was the final item. Smitty always likes to save the best for last, so when he pulled out a long black bat case with the name "Del Rio" emblazoned with cursive silver letters across the top of it, the entire room fell into a hush. Smitty opened the case and lifted out an old baseball bat. It was medium in length, probably about 33 inches; but its color was a much darker brown than most bats. Must have been its age, I thought—or maybe a different kind of wood. Smitty held the bat out in front of him with both hands.

"We're gonna wrap up today's auction with a once-in-a-lifetime opportunity to buy one of the most unique items that's ever come through our doors. This is a custom-made bat once owned by Hall of Fame slugger Domingo Del Rio. Del Rio used this bat for the last five years of his career. Its longevity was due to the fact that he only used it in occasional clutch situations. Although the exact statistics are not known, its been estimated that Del Rio's career batting average with this bat was well over .500. He had astonishing success with it, including two game-winning World Series homers. As you all probably know, Del Rio is the only player in major league history to actually hit a ball out of Yankee Stadium. He did it with this bat."

I glanced at Gus: his eyes were as wide as a kid's on Christmas morning. Del Rio was one of Gus' heroes, and I knew he was going to bid heavy for it. He didn't disappoint me either. After several minutes of spirited bidding, Gus finally got the better of a high roller in a business suit, landing the bat for an astronomical amount. Smitty slammed the little kid's bat down on the podium...

"Sold to Gus Cantrill for $27,000." The room burst into applause.

I looked at Gus. *"Twenty...seven...thousand...bucks?"* I half-whispered. "You gotta be outta your mind, pal."

He looked at me and grinned. "Some things you just have to have, kid."

I thought he was crazy, but it didn't matter to Gus. When you're still bringing home two million a year (and even that after a huge pay cut) a miniscule $27,000 is nothing more than pocket change. Domingo Del Rio was one of his idols, too. Del Rio, a Mexican phenom with an explosive bat and a cannon for an arm, played his entire career for Philadelphia. He died tragically 17 years ago when his private plane went down, splattering him and his brother all over the side of a mountain in northern Mexico.

Before we left Smitty's, Gus let me take the bat out and look it over. At first glance it didn't appear to be anything special, just an old, dull-looking bat. Yet, there was something unusual about its smoothness when I touched it. I suddenly realized there didn't seem to be any marks or nicks on it—none. I examined it more closely: it was perfectly smooth, no blemishes of any kind.

That's damn peculiar.

The trademark was odd, too. It had the usual oblong-circled border, but within it were odd letters or characters that I was totally unfamiliar with. I held it up for Gus to see.

"What the hell kinda writing is this?" I asked.

"Beats me. Looks like it might be Arabic or somethin'. I was stationed in Saudi back when I was in the service and that's kinda what this looks like." Gus looked closely at the trademark.

"There is one word in English, though," he said pointing to the trademark."

I leaned closer. "Yeah…what does it say?"

Gus squinted for a moment. "It says 'Al…haz…red'."

"Alhazred? What the hell is Alhazred?"

"Dunno, kid. The rest of it looks like Arabian gobble-di-goop." Gus put the bat up to the side of his face, stroked it affectionately, then kissed it—right on the trademark.

I looked at him and rolled my eyes.

"This one's a collector's dream, Brady," he said softly, an exuberant look in his eyes.

A minute later we were speeding back to the stadium in Gus' Ferrari, his new treasures locked in the trunk.

Portland, May 27th.

Today I was surprised to see the Del Rio bat, out of its case, sitting next to Gus in the dugout right before the start of the game.

"Isn't that a little too spendy to be lying around on a dugout bench?" I asked.

"I'm thinkin' about using it in the game."

"Now I *know* you're out of your mind."

"If it worked for Domingo Del Rio maybe it'll work for me." He picked it up and gripped it. "I'll use it in clutch situations…the same way he did."

I shook my head. "You're crazy to use a top-dollar collector's item in an actual game."

"Well, I sure need something with the way I've been hitting." Gus winked and smiled. "Don't worry, kid. I'll take good care of it."

Oakland, May 30th.

We opened a three-game stand in Oakland tonight. Although he still had yet to use it in an actual game, Gus brought the Del Rio bat with him into the dugout again, the third game in a row.

A 20-year old Cuban kid named Frankie Fernandez was on the mound for Oakland. Fernandez has one pitch: a 98-mile-an-hour fastball that very few hitters can catch up to. He was shutting us down pretty badly after seven innings. Gus struck out and hit into two double plays. Garber got really steamed after the second double play and I thought he was going to jump all over Gus when he got back to the dugout. He bit his tongue, though, and just gave him a good hard glare.

We were down 4-1 in the top of the ninth, but we managed to knock out a couple of leadoff singles. This caused some activity in the Oakland bullpen. I was up next. Fernandez, true to form, came after me with three consecutive fastballs; but he was getting tired and I nailed the third one for a deep fly ball to straightaway center. I thought I had all of it, but the centerfielder made a terrific leaping catch at the warning track and hauled it in. Fernandez was yanked at this point; Oakland brought in their closer, an ex-teammate of Gus' named Lou Chandler, who had done a five-year stint with San Francisco earlier in his career.

Gus' eyes lit up when he saw Chandler trotting out to the mound. He called back to Garber in the dugout, "I know what this guy's gonna throw before he even throws it."

Up to bat in front of Gus was our centerfielder, Tim Castleberry. Castleberry hit Chandler's first pitch into the ground for what should have been a game-ending double play. The shortstop bobbled it, though, and everybody was safe. The bases were loaded; Gus was up.

At this point Gus signaled the home plate umpire for timeout and trotted back to the dugout. He opened the Del Rio bat case and took out the aging brown bat.

"You're nuts," I said.

"Watch this," he replied, a subdued gleam of confidence in his eyes.

Gus trudged slowly back to the plate, flexing his grip on the bat as he walked. He settled into the batter's box and waited for the first pitch. Chandler started him with a fastball, low and away. His next pitch was a hanging curve.

Gus creamed it.

When the ball left the bat, I thought it actually had a chance of going out of the stadium, but it hit the Wheaties sign on the upper façade above the third deck and fell back onto the playing field—a grand slam. The Oakland crowd fell into a gigantic hush, but in the dugout we were screaming. Garber clenched his fist and punched through the air. You'd have thought we won game seven of the World Series. We all rushed out to congratulate Gus, who broke into a huge smile as he touched home plate. When we got back into the dugout he took me aside.

"Now that, kid, was a real bat-screamer." He pulled up the Del Rio bat and kissed it on the trademark.

We held on in the bottom of the ninth and won the game five to four.

Portland, June 17th.

Gus went four for five tonight, including two homers. We killed his former team, San Francisco, in an interleague contest, 9-3. The place went crazy when Gus hit his second homer—an upper deck shot in the eighth inning. You should have seen it. None of his hits involved the Del Rio bat, but since Gus has started using it, his offensive numbers have gone through the roof.

"One helluva night," Garber told Gus after the game.

Gus has only used the Del Rio bat three more times since hitting the grand slam against Oakland, but the results have been uncannily similar: two hits in three at-bats, including a solo homer and a triple. His only out was a drive to center that was caught at the wall.

It's been odd, though. Since he first started using the Del Rio bat, not only have his offensive numbers been steadily increasing, but his personality seems to be altering, too—a little bit each day. He's still the same old Gus, but everything seems more pronounced, exaggerated even. On his up days he's really up; on his down days he's really down. You don't want to be around after he strikes out.

It's queer.

Chicago, June 25th.

We had a strange incident inside the clubhouse today. Chicago edged us in an afternoon game, 3-2 in 10 innings. When we got back into the clubhouse, we were all surprised to find that three of the sectional mirrors around the sinks in the grooming room had been shattered. There was broken glass all over the floor. A couple of the clubhouse guys were busy cleaning it up. One of them walked up to Garber as he entered the room.

"Does this belong to one of your players?" he asked, holding out a long piece of dark brown wood.

It was the Del Rio bat.

"That's Cantrill's," Garber responded. He pushed his hat back and scratched his head. "Where the hell did you get it?"

"We found it on the floor," the clubhouse guy replied. "Somebody used it to smash the damn mirrors."

Garber got a perplexed look on his face. The clubhouse guys gave us the whole story. Apparently nobody saw it happen, but Duke Lawrence, one of the trainers, was in the training room and just about jumped out of his skin when he heard it.

"There were three loud bangs," Lawrence told Garber. "Real quick, too…*Boom! Boom! Boom!* It was so darn loud I just about crapped my pants."

Lawrence had ran into the grooming room a moment later, but the only thing he found was the Del Rio bat lying on the floor in the middle of all the broken glass.

"After the glass shattered I actually heard the bat hit the floor," Lawrence continued, "but there wasn't anything else…no voices, no footsteps…nothin'." He shook his head and got a puzzled look on his face. "It was really kinda creepy."

The incident happened right before the end of the game, so we all knew it couldn't have been Gus who did it. He had made one of his rare starts in the field and was playing first base at the time. Gus, who like many major leaguers never actually locks his locker, had a fit when he found out someone had taken the bat.

"The one damn day I don't take it into the dugout with me and look what happens," he said, gritting his teeth. I'll kill the sonofabich who did this!"

When we got back to the hotel everyone seemed to have forgotten the incident, but it stuck in the back of my mind—like a bad feeling you can't shake.

Portland, July 5th.

We just got the news: Gus was named Major League Player of the Month for June. He hit .426 with 10 homers and 25 RBI.

His overall average has soared—all the way up to .314. He's also been tapped as the Grizzlies' sole representative in the All Star Game a few days from now.

"I feel like a new man," he told me.

Gus' mood swings have continued, though. In fact they seem to be getting worse. Just the other day he went eyeball to eyeball in a shouting match with Heathcliff Thomas, one of our relief pitchers. They were ready to come to blows in an argument over who was better, Garth Brooks or James Brown. We literally had to hold Gus back when Thomas called Brooks a no-talent white-boy with a brick in his ass. Then just yesterday Gus chewed out one of the locker room boys for only having one can of Dad's Root Beer in the clubhouse cooler. Yet in spite of all this, the clubhouse seems to be a much happier place lately. We actually had a winning record in June, and that was due in large part to Gus.

Yet, as happy as I am for him I can't seem to shake this funny feeling in the back of my mind. There's something going on that I can't put my finger on. It all goes back to the Del Rio bat. I know Gus thinks it was helped his hitting and all that, but there's something about it, something that makes me think it should have stayed at Smitty's.

Kansas City, July 15th.

There was a freak accident during the game tonight.

We jumped on Kansas City for six runs early. By the end of five, the game had turned into a runaway with the Grizzlies out in front by a lopsided 12-3 score. With one out in the sixth and a man on second, Gus was walked intentionally to set up a double play. Our third baseman, Morris Freeman, hit a slow roller to the shortstop, who charged the ball hard, fielded it, and flipped to second for what should have been the start of an inning-ending double play. However, Gus—weak legs and all—got a decent jump off the bag and thundered into second. His 255-pound frame hit the infield dirt in a tremendous cleats-up slide that sent a cloud of dirt flying. The Kansas City second baseman, Freddie Simmons, was upended like a bowling pin, causing his relay throw to hit the ground about 20 feet short of first base. Freeman, one of the faster guys on the team, was called safe. Simmons then jumped up and started screaming at Gus. The second base umpire jumped between them before any blows could be thrown, but both players were red in the face from a heated verbal exchange.

Gus vented his wrath when he got back into the dugout.

"Stupid dumb sonofabich…what the hell does he expect me to do…hold his hand?"

"What'd he say to you?" I asked, a bit of a smile on my face.

"Well he called me a fat ass for one thing," Gus barked. "I won't repeat the rest." He glared out toward second base and muttered under his breath. "Asshole."

A number of the guys laughed, but I could tell Gus was pretty upset with whatever Simmons had said to him. I didn't think too much of it at the time, though.

When the top of the ninth rolled around, we were up by 12 runs—a real laugher. Gus was due up second in the inning. When he strolled out to the on-deck circle I noticed something unusual.

He was holding the Del Rio bat.

This surprised me because Gus had previously only used it in tight situations, usually with a game on the line. I got a curious expression on my face and looked over at Garber.

"What's he usin' that thing now for?"

Garber shook his head. "Dunno."

Gus took two breaking pitches inside for ball two. The next pitch was an outside fastball that Gus jumped on and drilled to the right side of the infield. It was a real screamer, one of those "blink your eyes and you'll miss it" type hits. Simmons moved in to field the ball on one hop, but when it hit the artificial surface it took a freak low bounce and streaked toward Simmons about a foot-and-a-half lower than he was anticipating. It nailed him right in the groin—a 100-plus-mile-an-hour screamer right into his manhood. There was a loud "pop" as the ball smashed into Simmons' protective cup (after the game we found out it had shattered into two pieces). Simmons collapsed into a fetal position, both hands clutching his groin. He just laid there, writhing in agony and moaning. Trainers and coaches went running out to help him. After a couple of minutes they tried to help him up so he could walk off the field in some sort of dignified manner, but he fell back to the ground and grabbed his groin again. He was carried off on a stretcher a couple of minutes later. Gus stood on first the whole time, staring blankly at what was happening.

Tim Castleberry nudged me in the dugout. "When was the last time you saw a bad bounce on artificial turf?"

I shook my head. "Never."

Garber, who had overheard what we were saying, looked over at us and shook his head, too. "Weirdest damn thing I ever saw."

I can't imagine that Simmons will be in Kansas City's lineup tomorrow.

New York, July 18th.

Gus did something weird after the game tonight, and frankly, I'm starting to really worry about him. His behavior is getting more bizarre each week, and it seems particularly worse for the next day or two after games in which he uses the Del Rio bat. It's gotten to the point where I'm thinking about talking to Garber about it. Because I'm his roommate, I see a lot more of it than anyone else on the team. I've tried to shrug it off for weeks now, but tonight's incident has me very concerned.

We opened a three-game series in New York. Nothing particularly unusual happened during the game, but I did notice something odd during the top of the eighth. We were down 6-1 when the bottom part of our batting order got a rally going and loaded the bases. At this point a couple of pitchers started warming up in the New York bullpen. This seemed to get Gus' attention. He strolled down to the far end of the bench and stepped up on one of the dugout steps, staring intently out toward the New York bullpen. I don't know if I was the only one to notice it, but he must have stood there totally motionless for a good two minutes—just staring. He finally snapped out of it when Garber called him into the on deck circle. The rally eventually fizzled, and we lost 6-3.

After the game, Gus and I showered and headed to the VIP parking lot where his limo was waiting for us. Gus is the only player on the team with enough stature (and a clause in his contract) to have limo service to and from the hotel on road trips. Everybody else on the team, including Garber, rides the team bus. Because I'm his roommate, though, Gus lets me "tag-along."

When the limo pulled out, Gus was very quiet. I tried talking to him, but he didn't say much of anything and sat with his head down, looking at the floor. I figured he was just tired. We were about halfway to the hotel when he looked up at Louie, our limo driver.

"Louie, I want you to take me to 2845 Old Park Boulevard in Queens."

Louie nodded and took a turn at the next corner. A short while later, we pulled up in front of an aging brownstone apartment building in a nice, but older section of Queens. Louie parked on the opposite side of the street. Gus immediately climbed out and walked mechanically across the street. When he got to the far curb, he stopped, stood on the curb, and looked up. Although his back was to us, he appeared to be staring at a dimly lit window on the second floor. This went on for three or four minutes. Louie finally looked over his shoulder and said something.

"What's he doin' out there, Brady?"

I shook my head. "Beats the hell outta me." I opened the side door. "Gimme a minute and I'll find out."

I trotted across the street. It had showered right after the game, and the asphalt, still wet, gave off that dingy big city street smell.

I stepped up on the curb. "So what's goin' on?"

At that moment I got a good look at Gus' face—I nearly cringed. He was staring up at the second story window as though in a trance, an ominous, repugnant look on his face. I had never seen Gus like this, even in his angriest moment on the playing filed; but it wasn't really anger, it was something else. There was a vicious look in his eyes. He looked like a predator contemplating a victim. The dim light seemed to accentuate this weird expression and it made his face look even scarier. I finally put my hand on his shoulder.

"Gus…what's going on?"

There was a long silence.

"Just lookin'," he finally said.

After staring a few more seconds, Gus quietly turned around and crossed back over to the limo. I climbed in behind him. Louie looked in the rearview mirror at us.

"Where to, Gentlemen?

"Take us to the hotel, Louie," Gus replied in a somber tone.

Louie revved the engine and pulled away from the curb. Gus didn't say a word on the way back to the hotel. When we got up to the suite he threw his clothes off and went straight to bed, still not saying anything.

I have a real feeling of dread inside me. Something is terribly wrong. Gus is starting to lose it, but how is it I seem to be the only one who is noticing it? How come nobody else on the team has said anything about it? Maybe they know and are just afraid to bring it up—like me. Garber needs to know about this, but I'm not sure if telling him is the right thing to do, at least not yet. Anyway, how does a rookie tell his manager that you think his best player, a future hall-of-famer no less, is on the verge of going completely nuts? I'm convinced it all has to do with that damned Del Rio bat.

It's supposed to rain tomorrow and I'm kind of hoping for a rainout, because it's not going to be easy getting to sleep tonight.

Portland, August 11th.

There's been another mirror-smashing incident, this time in our own clubhouse. It happened in the middle of the night. No one heard or saw anything, but the clubhouse crew came in this morning and found every mirror in the grooming room completely smashed out. I've never seen so much broken glass in all my life.

The Del Rio bat was found lying in the shattered glass again.

When Gus found out he became extremely livid and started cursing. You could hear him yelling all over the clubhouse—a real major league tirade. He quieted down, though, when he got over to his locker and found it was still locked.

"What the hell is this?" he asked, the anger on his face turning to a look of puzzlement.

When it became apparent that Gus' locker hadn't been tampered with, an odd silence fell over the entire clubhouse. Everyone knew that Gus had been locking his things up regularly since the first mirror-smashing incident, but the Del Rio bat case was laying open on the bench, as though someone who knew the combination had opened the locker, taken the bat out, then closed and locked it again. I looked over at Castleberry who, like me, had a bewildered look on his face.

"How did that thing get out of his locker?" I whispered in Castleberry's direction.

Tim shrugged his shoulders and shook his head. We all continued to dress down, but there was a lot of low talk between players and coaches throughout the clubhouse and then again during warm-ups. At one point I saw Garber and the clubhouse manager take Gus aside and talk with him for a minute. Speculation about the incident continued right up until game time.

In an afternoon contest we were thoroughly trounced by Oakland, 9-2; but even in the dugout the topic of the shattered mirrors came up a couple of times. At one point when Gus was batting, Garber pulled me aside and asked if I had spent any time with Gus the previous evening. I told him we'd been at the Pig's Trough right up until curfew. I guess it's a manager's job to be suspicious of everyone when something like this happens, but it would surprise me if Garber really thought Gus was the one responsible.

When we got into the clubhouse after the game, talk of the incident had pretty much tapered off. I took some extra time in the whirlpool and was one of the last players to leave. While I was dressing, one of our clubhouse guys, Tino, came over and sat on the bench next to me. Tino is a slightly built Latino in his mid-fifties with graying hair and is the team's head laundry man. He knows how to pop a towel better than anybody in baseball. Bob Reed challenged him to a towel fight earlier in the season and walked away with a couple of major league welts—one on his upper leg, the other on his ass. Reed actually had to see the team physician about it. Tino had a somber look on his face as he straddled the bench. He sat there for a few moments before finally speaking up.

"Déjà vu," he said.

I was a little baffled. "What do you mean?"

"Do you know where I worked before I came to Portland this year?"

"Nope."

"Philadelphia. I was a clubhouse boy there for a long, long time." He scooted over and got real close to me. "I was there 17 years ago."

I wasn't sure what he was getting at. "Okay…so what does it all mean?"

"Think about it, Brady…Philadelphia…17 years ago?"

I was still confused. Tino leaned toward me and spoke in a low voice. "Del Rio's last season…his last games. I was there."

I raised my eyebrows at this. "What are you trying to tell me?"

"Del Rio died in a plane crash a couple of weeks later, but not many people know what happened the last couple days of the season."

"Gus told me all about it," I responded. "Del Rio lost the batting championship by one percentage point. He was leading the league, but he got injured and had to sit out the last game of the season. Kirkland with Cincinnati went four for four in his final game to win the title."

Tino nodded in agreement. "They said Del Rio pulled a groin muscle."

"Gus mentioned that, too."

Tino glanced around the locker room, as though checking to see if anyone else was still around. "Want to know what really happened?"

I nodded slowly. "Sure…sure I guess so."

Tino took off his cap and ran his hand over his hair. "Del Rio had a beautiful wife, 12 years younger than him. She was nice…a real sweet lady…smart, too, for a younger gal. Better than Domingo deserved."

"What do you mean?"

"Domingo was a great player, but he could be a real asshole, too. He cheated on her…treated her like crap. Hell, he had different girls on every road trip. Then…the day before the end of the season, he found out she was having an affair with one of the guys on the team."

"You gotta be kidding."

Tino shook his head.

"Who was it?" I asked.

"I'm not gonna say. But he was smart enough not to be anywhere near the stadium the next day. Domingo and his wife had a hell of a brawl that night. She slashed his face with a steak knife. He ended up in an emergency room at midnight. The next morning he came into the clubhouse with a huge gash on his cheek and a couple dozen stitches. It was real ugly.

Needless to say, Domingo didn't want nobody in the stands to see his face like that, so he decided not to play the final game. At the time I think he was still ahead by three or four percentage points and I guess he must have figured no one was gonna catch him." Tino put his cap back on his head. "He was wrong, though."

"He sure was," I agreed.

"Our game hadn't been over more than ten minutes when the news about Kirkland came in from Cincinnati over the sports wire. Domingo went berserk. He was throwin' crap all over the locker room. It took us 10 minutes to get him calmed down. After that he showered and went into the grooming room to blow-dry his hair. That's when all hell broke loose. His wife cheating on him was one thing, but losing that batting title was way too much for a guy like Domingo. He looked in the mirror and saw that gash on his face and went crazy again." Tino's voice lowered almost to a whisper, "but quietly this time."

"Quietly...what do you mean?"

"He walked...real calm, like nothin' was wrong...over to his locker and took out the bat."

My eyes really opened up. "You mean—"

"That's right, Brady. The same damn bat Gus has been using. Domingo laid the case out on the bench, opened it, grabbed the bat, and then calmly walked back into the grooming room. Couple a' seconds later the place erupted. Domingo smashed out every mirror in the place. You should have heard it. Scared the livin' insides outta just about everybody in the place. I was standing right there when he walked out. He was wearin' a towel and carrying that bat. I remember his feet was bleedin' from walkin' on glass."

I got a queasy feeling in the pit of my stomach. "This is— unbelievable," I stammered.

Tino continued, "And two weeks later he was dead. Smashed right into the side of that mountain..." He slapped the heels of his hands together, "...*ka-pow!*"

I was nearly speechless. Tino got up to leave.

"Anyway…you're Gus's roommate. I figured you should know about all this. You know I'm really not a superstitious guy, but uh…I think Gus needs to *lose* that bat. I think he needs to lose it soon." He shook his head. "Something just ain't right with it."

Tino turned and walked out. I sat there, deep in thought, for quite some time afterward.

New York, August 22nd.

The culminating incident came two nights ago in the Big Apple. We flew in earlier in the day for a day-night double header that was a make-good for two rainouts in July. It's the kind of scheduling snafu all ballplayers hate. We just finished a nine-game homestand, and Monday was supposed to be a travel day before landing in Chicago for a three-game series starting Tuesday night. Sunday afternoon's game was a grueling 10-inning affair in 98-degree heat, and a side-trip to New York in between everything was the last thing any of us wanted. However, we were still mathematically in the hunt for a wild card berth. So the games had to be made up.

In the afternoon opener, New York creamed us 15-1. They slammed four homers off Bob Reed in the first two innings alone, landing him in the showers and sending him to a sooner-than-expected engagement with his favorite bottle of Jack Daniels. New York's ace, Leroy Johnson, humiliated us with a three-hitter. I went 0-for-4, including an embarrassing strikeout on a 60-mile-an-hour changeup in the third. Johnson actually winked and smiled at me as I trudged sheepishly back to the dugout. Gus, who was given the afternoon game off, sat on the bench and chuckled. He seemed to be in an okay mood. In fact, for about the last week there hasn't been anything too unusual about his behavior, and that has been something of a relief.

Our bats woke up in the evening contest. It was a tight game with a lot of offensive fireworks. I homered to right in the second and Gus hit a three-run shot in the fifth. When the eighth inning rolled around, the score was tied, 8-8. At the start of the inning New York announced a pitching change. Strolling out to the mound was a 39-year-old journeyman pitcher name Carlos Robles. Robles was a successful starting pitcher earlier in his career and actually played with Domingo Del Rio during his rookie season in Philadelphia. By this time, though, Robles, while still effective, had been regulated to the role of middle relief and occasional closer.

Gus was due up third in the inning. I led off with a single to right, but Robles—always known for having an incredible move to first—gunned a bullet to the bag and picked me off. As I trotted back to the dugout I saw Gus standing in the on deck circle, the Del Rio bat in his hand. Usually when I did something foolish on base or in the field he would at least look at me and roll his eyes, or bark out a lewd comment to help accentuate my stupidity. But this time Gus didn't look in my direction, not even a glance. He was completely transfixed on Robles, a queer look of blank intensity on his face.

Our next hitter was Castleberry, who grounded a 2-2 pitch to the shortstop for an easy play at first. Gus moved into the batter's box, clenched the Del Rio bat above his head, and waited for the pitch. Robles followed a moment later with a 91-mile-an-hour fastball on the outside part of the plate. Gus laid into it hard and hit a screamer right up the middle—a low line drive no more than five feet off the ground. Never before have I seen a ball leave a bat so fast and so hard. It was a true bat-screamer in every sense of the word. In a microsecond it smashed into the upper right of Robles' forehead just below the bill of his cap with an electrifying thud. At that instant, in an event like no other in baseball history, Robles' upper right head was literally crushed by the impact. The collision of ball, flesh, and bone was so tremendous that several chunks of Robles scalp, along with his cap, were torn off and sent flying into the air. It was the most sickening thing I have ever witnessed and it brought back memories of the same repulsive shock I felt when watching the movie, *JFK,* many years before, during which the actual film of Jack Kennedy's assassination had been shown in a courtroom scene. The grainy 8mm film shot by Abraham Zapruder actually showed the President's head explode as it was hit by Oswald's bullet. The real life scene before me had been frighteningly similar, with chunks of Robles' flesh and hair now scattered about the pitcher's mound.

A second later, pandemonium broke out. New York's second baseman, a gold glover named Bobby Williams, had instinctively broken toward the ball and literally fielded a piece of Robles' scalp in his glove. The rest of the infield scrambled to Robles' aid as he lay dying of a massive brain injury—the turf turning crimson below the massive, sunken wound in his head. Some lady in a top-dollar box seat right above the dugout started screaming hysterically. It was deafening. However, the most sardonically frightening image was that of Gus Cantrill circling the bases as though oblivious to what had just happened. The ball had come to rest only a few feet from Robles' crumpled body, but none of the New York players were even thinking about making a play on Gus, nor were the umpires paying any attention, they were all rushing to Robles' aid. So Gus mechanically circled the bases in a slow, deliberate trot, as though he had just smacked one out of the park. When he touched home plate, he stopped and turned toward the mound. I'm not sure, but for just an instant I thought I saw the slightest hint of a grin on his face. Then he did the unthinkable:

He looked to the stands and tipped his cap.

Strangely enough, from the crowd of 26,000 people there was only a smattering of boos. Everyone's eyes were riveted on Robles' limp form. A moment later Gus picked up the Del Rio bat and began walking slowly back to the dugout. As he came down the dugout steps he was greeted by the cold, stony silence of amazed stares of shock and disbelief. He said nothing; he looked at no one. After placing the Del Rio bat in its case, he calmly disappeared into the clubhouse runway. It was a bizarre postscript to one of the most horrific incidents in major league history.

The dugout was like a morgue. Players, coaches, trainers—nobody was saying anything. We all just sat there, staring out toward the pitcher's mound at a dying ballplayer who was being feverishly tended to by trainers and physicians. A couple of trainers ran onto the field with a stretcher, but I think we all pretty much knew there was no hope.

They had been tending to Robles for several minutes when the umpires gathered near home plate in a conference over what to do next. They were obviously trying to decide whether to resume play or not. The injury of a player, even a serious one, would normally never be enough to cause a game cancellation, but the magnitude of this incident was entirely out of the norm. Some of the people in the stands—especially those close to the playing field—had been so horrified that they ran from their seats to the exit tunnels within seconds after Robles was hit. We were all in shock. The head umpire soon made a call on a cell phone. Some kind of emergency hotline to the Commissioner, I figured. While the crew chief was on the phone, Robles was rushed off the playing filed. His face had turned stone gray and his pitching arm hung limply over one side of the stretcher. I cringed and turned away. It was an awful sight.

Several minutes later we got the word—the game had been suspended until further notice. The stadium announcer gave the word over the PA system a few moments later. The fans in the stands—who had let out a tremendous collective gasp a split second after Robles' skull was crushed in—filed toward the exits in an ominous near silence that was almost frightening. The faint, low sound of muttering, even some weeping, reverberated softly across the playing field.

After the announcement of the game's suspension, I was the first one to leave the bench and head back into the clubhouse. When I got into the locker room, I was surprised to see Gus already in his street clothes (he obviously hadn't bothered to shower) and heading for the outer door. Tucked under his arm was the black case containing the Del Rio bat.

"Gus…Gus, wait a minute."

He looked briefly over his shoulder, cast me a non-expressive glance, and kept on walking. In full uniform I followed him out to the private lot where our limo was waiting. I stood at the gate and watched him amble nonchalantly toward the vehicle. Even though I called his name several more times, he kept on walking.

Louie, our limo driver, was singing opera to the car radio as it blared away on one of New York's big classical stations. When he saw Gus approaching he killed the radio and opened the door for him. Louie was surprised to see me trotting up in full uniform.

"Going to a costume party are we?"

I just sort of grimaced at Louie and climbed in after Gus who was already sitting in the farthest back seat, the Del Rio bat case in his lap. Louie slipped behind the wheel and looked over his shoulder.

"Back to the hotel, gentlemen?"

I gave Louie a quick nod. A moment later we pulled out into the New York traffic. Louie was obviously unaware of what had happened in the stadium. I slid into a side seat a couple of feet away from Gus. He still wasn't saying anything and refused to even look at me. He just stared straight ahead. This went on for a minute or two before I finally said something.

"Gus—"

"Don't talk, kid. Just let me be," he said, cutting me off. There was a blank apathetic look on his face. We were about halfway to the hotel when he spoke up again.

"Louie, take us to 2845 Old Park Boulevard in Queens."

I was pretty sure it was the same address we had been to several weeks earlier. Louie looked in his rearview mirror and acknowledged Gus, then he looked at me. His eyes seemed to be saying, "is everything okay?" I just shrugged my shoulders. Louie kept on driving.

A few minutes later we pulled up in front of the same brownstone apartment building we had visited before. Gus immediately got out of the limo carrying the bat case with him. He laid it on the hood and opened it right in front of Louie, who by this time had to be wondering what the hell was going on. Gus must have stared into the case for a good 20 seconds before pulling out the Del Rio bat. Clutching it in both hands, he proceeded to cross the street. It was a pretty dark evening and there weren't many street lamps in this older New York neighborhood, but even in the dim light I could see Gus flexing his grip on the bat as he slowly crossed the boulevard. He was "ringing out" the bat, much in the same way he did while standing at the plate looking for a pitch to crush. I got out of the car.

"Gus. Wait a minute. Gus!"

I trotted around the car and started to follow. Louie rolled down his window and spoke to me.

"Brady, what's goin' on. What's up with Gus?"

"I don't know…something really strange. Maybe you should come with me."

Louie climbed out of the limo. We crossed the street and found Gus standing on the sidewalk staring up at the same dimly lit window on the second floor that he had eyed so intently just weeks before. Louie and I approached him slowly.

"What do you see up there, Gus?" I asked.

Gus didn't flinch. He kept on staring at the window as though he hadn't heard a thing. Louie put his hand on Gus' shoulder and gently tried to shake him, the same way you might try to bring someone out of a light sleep. This also failed to get his attention.

Down the street we could hear a car approaching. I looked over and saw a taxi pull up to the curb a few yards away from us. The cabbie got out and opened the curbside rear door. Climbing out of the cab was a very attractive Hispanic woman in a slick-looking dress carrying a small shopping bag. She was older—probably near 40—but still a knockout. She glanced at us as she walked by. Gus stiffened up when he saw her. She proceeded up the steps to the building and disappeared inside. Gus looked at Louie, then me.

"You guys wait here. Everything's gonna be just fine. I'll be back in a few minutes."

With that Gus walked up the stairs to the outer vestibule just before the entry door to the building. He rang one of the tenant buttons. A moment later a voice came over the intercom. It was female, but we couldn't make out what it was saying. We could hear bits of what Gus was saying, though.

"Hello, Dolores...*(inaudible)*...with the ball club... *(inaudible)*...some news about Carlos...*(inaudible)*...an incident at the stadium..."

The female voice came back on. It was still distorted, but it was much louder and had an agitated sound to it. Gus spoke again, but this time more softly. Neither Louie nor I could catch anything he said. This was followed by a few seconds of silence. Then the door buzzer sounded. Gus gently pushed it open and walked inside, still clenching the Del Rio bat in his right hand.

He hadn't bothered closing the door behind him, so Louie and I crept up the stairs and peeked inside from the outer vestibule. All we could see was Gus walking up a flight of stairs at the far end of foyer. There was an old fashioned heating radiator next to the wall at the bottom landing. Next to it was an ancient-looking elevator. At the top of the stairs was a large upper landing that appeared to have connecting hallways on either side. Gus turned to the right when he got to the top and disappeared down one of the hallways. Louie and I moved closer to the door to get a better look inside. The foyer was spacious and luxurious in appearance, with hardwood floors partly covered by expensive looking rugs. There were lavish pieces of furniture scattered strategically about, a few of which were nestled up close to a beautiful brick fireplace. There was no one else inside, so we stepped in.

Louie spoke to me in a soft voice, "What is he doing up there? What's this all about?"

"I don't know…but I'm scared about this, and I mean *scared*. We should probably follow him." I looked Louie right in the eyes. "I think he killed Carlos Robles on the mound tonight with that bat."

Louie's mouth flew open. "What the hell are you talkin' about?"

"He hit a liner in the eighth…took Robles right in the forehead. It put him down, Louie. There was blood everywhere. They hauled him out on a stretcher and suspended the game."

"Good lord!"

"That's why I came after him while I was still in uniform. He just threw his clothes on and walked out of the clubhouse like he was in some sort of a trance. I think…I think he's gone crazy on us."

Louie stood there dumbfounded.

"But it's more than just Gus goin' crazy. It's…it's that damn bat of his. I know this sounds crazy, Louie, but there's something wrong with it. I don't know what kind of weird crap Del Rio was into, but that bat isn't any regular bat. It's got some kinda' power to it. Something supernatural, something…something unholy."

"What do you mean?"

"I'm not sure, but whatever it is, it's got a hold of Gus. We got—"

A blood-curdling scream cut me off. It came from upstairs. There was the sound of a loud ruckus followed by more screams. I thought I heard Gus' voice shouting. Louie and I started across the foyer, but even before we moved a few feet a screaming woman appeared at the top of the upper landing and came stumbling down the stairs in high heels. It was the same Hispanic lady we had seen a few minutes earlier. She had a look of total terror on her face. It was one scream after another. She was holding her ear as she ran; blood was running down her neck. Then Louie and I saw something that stopped us dead and made us stagger backwards.

The Del Rio bat was chasing her.

It was bouncing up and down on the handle end, coming down the stairs like a pogo stick from hell. For a moment I think I actually laughed in disbelief. It was nuts—a baseball bat chasing a beautiful Hispanic babe. The woman stumbled into Louie's arms, but he pushed her behind him and went for the bat. I was still standing there, shaking my head in disbelief. It was almost too ridiculous to be frightening.

Then it smashed Louie in the jaw.

As Louie had reached wildly for the bat, it bounced up and twirled like a baton in mid-air, then smacked him right on the kisser. Louie went down, flat on his back completely unconscious.

"Louie!"

I hurried over to the fallen limo driver. The woman, who had collapsed to the floor just behind him, jumped up and scampered for the open door. Then, in what was perhaps the most frightening moment of all, the door—on its own— slammed shut. The woman tried the knob, but the door refused to budge.

She turned around—the bat was almost upon her.

I broke toward her. She held her hands in front of her face and started screaming again.

"No, Domingo! No!"

A split second later the bat did another devilish twirl and crashed down on top of her head. Her back was against the door and she sunk to the floor, still screaming. I leaped for the bat and snagged it in mid-air. I might as well have grabbed an out-of-control fire hose. It jerked me hard in every direction. Behind me I could hear footsteps coming down the stairs.

It was Gus.

One side of his face was covered with blood. Seconds later the bat broke free, bounced up, and went into one of its twirls. I tried to duck, but it caught me flush on the side of the head. I went down on my ass. (Now I knew how Johnny Roseboro had felt back in '65) I was flat on my back looking up, completely dazed—everything was spinning.

The bat bounced back toward the woman and landed a couple of hard shots to her body. It went into another twirl, but Gus grabbed it in mid-air and threw his body on top of it. He struggled on the floor with it for a few moments. Then, with his hands still locked around it, the bat actually pulled him up off the floor and almost into the air. Gus' incredible hand and arm strength was the only thing that kept it from breaking fee. Then, as if sensing its struggle was fruitless, the bat stopped trying to jerk free and commenced poking Gus in the face—hard—even while he was holding onto it. Gus looked like he was literally beating himself in the face. It was an outlandish sight. During the next few seconds Gus managed to stumble over to the radiator next to the wall. With a massive effort, he was able to wriggle both hands down onto the handle part of the bat. He then reeled back and began taking monster home run swings at the radiator. I closed my eyes and heard the sound of wood smashing into iron over and over again. I don't think Gus had ever swung a bat so hard in his life. On about the tenth swing, I heard the hiss of steam coming out of the radiator. A few swings later I heard the sound of wood splintering. Gus kept beating away—harder and harder. The wood splintering sound continued. I heard a weird roar, then I faded out completely and woke up in the hospital yesterday morning.

Portland, October 15th.

It's funny how things turn out. The season has ended, and as strange is it sounds, Gus is something of a hero. The people of New York will forever be haunted by the image of Carlos Robles being fatally struck in the head by a screaming baseball. They'll never forget Gus circling the bases as Robles lay dying. They must have replayed the shot of Gus tipping his hat a thousand times on all the sports networks. Gus seems to have been largely forgiven, though. He truthfully stated to the press that he had no memory of the incident at all. So his unforgivable actions immediately following seem to have been widely regarded as those of a person in shock. What really redeemed Gus, however, was the media account of his saving the life of Robles' wife, Dolores, from an unknown assailant. Yeah, that's right, an unknown assailant. According to the media Gus and I went to Dolores Robles' high-priced apartment building immediately following the game to explain what had happened and to offer our condolences. According to the media Gus had encountered a burglar brandishing a large wooden club who was assaulting her. According to the media a large scuffle had ensued in which Louie and I were struck and injured (I did miss the next seven games; Louie had a fractured jaw) after which Gus tangled with the assailant and chased him from the building.

According to the media.

What the media didn't tell anyone is that Dolores Robles was formerly the widow of baseball great, Domingo Del Rio. They mentioned nothing about Gus' coming to the apartment with the Del Rio bat. No mention was made of a busted radiator. No mention was made of the torrid affair between rookie pitcher Carlos Robles and Dolores Del Rio 17 years earlier. No mention was made of the screeching sound from hell I heard while fading from consciousness as Gus hammered the unholy life out of that devilish bat.

But frankly, the media reported it that way because that's the story they were given by the authorities. That's also the story that Gus, Louie, and I were *told* to say. Never mind the truth, give the public something they can handle. I look at it this way, though, no matter how you spin the story, Gus wasn't really responsible for the death of Carlos Robles; but he certainly was responsible for saving the life of Robles' wife. Gus later told me he didn't remember anything from the time Robles came into the game until he found himself standing in a strange apartment watching the Del Rio bat taking swipes at a screaming Hispanic lady.

I don't know what happened to the Del Rio bat, and Gus won't talk to me about it. It doesn't seem to matter to him, though. A few days later he was back in the lineup, playing with the enthusiasm of a 10-year old.

The Grizzlies ended the season only four games under .500—a terrific year for an expansion team. Garber got a three-year contract extension because of it. Gus' hitting tailed off a bit the last few weeks (the loss of the Del Rio bat maybe?) but his stats are still good enough that he's practically a shoo-in for the Comeback Player of the Year award.

And what a year it was for me. There was the excitement of making a major league club; my first big league hit; the supernatural mystery of the Del Rio bat; the death of Carlos Robles—all these things I will carry with me the rest of my life. But most of all I'll remember Gus Cantrill. In an age when most players are far more concerned about their egos and the size of their paychecks, Gus still plays baseball for the pure joy of it. Not that Gus isn't interested in making a buck, but I truly think he'd play for free if he had to.

You'd think with a long season finally coming to an end that an older ball player would want to take some time off and do nothing, but not Gus. There's an autumn peewee league here in the Portland area, and Gus has already shown up at a couple of local practices. Just the other day there was a knock at my door. When I opened it, there was Gus, leaning against the outside rail with an impish smile on his face.

"Grab your cleats and come with me, kid. I'll show ya some real baseball."

THE END

SCHIZOID CREATOR

By Clark Ashton Smith

When a modern psychologist gets mixed up with ancient grimoires, there's bound to be the Devil to pay. But sometimes, the Devil comes in ways not precisely covered in the legendary warnings for handling him.

In the private laboratory that his practice as a psychiatrist had enabled him to build, equip and maintain, Dr. Carlos Moreno had completed certain preparations that were hardly in accord with the teachings of modern science. For these preparations he had drawn instruction from old grimoires, bequeathed by ancestors who had incurred the fatherly wrath of the Spanish Inquisition. According to a rather scurrilous family legend, other ancestors had been numbered among the Inquisitors.

At one end of the long room he had cleared the cluttered floor of its equipment, leaving only an immense globe of crystal glass that suggested an aquarium. About the globe he had traced with a consecrated knife, the sorcerers' arthame, a circle inscribed with pentagrams and the various Hebrew names of the Deity. Also, at a distance of several feet, a smaller circle, similarly inscribed.

Wearing a seamless and sleeveless robe of black, he stood now within the smaller, protective circle. Upon his breast and forehead was bound the Double Triangle, wrought perfectly from seven metals. A silver lamp, engraved with the same sign, afforded the sole light, shining on a stand beside him. Aloes, camphor and storax burned in censers set about him on the floor. In his right hand he held the arthame; in his left, a hazel staff with a core of magnetized iron.

Like Dr. Faustus, Moreno designed an evocation of the Devil. But not, however, for the same purpose that had inspired Faustus.

Pondering long and gravely on the painful mysteries of the cosmos, the discrepancy of good and evil, Moreno had at last conceived an explanation that was startlingly simple.

There could, he reasoned, be only one Creator, God, who was or had been primarily benignant. Yet all the evidence pointed to the co-existence of an evil creative principle, a Satan. God, then, must be a split or dual personality, a sort of Jekyll and Hyde, manifesting sometimes as the Devil.

This duality, Moreno argued, must be a form of what is commonly called schizophrenia. He had a profound belief in the efficacy of shock treatment for such disorders. If God, in his aspect as the Devil, could be suitably confined and subjected to treatment, a cure might result. The confused problems of the universe would then resolve themselves under a sane and no longer semi-diabolic Deity.

The glass globe, specially constructed at great expense, contained at one side electrical apparatus of Moreno's own devising. The machine, far more complex than the portable apparatus used in electric shock treatment, could release a voltage powerful enough to electrocute simultaneously all the inmates of a state prison. Moreno considered that no lesser force could effect the shock necessary for the cure of a supernatural personage.

He had memorized an ancient spell for the calling up of the Devil and his confinement within a bottle. The globe would do admirably for the aforesaid bottle.

The spell was a bastard mixture of Greek, Hebrew and Latin. Its exact meaning seemed doubtful. It was filled with such terms as Eloha, Tetragrammaton, Kis, Elijon, Elohim, Saday and Zevaoth, the names of God. The word Bifrons recurred several times. This was no doubt one of the Devil's numerous names. But there could be only one Devil.

Moreno disregarded as childish those old demonology's that peopled Hell with a multitude of evil spirits, having each his own name, rank and office.

All, then, was in readiness. In a firm, sonorous voice, which might have been that of a priest chanting the Mass, he began to recite the incantation.

When the summons came, Bifrons was busily engaged in amorous dalliance with the she-imp Foti. Like Janus, he was two-faced; and he possessed multiple members. Since Foti herself was somewhat peculiarly formed, their lovemaking was quite complicated.

Bifrons began to withdraw his members from about the she-imp, explaining, "Some damned sorcerer has gotten hold of that ancient spell containing my name. It's the first time in two hundred years. But I'll have to go."

"Hurry back," enjoined Foti, pouting with her four lips, two of which were located in her abdomen. "If you don't you may find me otherwise occupied."

The air sizzled behind Bifrons in his exit from the infernal regions.

Dr. Moreno felt surprised and even appalled when he saw the being that his incantation had called up in the globe. He had scarcely known what to expect, and had paid little attention to old pictures and descriptions of the Devil, seeing in them only the dementia of medieval superstition. But the teratology of this creature seemed incredible.

The two faces of Bifrons bloated alternately against the globe's interior; and his arms, legs, body and numerous other parts squirmed and flattened themselves convulsively in a furious effort to escape. But through the thickness of the glass, or the power of the surrounding circle, Bifrons was bottled up as helplessly as any djinn imprisoned by Solomon. He resigned himself presently and began to relax, floating awhile in mid-air, and finally seating himself on Moreno's electrical machine. As if feeling more at home, he looped some of his parts around the various pairs of forceps, ending in electrodes that projected from the huge and intricate device.

"What the devil do you want?" he bellowed. The glass muffled his voice, which was still sufficiently audible. His tones bespoke anger and resentment.

"I want the Devil," said Moreno. "And I presume that you are he."

"*The* Devil?" queried Bifrons. "It's true that I'm *a* devil. But I'm not the Old Man himself. There are many thousands of us, as you should know if you've read the demonologists. I'm no infernal prince but merely a subordinate, though with special powers of my own. Again, what do you want? Money? Women? A Senatorship? The Presidency of your cock-eyed republic? Name it, and I'll grant the wish. I'm in a hellish hurry to get out of here."

"You can't fool me. I know that you are the Devil—the only one in the universe. And I don't want any of your gifts. All I want is to cure you."

Bifrons was startled. "Cure me? Of what? Say, what kind of a sorcerer are you anyway?"

"I'm not a sorcerer but a psychiatrist. My name is Dr. Moreno. My hope and intention is to cure you of being the Devil."

This madhouse doctor must be crazy himself, thought Bifrons. He cogitated. The trend of his cogitations was betrayed only by a sardonic one-sided twist of his left-hand mouth.

"All right, I'm the Devil," he agreed finally. "But let's get this over with. What do you mean to do with me?"

"Subject you to shock treatment," announced the doctor. "A very special high-voltage treatment. It should be the best thing for schizophrenia like yours."

"Schizo-what?" roared Bifrons. "Do you think I'm a lunatic?"

"Let me explain. I am using the term schizophrenia in its literal sense, meaning split personality—not as commonly applied to several types of psychic disintegration or regression. I think that you are really a sick Deity. Your illness consists in being Satan part of the time. A genuine case of dual and alternating egos. The Satanic self dominates at present, otherwise I shouldn't have been able to call you up. But we'll soon remedy all that."

The demon thought it well to conceal his consternation. He must get back to Hell as soon as possible and make a report. Satan, he felt, would be interested in Dr. Moreno.

"Get on with your treatment," he enjoined. "What is it, anyway?"

"Electricity."

Bifrons assumed an expression of double-faced dismay. "That's a highly dangerous and destructive force. Do you wish to annihilate me?"

"The result should be different in your case," said the doctor in his most soothing professional voice. "Are you ready?"

Bifrons gave a bi-cephalic nod. Moreno stepped cautiously from the circle and went over to a panel of switches and levers set in the laboratory wall. Watching the demon closely he began to manipulate one of the levers.

The numerous forceps of the machine, on which Bifrons had so conveniently seated himself, closed themselves on various parts of his anatomy, applying their electrodes to his skin. A pair, hitherto concealed, sprang forth and seized his temples tightly.

Moreno grasped a switch firmly and turned on the full voltage. Then, still cautious, he returned to the protective circle.

A shower of sparks and short blue bolts issued from the machine within the globe. In spite of the many forceps that had tightened upon him, Bifrons writhed and tossed like a harpooned octopus. Smoke seemed to pour from his head, body and members, muffling the apparatus that held him captive. Soon a dark-brown cloud, seething and swelling, had filled the globe's interior, concealing everything from view. The cloud was something that Bifrons could emit at will, like the fluid of a cuttlefish.

As a matter of fact, since his nature was itself electrical, he had absorbed the terrific voltage with merely a mild discomfort. The dark cloud was a necessary screen for the tactics that he now intended to use.

Perhaps, Moreno thought, the treatment had been sufficiently prolonged. He could repeat it if necessary. Emerging once more from his magic shelter, he turned off the switch and reversed the lever that had served to manipulate the forceps. Once again he went back to the circle.

After an interval of silence there issued from the clouded globe a voice, which had no resemblance to that of Bifrons. It was both thunderous and mellow. To Moreno's inexperienced ear, it sounded like the Voice that spoke to Moses on the mountain.

"I am cured," it announced. "You have restored Me to My Divinity, O wise and beneficent doctor. Pronounce the formula of release and let Me go. I will return straight to Heaven. Hell is henceforth abolished, together with all evil, sin and disease. The Devil is dead, God alone exists. And God is good."

Moreno was enraptured, believing that he had realized so quickly his fondest professional hope. Scarcely knowing what he did, he uttered the formula that served to release an imprisoned spirit.

Afterwards he asked, "Now will You reveal Yourself to me? I would behold You in all Your glory."

"It cannot be," the Voice thundered. "My glory would blast your eyes forever. Therefore the cloud with which I have surrounded myself."

A moment later the globe was burst asunder in flying fragments, like some gigantic bottle of new champagne. The released cloud, billowing vastly and voluminously, seemed to overspread the whole laboratory in an instant. Bifrons, raging behind it but still invisible, proceeded to wreck all of Moreno's equipment like a dozen baboons gone berserk. Tray-laden tables were overturned and smashed into splinters, shelves were pulled down with a crashing of countless vials and carboys. Coiled tubings were twisted and bent and ripped apart, heavily insulated wires snapped like twine. The old volumes of magic, piled in a corner, sprang into flame and burned to ashes in a few seconds. A violent wind, coming as if from nowhere, took up the ashes and scattered them throughout the room.

Moreno, protected by the circle, alone escaped the demon's wrath. He crouched at the circle's center, cowering and gibbering, while the cloud passed away through windows from which every pane had been broken.

Several of his colleagues, coming to consult him that evening found him still crouching on the wreckage-littered floor. He did not seem to recognize them, and had obviously become deranged. His mouthings appeared to indicate a sort of theological mania.

The colleagues held an impromptu consultation of their own. As a result, Moreno was removed gently but forcibly to the same type of institution as that to which he had committed so many of his patients. His friends and fellow-psychiatrists deplored the interruption, perhaps the ending, of an illustrious career.

The wrecking of the laboratory remained a mystery. Had there been an explosion caused by one of Moreno's experiments? Had the doctor himself destroyed his equipment in a state of violent mania? Or—should the occurrence be classified as an act of God?

Fuming at the interruption of his tryst with Foti, Bifrons nevertheless thought it incumbent upon himself to report at once to Satan when he returned to the nether realms.

He found the Master of that picturesque region occupied in caressing a half-flayed girl. The flaying had been done to render the caresses more intimate and more exquisitely agonizing.

Satan listened gravely to the demon's account of Dr. Moreno. His tapering artistic fingers, with long-pointed nails of polished jet, ceased their occupation; and a furrow appeared like it black triangle between his luminous marble brows.

"This is all very interesting—and rather unfortunate," he said. "However, you have acted with admirable aplomb and presence of mind. The situation should be well under control as long as Moreno remains in the madhouse where you and his colleagues have landed him."

He paused, and his fingers resumed in an absent-minded fashion their gentle raking of his victim's lumbar regions.

"Of course, as you understand, Moreno was quite mad from the start. But lunatics with a speculative bent can sometimes stumble overly close to certain guarded cosmic secrets and there are spells that even *I* must answer and obey...not to mention the Unspeakable Name, the Shem-hamphorash, which coerces and compels Jehovah. After he recovers from his present state of shock, Moreno might be adjudged sane—and released to continue his researches and experiments.

"Such an eventuation must be forestalled permanently. My good Bifrons, you must return immediately to earth and watch over him. I have full trust in your abilities, and I confer upon you plenipotentiary powers. All I ask is that you keep this doctor well bedeviled and legally insane until the hour of his death."

When Bifrons had departed, Satan summoned his chief lieutenants before him in the halls of Pandemonium.

"I am going away for awhile," he told them. "There are certain obligations of a pressing nature that call me—and I must not neglect them too long. In my absence, I consign the management of Hell to your competent hands."

Bowing reversely, Gerson, Goap, Zimimar and Amaimon, lords of the four quarters, went out one after one, leaving their prince alone.

When they had gone, he descended from his globed throne and passed through many corridors and by many upward, winding stairs to the small postern door of Hell.

The door swung open without touch of any visible hand. A long white robe seemed to weave itself swiftly from the air about Satan's form. His infernal attributes withered and dropped away. And the long white beard of the Elohim sprouted and flowed down over his bosom as he stepped across the sill into Heaven.

THE END

SEE ME IN BLACK

By Robert Beine

How did the stranger know so much about Hickman? Then Hickman found out—and wished he hadn't!

IT was at 10:04, on the morning of December 28th that the man in black walked into Daniel Hickman's life, a man of most unusual aspect, at once ludicrous and appalling—a man you would do well to remember.

Dan Hickman was a pleasant young man, bright and glib, a good salesman, a Buyer-to-be (shirts and ties) for Hasker's, just off Broadway.

On this particular morning, Dan was bored and sleepy. By ten o'clock, he'd had only two sales—a "clearance" shirt and a two-buck tie. Now, he stared through the doorway at the whirling gusts of snow that broke funnel-like in the narrow window lobby of the store, idly pondering the challenge of the storm to his mid-morning appetite for coffee and toast.

Occasionally, a huddled, coat-heavy pedestrian would swerve into the lobbyway, pause, shaking and stamping, and then push resolutely back onto the street. But no one bothered to look into their big window, now mockingly dated with its huge, avuncular Santa.

After some few moments, Dan turned and walked back to his counter. He picked up his sales book, glumly flipped the pages, laid the book aside again, then dropped to his knees behind the counter and sorted through the bottom row of ties, the two-dollar line.

AND then it happened. Even while he was stooped behind the counter, Dan knew that someone was looking at him. Rather, looking *for* him, since he was completely hidden behind the counter.

He straightened quickly, puzzled to see no one standing before him. Then his eyes, turning to the doorway, widened suddenly.

A man stood looking at him, surprise and recognition in his expression. A man Dan never had seen before.

Dan dropped his eyes instantly, embarrassed by the intimate directness of the man's gaze. The stranger's image hung startlingly bold in his mind. The man was dressed entirely in black—hat, coat, shoes, muffler, even gloves. That in itself was not so remarkable, but the man had an extraordinary pallor, a sickroom whiteness that struck a fearsome contrast with the unrelieved blackness of his clothing.

The stranger's face was almost lost in the whiteness. Stranger? Yes, definitely a stranger.

"Dan? Dan Hickman?"

Dan looked up.

There he was, smiling a hideous greeting, a man he had never seen before.

"Why, yes. I'm Dan—"

"Dan Hickman," the man repeated. "You're a long way from home."

Dan looked at the man. He had quite a face—with its long, even nose, high, almost sacred cheekbones, almost no eyebrows, and eyes, black—by God—black eyes, pitted in the white clay of his flesh. The face looked about forty years old.

Dan knew he could never have forgotten this face. The man was definitely a stranger, a stranger who knew his name was Dan Hickman, and that he was, indeed, a long way from home.

The man proffered his hand, chuckling. "I never expected to see you in New York, Dan."

Mutual, Dan thought, desperately searching his memory for some clue to the man's identity. He decided that his odd visitor had him confused with another Dan Hickman and was about to suggest a coincidence when the man asked, frowning, "How is your family, Dan?"

"All right, thank you," Dan said hesitantly. "Mother was operated—"

"Yes, I knew of that. She's on her feet now?"

"Yes." Who *was* he?

"And your dad?" the stranger asked, his smile working again. "Still with the Joplin school board?"

A friend, then.

"Yes," Dan laughed, "no one dares suggest retirement around our house. He still thinks he's indispens—"

"Does Bernice still call you 'birdie'?"

Dan blinked, startled. Impossible. No one but close friends and his family knew of this dreaded intimacy—his sister's childhood taunt.

THE man was chuckling again, his black eyes fastened on Dan, his hands folding and unfolding like long white spiders on the top of the counter. "If you two weren't..." the man continued, trailing off into a clacking laugh that made Dan shudder with embarrassment. "How long have you been in New York, Dan?"

"About a year and a half," Dan said, unable to meet the stranger's gaze. "Are you living in New York?"

"Just passing through. Have to leave tomorrow, in fact. Back home for me."

"Oh," Dan nodded vaguely. "Back to...?"

"...the same old place. Oh, yes."

Abbott and Costello, Dan thought, trying to remember which one was Abbott.

"Well, I'm glad to see you've got a nice job, Dan," the man said, tilting his gaze along the wall. "Say—what time do you get through here?"

The question hung like a threat.

"Oh, about six," Dan said ineptly. "But it—"

"Wonderful! Then you'll have dinner with me?"

Ass, ass! Dan cursed himself.

He braced himself for the kiss-off. "I'm sorry, Mr.—ah—but the truth is, I can't remem—"

"You're not busy for dinner?" Blue lines of disappointment appeared suddenly in the white face.

"Well, not exactly," Dan began nervously, "but the truth is—"

"Then you'll come. As my guest, of course, Dan. What a marvelous break this has been—my finding you here in the middle of New York City. I know a little place—in the lower part of town—we'll have a quick dinner and you can hurry right along if you have things to do."

"Well, that's very nice of you, sir, but I don't think—"

"Nonsense. I want to do it. I'll meet you here at six. All right?"

"All right," Dan said, defeated, adding unnecessarily, "if you insist."

DAN looked at himself in the mirror over the counter, hating himself, people in black clothes and the cup of watery coffee he was drinking. He sternly reviewed his "meeting" with the man in black, but the absurdity of the conversation gave the whole situation a silly, dreamlike inconsistency. He wondered for a moment if he weren't the victim of some fabulously impractical joke. But in that case, he reasoned dismally, it would have to have been an imported joke.

No one, certainly, in New York knew about his nickname, "birdie"—except probably Bill Cooper, his best friend. The man obviously knew him and knew him well. He was stuck, and it was his own damn fault. He should have spoken up in the beginning, professed his ignorance—or rudeness, as it was—and admitted that he didn't know his visitor.

Now he'd best try to bluff the evening through, catch or determine the man's identity if he could, conduct himself gracefully if he couldn't. But oh, God…what did you call a "stranger" who apparently has known you from the crib? *Mister? Sir? This is a dandy little place, mister! Say, boy, this is some steak! Yes, sir! Yessiryessir.*

Dan threw a dime on the counter, dug his arms into the sleeves of his storm coat and shuffled miserably out into the storm and across the street to the store...

"There's a note for you in your book, Dan." Mr. Treddup, the store manager, called from the back of the store when Dan had hung up his coat. "Some fellow called. About two minutes ago."

"Thanks, Mr. Treddup," Dan said, waving. He moved to his counter and picked up a yellow slip with the message, *Call Cooper.*

WITH a small stir of excitement, Dan hurried to the phone in the stock room. Maybe Cooper had something lined up for the evening, some dark little intrigue with girls that would salvage the later hours of a doomed dinner.

"DeWitt Airlines," announced a tinny voice at the other end of the line.

"Mr. Cooper, please," Dan said and waited.

"Yes?" a deeper voice inquired after a moment.

"No."

"No what, my simple friend?"

"No, I won't tell you my secret of eternal youth."

"I already know it—sleep. Listen, I didn't call you for secrets *or* advice, I've got a neat proposition."

"Shoot."

"My folks are going to be in town this weekend."

"Hey, that's wonderful. When'll they—"

"Lemme finish. For some obscure reason, they'd like to see you. In fact, they insist that I ask you out. Saturday night. Dinner, drinks, the works. We'll probably be going to a fairly nice spot, so wear your socks."

"Okay, buster, I'll even shave. What's new with them?"

"I'll let them tell you. Incidentally, your mother sent along a few things with them—towels, sheets and fluffy slippers to keep your darling feet warm. Said to be sure to tell you that your dad bowled 243. Also, you're supposed to write."

"I never left home," Dan said, feeling wonderful. "Hey, what's the deal then for Saturday night? Do I meet you?"

"We'll pick you up at your place. About eight. And, please, send the girls away before we get there."

"All right, old man. Sounds good."

"Good."

"Stay clean."

"Clean."

Dan hung up. He felt great. A weekend with the Coopers, his favorite people. He began to whistle. Then he remembered his date with the man in black and all joy left him.

THE 905 Club was a surprise. Dan had been expecting a paper-doilied tearoom, filled with nondescript, respectable men and dusty, aging widows. Pocketing his claim check, he looked through the archway into the bluish haze of a mirrored lounge, busy and exciting with the intimate buzz of cocktailers. His glance measured a covey of unattached girls at the bar, all of them astonishingly pretty in the dim light. He was in the process of making a mental note of the location of the place when he felt a touch on his sleeve and turned to find his nameless host, a smiling shadow in the blue fringe of the bar's light.

"Shall we?" the pale man suggested and the two of them worked their way between crowded tables to a small table in the dining area of the lounge.

For a moment after they were seated, they took separate measure of the room. The bar itself was not huge—a neat, blondwood horseshoe counter—but cocktail drinkers were standing between the stools, adding their noise to the sounding activity of the room. The two men turned to the sudden shadow of the waitress.

"A drink, Dan?" asked the man in black.

Dan hesitated, smiling. "Well, it might take some of the sting out of that wind."

And some of the gloom out of this meeting, he added to himself. On their way over in the cab, Dan had said very little—a few guardedly inquiring comments that failed to elicit the man's identity. He lived, or had lived, in Joplin. That was all Dan knew.

"A martini, then?"

"Fine," Dan said, adding belatedly, "are you having one?"

"Why, yes," the man said, clasping long fingers together on the table. "Two martinis."

While they were waiting for their drinks, the pale stranger spoke quietly of "home"—friends, neighborhoods, country that Dan knew well. The drinks came and Dan turned gratefully to his glass.

He was vaguely conscious of the man's persistent stare, but managed to convince himself that he didn't give a damn. *Funny duck,* he thought, as the gin started its thaw of his wind-reddened face and limbs. *A nice enough guy—quiet, gentle, embarrassingly sincere.*

But something was *wrong* about him, something more than his funereal aspect. The man impressed Dan with his loneliness— really an emptiness, left by disappointment or, perhaps, by tragedy. At certain times, Dan would find himself catching at certain phrases or intonations in the man's speech that stirred familiar echoes in the halls of his memory. *There! I do know him. I've heard that voice before...* But, upon looking again at the thin, pale face, Dan knew with uneasy conviction that he could never have known this man.

They finished their drinks, ordered another pair, and Dan relaxed with an inner shrug. So he didn't know the man—he could still enjoy himself, couldn't he? Fine drink, yessir, fine drink. They drank.

EARLY in his fourth martini, Dan suspected he was drunk. He was not disturbed by the realization—rather, surprised and pleased. He contemplated saying to the man, "Say, Blackie, just who the hell are you? What's with the midnight suit?" Or maybe, "Spider." Spider was better than Blackie. "What's the trouble, Spider? Do you need sex or sunshine?" Somebody giggled and Dan recognized his own voice. The giggle soared suddenly into a shrill scale of laughter—then into a violent fit of coughing that left him shaken and tearful, clutching his half-spilled drink.

"'M sorry," he mumbled without looking up. He reached for his napkin and dabbed his eyes and mouth before trusting himself to look up again. The man was looking at him, his half-smile reassuring. Dan opened his mouth to speak, but held his words as he saw the other man's lips move.

"We're having fun, aren't we, Dan?" the man said in a low voice. He raised his martini and Dan joined him, draining his glass. From that point on, things became wretchedly confused for Dan. At one remembered moment, he discovered an empty plate in front of him with no recollection of having eaten. At another, he found himself by the bar, drinking something stinging hot from a small glass. He turned his head slowly—the move seemed to take forever—and found his unknown friend sitting beside him, nodding and smiling his ghostly smile.

Time was acting funny, too. First it would freeze, strangling sound and motion for an eternal, displaced second. Then it would jerk rudely forward, and Dan would find himself anticipating small noises and scraps of conversation in the half-second before they reached his ears. And then, suddenly, they were on the street, the two of them, the younger man weaving dangerously on the curb, his companion dark and silent by the street light.

DAN stood by the curb for several seconds, lost in a bright, anonymous haze of lights and voices. Presently, however, the slicing wind cut through the fog of his drunkenness and he turned, with clearing vision, to see the man in black a few feet behind him.

"'Fraid I got li'l high," Dan said slowly, straightening his back against the wind. "'M awf'l sorry, Mr. Black." Instantly he realized his slip and started to compose an apology, but the man had taken his arm firmly at the elbow and was leading him to the corner.

"'M all right…" Dan mumbled, drawing his arm away with drunken dignity. The next moment, one foot was skidding and he found himself genuflecting in a snow bank. He rose again quickly, brushing himself, and walked the few steps unsteadily to his companion's side.

"...cap at my place."

"What?" Dan screamed into the high wind.

"How about a nightcap at my room?"

As soon as Dan had put the words together in his own mind, he nodded thoughtfully. "'S nice idea."

There was a cab ride, then a long flight of stairs—parts of each Dan could remember. He was surprised, however, to find himself seated in a huge leather chair, in a room he had never seen before—and could only partially see now. The room was silent and Dan leaned forward stupidly, trying to see beyond the silver haze of his drunkenness.

The next moment, he fell sharply back against the cushion, dizzy in a spinning, sickening way. He blinked several times, but his eyes refused to focus. Suddenly, he became conscious of a slow, silent movement beyond the liquid circle of his vision. "Whoosair?" he hooted to the unseen walls and, for an instant, the silence in the room was infinite.

And then, as if a curtain of nightmare had been drawn suddenly aside, the room cleared shockingly to Dan's straining eyes. He saw the man standing before him, his arms raised imperiously in front of his chest, one hand performing a delicate but terrifyingly deliberate circular movement, the other holding a long, silken, formless *something* that became nothing as the walls turned to flashing mirrors. Then Dan was falling backward into a whirling, glowing rush of silence, backward, it seemed, through time itself, into a sudden, splintering whiteness and a final crush of some dark, enraged force that tore the bright fragment of memory from Dan's agonized mind.

HE awoke with a start, then closed his eyes quickly, waiting for the shock of daylight to announce his hangover. When nothing happened, he tilted his head slowly back upon the top of the chair and opened his eyes with great deliberateness. He stared at the ceiling for several seconds, trying to organize his thoughts.

Gradually, they attained form. He jerked forward as the memory of the man in black touched some inner nerve.

The room was empty.

Empty and unused, Dan observed, staring around at the dull brown walls, thick with dust and cobwebs, at the unmade bed.

A moth caught his eye at the window and, as his focus shifted to the street beyond, he saw with great relief the familiar towering clock of a downtown bank. He was only a few blocks from work! And over an hour late. He jumped to his feet.

The next moment he almost fainted.

He stared at his feet, a fist of panic tightening in his stomach. *His shoes were black! His trousers were black!* Not the navy blue of his regular suit—*black.* The rest of his outfit—shirt, tie, socks—he had seen only once before. On the strange man from nowhere.

Dan turned and rushed over to the closet. He found what he half-suspected would be there—two coats, a suit coat and an overcoat. Both black. And without labels.

A quick search in the pockets of the coats produced nothing except—oddly—two twenty-dollar bills. Dan frowned, forcing a swallow past his throat. His theory of robbery was shot. He'd had only eleven dollars when he left the office the night before.

Already, a new theory was beginning to form in his mind, a theory so fantastic and involved that, for a moment, he refused to acknowledge it. Still, it seemed the only explanation for the extraordinary deception. The man in black was in trouble, a marked man—or, perhaps, he was trying to get away from someone. This would account for his evasiveness the night before. He needed a new identity, new papers—driver's license, personal cards, everything. And, of course, different clothes. Why not acquire them all in one easy operation?

Get a fellow drunk and rob him right down to his skin. First, though, learn something about him, lure him into confidence, then get him blind in some dingy hotel room and pull the switch. In New York City no one would know there were two Dan Hickmans walking around. There were big question marks in the theory, to be sure. Why should Mr. X bother to dress his victim after the switch? But then, the guy was a little mad anyway—Dan had sensed instability from his first startled glimpse of the man. The man was sly—but mad.

Dan felt a powerful urge to get out of the room. He stepped quickly to the door and, without looking back, moved into the short, narrow hallway that led to the stairs. He started down the steps, then grasped the rail for balance as a sudden rising vertigo washed coldly through him. It was a strange feeling, like falling into a great swallowing emptiness. He was shaking slightly, as he continued down the stairs and then outside.

ALTHOUGH the sky had lightened considerably, there was still a great deal of snow in the air, hurled by the wind in bold, stinging sweeps. Dan made his way to the corner, heading for the store. Halfway across the street he collided with a small hunched figure and, looking down through the peppering snow, he saw an old woman, gray-faced, incredibly wrinkled. "Keep your head up," he mumbled and pushed on, wondering what in hell an old woman would be doing out in the storm.

He quickened his pace in the next block, anxious to get to the store and describe his misadventure.

Then something happened.

It was too slight to notice at first—a mere flutter in his mind, then a whisper, then a warning, burgeoning suddenly into terror—a spontaneous terror he had never known before. He was seized by something he could not identify, something like the panic of being followed on a dark street.

Instinctively, he looked over his shoulder, seeing nothing, but there was still terror in his mind. He began to run with the speed of desperation at first, finally in agonized breathless pain as he reached the corner near the store. He stopped only a moment, fighting for each burning breath of snow, his head pounding savagely. And then he was running again, not understanding why he ran, knowing only that he had to reach the safety of friends.

He steadied himself against the street window as he reached the store, half-stumbling into the narrow lobby. For a moment, he thought he was going to pass out. His chin dropped down to his chest. He stood a moment longer, resting against the side window. Then he walked to the door and reached for the knob.

The icy sting of the brass against his palm was the only thing that kept him on his feet. As he stared at the horror confronting him on the other side of the glass door, his only conscious impression was the cold burning of his hand.

For there, standing behind his counter, sorting his ties, was himself—the face he saw in the mirror each day—the hair, the ears, the smile, the awkward, slightly stooped posture—and, of course, his clothes. Himself. This, then, was his terror.

Even before he turned to the black mirror siding of the doorway, Dan knew what he was going to see—a hollow face with a long even nose, eyes, black with a timeless, inner rage, skin so white it belonged to the grave. It was all there and, as Dan looked into the lifeless eyes, he knew the secret of the black rage. He was in a body without a soul.

He didn't question the source or certainty of his revelation. This was truth, absolute truth like instinct. He was trapped in a *shell*, an accident of nature—or a product of unspeakable sin—doomed to walk the eternity of an endless day, without hope or redemption.

Dan moved with short steps toward the street, holding his forehead awkwardly as he went, as if the slight, familiar pressure of his fingers might keep the wild claws of his panic from tearing away his mind. What would happen? What did this body *do?* Did it know pain? Or anything else *but* pain? What would the—end—bring?

A THOUGHT came from out of nowhere.

Surely, *love* could conquer the evil of his being! Love and faith. He seized the thought, hope surging in his chest.

But...

Was he *capable* of love and faith—now?

Yes! shouted in his mind. The very fact that he could *think* of love and faith—conceive such a hope—proved him still capable of realizing goodness.

His thought soared. He had to find friends, quickly, someone who would listen to his story and believe him, understand how he had been victimized. Someone who would pledge faith—and help.

The answer came at once—Cooper.

Dan ran into the street, paused a moment, looking about, then hurried to the near corner where a cab stood idling, "DeWitt Airlines," he called to the driver and dropped into the back seat.

Dan leaned back and closed his eyes, fighting to clear his mind for the difficult scene ahead. The next moment, it seemed, the cab had stopped, and he was moving across the sidewalk toward the long, modernistic offices of DeWitt Airlines, where his friend Bill Cooper worked.

His heart throbbing in his throat. Dan pushed open the all-glass doorway and stepped into the ticket office. A number of young women poked solemnly at their typewriters beyond the counter, undisturbed by the large, swinging mobile immediately above them. Dan glanced about the room, stiffening with nervous dread as he saw a tall, blond young man move back from one of the lower files on the far wall.

"Cooper!"

The tall young man swung sharply around, a frown biting his eyes as he caught sight of the figure in front of the counter. His glance shifted to the doorway, then back to the lone figure. Finally, he moved forward with a long stride, his head tilted inquiringly.

"Bill Cooper," Dan said, and suddenly he knew everything, and he wanted to laugh like mad and tell his friend what a hell of a world it was. Instead, he concealed his mirth behind a frown and said, "Bill Cooper—you're a long way from home."

THE END

82

HOUSE...WIFE

By Boyd Ellanby

It was a new and frightening angle to the eternal triangle.

UNTIL that Saturday afternoon in August, Iris was not even uneasy.

She felt only the normal concern of the harassed young housekeeper as she watched the television repairman on his knees with his ear to the cabinet, head cocked, listening. He moved the dial an eighth of an inch to the right, and immediately the flickering waves on the screen solidified into the scene of a ballet. At the foot of dark mountains, feather-capped dancers glided in the patterned figures of *Swan Lake,* and music flowed into the living room.

"But I don't understand it, Eric," said Iris.

She looked at her husband. He was leaning against the mantel by the fireplace, eyes closed, his sullen mouth slowly relaxing into a smile. She was astonished to see how quickly the music was smoothing the petulance from his face, and for the first time she was vaguely alarmed.

THE repairman stood up, flicked off the switch, and thoughtfully dusted his trousers as *Swan Lake* faded and the music died. "I don't see what you folks keep complaining about, Mr. Beauchamp," he said. "This TV set is in perfect condition, and so is the radio."

Eric opened his eyes. "It does seem to be all right. But Mrs. Beauchamp insists that it's been behaving very oddly, and that it frequently picks up the wrong station."

"Well," said Mr. Braun indulgently. "Lots of times I've been called out to adjust things that didn't need it, just because the lady of the house got excited and forgot to punch the right button."

"I was *not* excited," said Iris. "I was perfectly calm, until that thing—"

"Now, now," said Mr. Braun. "Ever have any trouble with it yourself, Mr. Beauchamp?"

"No. When I use it, it always works perfectly. But of course, I only turn it on once in a while in the evening, or maybe over weekends. And even weekends, I'm mostly upstairs at my painting, and I don't pay much attention to the programs."

"That so?" said Mr. Braun, putting his tools back in their case. "Painter, are you?"

"Only on holidays. But I think I may flatter myself that, even so, my work isn't too bad."

Eric had changed, Iris thought. A few months ago he wouldn't have sided against her in an argument with a repairman, and he wouldn't have worn that smug smile in speaking of his work. Once, at least, he had painted honestly; but the pictures he was turning out now were as pretty and as meaningless as the ones you saw on calendars.

But Mr. Braun seemed impressed. "I've always thought I'd like to be a painter myself, if I only had the time. What do you paint?"

"Portraits and figures, mostly."

"Why, Eric," said Iris.

He scowled at her. "What do you mean, 'Why, Eric?' Do you have to object to everything I say? I paint portraits and figures."

"All I meant was, you don't any more. It's been weeks since you asked me to pose for you."

HE ignored her, turning to Mr. Braun. "Well, just recently, as a matter of fact, I've been doing landscapes. They're easier when you don't have many free hours, and the company keeps me pretty busy except for Saturdays and Sundays."

"And when you get started painting, you don't even hear the radio," said Iris. "But I'd like to be able to have it on during the day."

"Can't find a thing wrong with it, TV *or* radio," said the repairman. "Try it for yourself, Mrs. Beauchamp, and let's see how you handle it."

Iris turned the switch. Again the music sounded clearly, and white-gowned dancers emerged to glide on in their graceful routine.

She could feel her face burning.

"I don't know how to explain it, Eric. Something always seems to go wrong. This set is working all right now, but when you're away at the plant and I'm here all alone, I swear sometimes it simply goes crazy—especially when I play the radio by itself. It doesn't play what the papers have scheduled—the stations get mixed up. When I start to dust in the morning, feeling happy and in a mood to sing, I usually look for a station that's offering lively, gay music. But likely as not I get a program consisting of Gregorian chants, or quarter tone stuff that drives me right out of the house. Or if I feel like reading poetry after my work's done in the afternoon, I tune in expecting to hear a Bach organ fugue, for example—and what do I get? A third-rate disc jockey playing a jig or a polka or a waltz so infectious that all I can think of is *one*-two-three, *one*-two-three."

Neither Eric nor Mr. Braun commented, but the way they looked at her made her angry. Twisting away from their skeptical eyes, she was startled by her reflection in the wall mirror. Ordinarily she was a pretty girl, she knew, with gleaming black hair banged straight across her forehead, her gray eyes wide under long lashes, her mouth a full curve. But now her frown seemed to shadow her whole face, to narrow her eyes, turn her skin sallow, and make even her red lips seem thin and uninviting.

SHIVERING, she turned off the set and stared at the men defiantly. "Do you think I'm imagining it?"

Mr. Braun lit a cigarette and looked around uncertainly.

"An ash tray?" said Iris. "Now where...? Just this morning I put one..." Reaching behind the cushion of a chair, she drew out a copper tray and handed it to Mr. Braun. "They're always disappearing," she said. "They do slip off so easily."

Mr. Braun took a meditative puff. He said slowly, "Now look here, Mrs. Beauchamp. This is the third time you've called me out here to adjust the TV combination, and this is the third time it doesn't need a thing. To say nothing of the minor complaints you keep making, like the time the vacuum cleaner wouldn't give you any suction, and it turned out the hose was plugged up. I don't know what the Housing clerk is going to say to me when he finds your name on my time sheet again."

"But things keep getting out of order!"

"Or maybe you're not used to keeping house," Mr. Braun said. "Maybe you'd be happier back at the hotel, where there're lots of people. The company wants its employees to be happy here, and nobody's forcing you to keep house. When they moved the plant out here to Concordton, they knew they'd have a housing problem—that's why they built the hotel, and why they took over all these old houses and went to the trouble of modernizing them. But there still aren't enough houses to go around, and you folks are lucky to have been assigned one so soon."

"That's what we thought," said Iris, "but I never expected a house to give me so much trouble."

Mr. Braun sighed. "For the life of me, I don't see how you can keep finding fault. Of course, this is an old house, but it's a lot better than these cracker boxes they put up nowadays. Take the things in this living room, now. Those old rockers and the sofa and tables have been here since the place was built, and you won't find anything better outside an antique show. You've got an authentic old New England cottage, but fixed up with every modem convenience from indoor plumbing to air conditioning. These old Colonial houses were well made, and they're still sound, as tough as the people that built them. Take this one, for instance..."

HE looked around at the Persian prayer rugs and the red Bokharas scattered over the wide boards of the floor, at the many-paned windows, the red brick fireplace with the dutch ovens at the sides, the pine rafters of the ceiling.

"From looking at her, I'd say she might have been built—oh, say two, maybe three hundred years ago, for the wife of a Boston sea captain, or maybe a whaler. Life wasn't easy in those days, and people thought it was practically a sin to laugh out loud, but they couldn't see any harm in being comfortable when they could afford it. Matter of fact, this house'll probably outlast some of the gadgets that the company put in her. Your furnace work all right?"

"I suppose so," said Iris. "We only moved in at the beginning of the summer."

Her head was aching. She wished the man would stop lecturing, pick up his bag, and go away, and give her a chance to talk things out with Eric.

"Air conditioner reliable?"

She nodded.

"How about the kitchen equipment? Electric stove okay? Oven thermostat set properly?"

"I guess so. But it's hard to get used to the stove. I never claimed to be the world's best cook, but I seem to get worse instead of better. Half the time the meals I turn out aren't even a reasonable facsimile of the ones I was trying to make. The hollandaise sauce gets scorched, or the turkey is underdone."

"Be reasonable," Eric burst out. "You can't blame the stove for that. Listen to what happened just last week, Mr. Braun. I'd particularly asked to have baked beans that night, and I even looked up an old New England recipe for her to use. Well, around dinnertime we smelled smoke. We rushed to the kitchen and dragged the bean pot out of the oven, but it was too late. They were a smoking mess, burned to a crisp, and there was nothing to be done with them but dump them in the disposal. And why? She said the thermostat was wacky. I say she forgot to keep adding water. Result, no dinner. Then *I* took over, and I produced a cheese soufflé that was straight out of Escoffier. And she blames the oven!"

"THAT'S not the only thing," said Iris. "Even you will have to admit that the dishwasher breaks a good many dishes. I hardly dare use my good china any more, and my wedding silver is badly scratched."

"Any dishwasher'll break a few dishes now and then unless you use plastic," said Mr. Braun. "Doesn't mean a thing. You just have to be careful how you stack them. Any other complaints before I leave?"

Iris rubbed her forehead, frowning. "There *was* something else... Help me remember, Eric. What else was it needed fixing?"

"Nothing. I don't think we should waste any more of Mr. Braun's time."

"If you can't think of it, it can't be too important," said Mr. Braun. "Now, I don't want to be too rough on you, ma'am. Lots of women get nervous, lonesome-like, being away from the city for the first time—but they just have to get used to living in a village. You haven't been here very long, have you?"

Iris's lips were quivering so that she did not dare answer. She shook her head, feeling thoroughly browbeaten.

"Only a few months," said Eric. "I joined the company in June, right after I got my doctorate."

"Then you're lucky to have this place at all, being newcomers. Why, some people have to wait more than a year before the Housing bureau can locate them. And yet you complain about your radio and everything else."

He moved toward the door. "Well, Mrs. Beauchamp, I hate to say this, but I'll tell you frankly—I'm not coming out here again. If you can't learn to adapt yourself, the best thing for you to do is move back to the hotel, because Housing has a waiting list a mile long of people who'd jump at the chance to have your place. You want to cancel your lease?"

"Yes. Oh, Eric, let's move out."

"Move? I should say not." His eyes were angrier than she had ever seen them. "In the four years we've been married, we've lived in one cramped little shoebox after another, with no privacy and hardly room to swing a cat. I'm sick of it. This is the most comfortable place we've ever had. It suits me fine. We're staying."

"That's the spirit, Mr. Beauchamp," said the repairman. "It doesn't pay to coddle nerves. Well, I'll be going now, and let you get back to that painting. Got a fine view of the woods from here. Maybe some Sunday I'll come out and have a try at it myself."

WHEN the door had closed, Iris sat down, too disturbed to think clearly. Waiting for Eric to speak, she watched him stride about the room, looking at anything rather than her.

The late afternoon sun coming through the window turned his yellow hair to gold, and highlighted the planes of his face to the rugged nobility of a bronze hero, as he prowled from the fireplace to the TV cabinet, back to the fireplace, and over again to the window whose starched white curtains, neatly belled at the sides, gave an odd air of primness to such a pretty room. As he stared through the window at the pine woods beyond, his fingers drummed against the glass to evoke a drone like the purr of a stroked cat.

"Look here, Iris," he said abruptly. "Do you know what's the matter with you?"

"No. Do you?"

"Yes, I do. You won't like to admit it, but here's the truth— you're jealous."

"Jealous? Of whom?"

"Of me! You're jealous simply because it was me who found this house, and not you. That's why you keep finding fault with it—because your silly pride is hurt. Well, you'll have to get over it, that's all. We're more comfortable here than we've ever been in our lives, except when you spoil it all with your complaining, and I'm not going to give it up just to please you. You tried to find a house for us, and couldn't. Then I went house hunting, and here it was, waiting like a ripe cherry, ready to fall into my hands. So you turn into a jealous female, and I must say it doesn't make you any more attractive."

Iris was too stunned to reply. She lit a cigarette, but it tasted stale. Snuffing it out, she dropped her hands to her lap.

"And now I'm going to try to get a little painting done," said Eric. "You've already made me waste half the afternoon on this business. Some wives would show a little consideration for their husbands."

AFTER the door slammed, Iris sat on alone, trying to understand what was happening.

Until lately, Eric had been as affectionate a husband as a girl could want: light-hearted, amiable, full of jokes. He even had a pet name for her—"my little pigeon," he used to call her. Now, her very presence seemed to irritate him.

Was Eric right? she wondered. Was it jealousy that made her dislike the house? No, that was ridiculous, it was something else, something she could not quite recognize.

The sun moved lower in the sky; the beam of light that had made the room seem snug shifted from the window, and the air was colder.

She considered the room she sat in, and reluctantly admitted the truth. It made her feel ill at ease, as though she were an uninvited guest in a stranger's house. She had never liked the way the furniture stood, of course, but she had never been able to rearrange it in a way that seemed pleasing. The stiff white curtains, too, seemed to drain the life from the room; but though she had twice replaced them with brightly colored draperies, they had all faded so quickly that in the end she had been forced to go back to white.

But it was not the furniture alone that made her feel unwelcome.

She had never heard the house so still. As the minutes crept by, the silence became so inimical that she wanted to scream, just to hear a recognizable noise.

Perhaps if she could get *Swan Lake* again...

She sat up suddenly. The radio! Staring at the mute cabinet, she stood up, crept forward on tiptoe, and paused before the dial. Tentatively, she raised her hand, hesitated, then quickly turned the switch.

A wail of disharmony shrieked into the room, battering at her mind with the implacable force of a wild northeaster. She clapped her hands to her ears, but the sound blasted against her skin like cold sharp sleet driven by a furious wind. Gasping, she flicked off the set. The silence terrified her. She whirled toward the door and stumbled out of the room, out of the house, and into the garden where she sank down under the maple tree, with her back to the house.

So Mr. Braun insisted that everything was all right? And Eric thought her a jealous, neurotic, fool of a woman?

She was beginning to understand. Until this afternoon she had been an ordinary, conventional young housewife, secure in a commonplace world. But now, as her mind checked back over the past few weeks and assembled data and arranged patterns, she watched her world shift and reform into a monstrous shape that was—reality.

Feeling dizzy, she rested her head on her knees.

So Eric had found the house waiting for them, like a ripe cherry? No—it had not been waiting for Mr. and Mrs. Beauchamp. It had not counted on Iris at all. It had seen Eric and wanted him, but Mrs. Beauchamp had been a surprise. And now it meant to drive her out.

She remembered the day he had found the place, nearly three months ago.

IRIS had been asleep in their room at the company hotel, exhausted by days of futile house hunting, when Eric clattered in triumphantly:

"Wake up, Iris! I've found us a house!"

"Then you must be a magician," she said drowsily. "What charm did you use, darling?"

"Nothing but my bright blue eyes."

"Tell me."

He had been strolling through the quaint, old-fashioned streets of Concordton, he said, admiring the trim houses behind their neat white fences. He'd got close to the edge of town, where the woods began, and was turning to go back when he noticed the house. The moment he saw it, with the afternoon sun winking from its windows, he had known it was exactly what they wanted. He had hardly dared believe his luck when he found the sign, half hidden by the bushes at the gate: TO LET, TO RIGHT PARTY.

The house stood apart from its neighbors, a prim little two-and-a-half story white cottage, set in a garden ornamented with pink roses and bleeding-hearts, and rows of pink hollyhocks bordering the path to the door.

The gate in the picket fence opened at his touch, and he had walked into the garden and around the house. Green shutters bracketed the windows, through which he could glimpse the starched curtains, the cushioned rocking chairs, the stone hearth before the fireplace. The second floor was many-windowed, and in the sloping roof of the attic there was even a skylight to make it ideal for his painting.

He had rushed back to the company's Housing bureau, afraid to risk delaying even the extra hour it would have taken to go back for Iris and get her approval.

Now, chuckling, he repeated to Iris his conversation with the skeptical Housing clerk:

"'You again, Mr. Beauchamp?   We haven't a thing for you...*Where* did you say this house is?...But I'm absolutely positive there isn't...But it's not on our list...Very well, we'll check with our master file if you insist, but I tell you again...H'm...Well, now, *that's* odd...'

"'Then it is for rent?'

"'Apparently it is, though how it was overlooked when this list was compiled is more than...   Why, if you hadn't called our attention to it the place might have sat there empty for goodness knows how many years.'

"'You mean I can have it?'

"'I hardly know what to say, Mr. Beauchamp.   Your name's near the bottom of our waiting list, of course—but since you found it by your own initiative...'

"And that was that," Eric concluded.   "Want to see the lease?"

She was glowing.   "Eric, you're wonderful.   When can we move in?   It sounds perfect, with a garden, and all the north woods for our backyard.   Wait a minute.   *Where* did you say this place is?"

"You sound just like that clerk," said Eric.   "I told you.   On Maple Lane."

"It can't be.   I canvassed that street myself, two days ago—there wasn't a single vacancy sign."

He grinned at her, smugly: "You just overlooked it, my little pigeon.   Obviously, it needed a man."

And so it had, Iris thought...but you put it the wrong way around, Eric.   You didn't find the house.   It—*she*—found you!

IT was nearly dark when she stood up and brushed her skirt. Slowly, she walked up the path to the front door, turned the knob, and entered the living room.   The reflection of her face in the mirror was a shadowed distortion; she ignored it and sat down in the gathering dusk, still thinking.

Above, she heard the door of Eric's studio open, heard him on the stairs, and then in the library next to the living room.

The house was her enemy.   And the house was not neuter.   The house was a woman who meant to take Eric and to evict his wife.

Iris tried to picture her: a middle-aged, tight-lipped pioneer housewife, who had tried to deny her body's curves by hiding them in boned corsets. A woman afraid of passion—she had allowed herself pink roses in her garden, but there were no red ones. An avid woman who made her house an embrace, and evaded self-reproach by curtaining her windows in starched, uncompromising white. She must be a widow; perhaps the widow of a sea captain, alone for months at a time, and then left alone forever, still unsatisfied, with nothing but her house. A woman unyielding in her virtue, but tormented by an urge to—to mother attractive young men?

The room was quite dark. Iris straightened her shoulders and switched on the reading lamp. Now that she realized what threatened her, she thought, it ought not be difficult to fight back—and to win. The house was a formidable personality, but what was a thing of wood and stone against a live, warm woman?

First, she must decide how to defend herself.

There was no use appealing to Eric, the house had made that impossible. With sly female subtlety, it had contrived by tampering with the radio, the oven thermostat, the dishwasher, to discredit Iris completely. No, she could not confide in Eric.

But she could try to re-establish an atmosphere of friendliness. Eric spoke so often of the comfort of the house. Well, she would make him comfortable herself, in ways she had been neglecting. Tonight, she would bring him his slippers, and light his cigarette, and...

No, she hadn't realized it before, but it had been weeks since he had smoked.

Well, she would offer him a drink, then, and she would stop complaining. As for the radio, she would not use it. As for the kitchen, she would not use the oven, and she would use plastic dishes.

And most important of all, she must be alert to counter the tricks of the house, and not let herself be maneuvered into a situation that would show her to disadvantage.

Iris smiled. She was no longer the unwary wife, she assured herself: She had been warned.

HEARING Eric in the next room, she felt safe from attack for the moment, knowing that the house was always on its best behavior when he was there to notice. Almost as a deliberate challenge, she walked to the cabinet and dialed her favorite station, smiling as the radio docilely began to play the Brahms-Handel variations, exactly as the paper had listed.

When Eric came into the room, she was relieved to see that he was no longer angry.

"Nice music," he remarked. "Have you started dinner yet?"

"Not yet. It won't take me ten minutes. Why don't we relax a while first? Let's have a drink before dinner, the way we used to."

"If you want one," said Eric.

"Will you fix them? I'll have a Martini, as usual."

She followed him into the kitchen and waited as he opened the freezing compartment of the refrigerator.

"Damn," said Eric.

"What's the matter?"

"No ice. You've been defrosting again."

"But I' haven't. I defrosted on Wednesday."

"You can see for yourself, Iris, there's no ice."

The trays were full of water; the whole icebox was at room temperature.

Then she remembered: "Oh, Eric! That's what—"

He interrupted angrily. "Every time I want some ice, it turns out there isn't any because you've been defrosting. The same thing happened nearly a month ago, when I tried to fix a drink. I notice there's always ice when you want iced tea, and the refrigeration is perfect when you want ice cream—but when *I* want ice, the cubes are *always* melted. You'd almost think it was done on purpose."

"It was not," she flared. "You know very well that crazy icebox does it all by itself. Remember this afternoon, when Mr. Braun asked if there was anything else that needed fixing? It was the refrigerator I was trying to remember to tell him about."

"Then why didn't you tell him? What made you forget?"

Stalking back to the living room, he slipped off his sandals and propped his feet onto a cushion. She followed angrily.

"You're getting to be a careless housekeeper, Iris. You admit that the defroster has been erratic ever since we've been here, and yet you've done nothing about it. You'd think that in more than two months time, with nothing to do but take care of a house that practically runs itself, you could at least get the icebox fixed."

He settled lower in his chair, yawning.

IRIS tried to keep calm. "I'm sorry Eric. Couldn't we do without ice for once? Bourbon and branch water isn't bad."

"You mean you still want a drink?"

"Of course I do."

"Then why can't you take the trouble to get the refrigerator repaired?"

"I *will* get it repaired—but I can't do it tonight. What's the matter with you, Eric? I'd never have believed the day would come when I'd have to coax you into being my drinking partner..."

"Nagging again," he said.

Iris was alarmed. She had not meant to quarrel. Placatingly, she put her hand on his. "Sorry, Eric. I'd forgotten how tired you must be, after several hours of work. You sit here and take it easy, and I'll fix us some Bourbon."

Shaking his head sulkily, he shuffled his feet back into his sandals. "No, you asked for Martinis, and that's what you're going to get."

"Then I'll come along to keep you company."

Following him into the kitchen, she perched gaily on the table, swinging the shapely legs he had always admired, hoping he would notice them again; but he was intent only on mixing the drinks.

Methodically he assembled the ingredients: glasses, bottles, bitters, shaker, olives, ranged in a neat row on the shelf. Holding the jigger up to eye level, he squinted as he poured. The jigger filled to the brim, suddenly overflowed, and splashed from Iris's swinging legs onto the floor.

"Damn," said Eric.

"Your technique seems to be showing," she said, mopping at her legs.

"You'd make anybody nervous, watching like that."

Without comment, she got out the mop and dried the floor.

Doggedly, he emptied the jigger into the sink, rinsed it, dried it, gripped the bottle tightly, and began to pour again.

Crash! The bottle slipped from his hands, bounced against the sink and smashed on the floor, the shattered glass glimmering in a spreading lake of gin.

Staring down at the wet pieces, Eric looked as astonished as a small boy who has been slapped without warning for a crime he did not commit.

SHE tried not to laugh as she got out the broom and dustpan. "Don't look so upset, Eric. Your hand must have been wet. Get another bottle and stop worrying."

Bringing out a second bottle, he uncapped it and poured. His hands were trembling so that she was scarcely surprised when it, too, crashed to the floor.

"I didn't want a drink anyway," he shouted. "A drink's no good without ice! If you want one, fix it yourself."

"There's one more bottle," she said. "I'll try."

This time, the bottle behaved normally. She ignored his resentful expression as she performed the rite, arranged the tray, and carried it into the living room. There she softened the lights, tuned in a program of Strauss waltzes, and sat down beside him to sip her drink.

Eric was right, she mused. This was a comfortable house, if it could just be kept in its place. And that should be a simple matter. It was only a question of who was to be mistress; that was all. Silly of her to have been so frightened this afternoon.

Absently, she held out her glass for a refill, lulled by the sentimentality of the music, not noticing Eric's silence.

"I'm ready for another," she said dreamily. "Will you...Why, Eric... You haven't touched your drink."

"No. I'm not going to."

"But why not?"

"I told you in the first place I didn't want one."

"But I didn't think you were serious."

"You didn't care whether I was serious or not. I come down after an afternoon's hard work, tired and hungry, and you insist on carousing. Have you even started dinner yet?"

"It's all cooked. It can be heated in ten minutes time, and the salad is all ready for the dressing. Is there any rush? You always used to enjoy the cocktail hour so much, I didn't think you'd mind delaying a while. I didn't realize you were *that* hungry."

His eyes were accusing, his voice bitter: "I don't ask much of my wife, Iris. I'm not an unreasonable man, I hope. This house has so many conveniences that you have very little to do. But you neglect even that little. Apparently you think more of your liquor than you do of your husband. Is it too much for a man to ask his wife to keep sober enough to remember to cook his dinner?"

The lilting melody of One Heart, One Mind galloped derisively through the room, nudging her mind with treacherous sweetness, taunting her, as Iris studied her husband's grim face. She tried to control herself, but the mocking waltz unnerved her.

"You've changed, my dear," she said tautly. "That wasn't a nice thing to say, even as a joke."

"I'm not joking. I'm just stating an obvious fact. And apparently I must remind you that I'm still hungry."

Deliberately, she reached across him for the shaker.

"Fix your own dinner," she heard herself saying, hardly believing what she heard. "Get your own dinner. *I'm* going to get drunk."

IRIS was alone in the bed. She turned her head to avoid the light of the morning sun stabbing through the window, and winced with the pain. Eyes closed, she tried to remember. Last night...the drinks...the waltz...the fight...

You've won another round, she thought drearily. *You, you— unscrupulous antediluvian predator!*

It had seemed a wonderful idea to show Eric that his wife wanted to make him comfortable; but she seemed to have emerged from the demonstration cast in the role of a dipsomaniac, a sore trial to a water-drinking husband. That was especially odd, for Eric had always been a more enthusiastic tippler than she...

Sudden illumination made her sit up.

So *that* was the answer!

Quickly, she ran over the data: the refrigerator that would let you have ice for tea or ice cream, but which defrosted itself when asked to provide ice for cocktails or highballs; her inability to remember to mention it to Mr. Braun on his frequent visits; the smashed gin bottles; Eric's self-righteous refusal of his drink.

Of course!

This was an early New England home.

The house was a teetotaler.

It approved of comfort, of a sort. Witness the cheerful living room, the flowers in the garden. But it was a Puritan. Witness the vanishing ashtrays, the quick fading of the colored draperies, the way the dishwasher broke her pretty frivolous dishes.

Decent comfort, decreed the house, but no self-indulgence. No tobacco. No liquor.

The house wasn't content with taking Eric away from her—it intended to reform him as well. It would take care of him; but it was a prudish house, and would not permit him any pleasures it considered immoral.

Iris thought nostalgically of the gay young man she had married, his sprightliness, his easy tolerance of human frailty; and then forced herself to envisage the complacent, strait-laced posturer he was becoming. She shuddered.

You may get him yet, she thought grimly. *But not without a fight, ma'am. Not without a fight.*

Jumping out of bed, she hastily put on some lipstick, threw on her robe, ran down the stairs...and stopped in the doorway.

The morning sun sparkled through the window onto the breakfast table where Eric sat, stirring his coffee, munching toast. His yellow hair was gold in the sunlight, his blue eyes wide with abstraction, the rugged features of his face were smoothly peaceful.

He didn't even miss her, she thought. He looked utterly contented with the companionship of the cozy breakfast nook, the blue morning glories of the window curtains, the winking silver of the coffeepot.

THE clatter of her mules as she walked to the table shattered the peace of the room.

He put down his spoon, frowning. "You're late, Iris."

"I know. I'm sorry." She sat down.

He eyed her critically. "Your hair's not combed."

"I know, darling. I was in such a hurry to get down to you and tell you I'm sorry about last night."

"And your robe isn't properly fastened. The collar's all wrinkled, and your skin shows through."

"Does it?" She smiled placatingly and held out her cup. "You know what you look like? You look exactly like a freshly scrubbed, mischievous cherub of a boy—the kind old ladies smile at in the streets, and want to pat on the head. I'm sorry I made you cross by sleeping so late, but I didn't think it mattered on a Sunday. Why didn't you call me?"

"I did call you," he said, reaching for the coffeepot. "I called you three times, but you pretended not to hear me."

"Pretended? But I didn't hear you. You know, Eric...this makes several times now that you've called to me and I haven't heard you. Do you think maybe there's something wrong with the acoustics of this place?"

"Always complaining about the house. Always finding fault with it one way or another." Petulantly, he tilted the pot over her extended cup.

The amber stream struck the rim, and at the automatic jerk of his hand, hot coffee splashed over the table and onto Iris.

She jumped up, trying to laugh. "Are you trying to scald me to death? Just look at my robe..."

"That's right, blame everybody but yourself," he said, slamming down the pot. "Blame the acoustics because you're sound asleep, blame me because you've got such a hangover you can't hold your cup steady. You wobble it all over the table and then complain because I can't follow it around with a pot of hot coffee. I never liked that robe anyway."

Tears filled her eyes as she stared at him, open-mouthed. "Why Eric. This is your favorite robe. Remember, when we were in Paris on our honeymoon, how you used to tell me I looked just like a red rose in it, and I should always have one just like it?"

"Then I must have been crazy."

"What's wrong with it?"

"It's too bright. Somehow, in this light, it's sleazy and flashy, cheap looking."

Iris fingered the stained robe, her mouth quivering. With sudden fury she tore it open, ripped it off her body, flung it to the floor.

"I'll never wear it again, then. I'll never wear it again!"

HE looked away, fidgeting. "That suits me fine—but you might at least put on something to cover yourself. You can't stay here like this without a stitch on except that gaudy lipstick."

"Why not?"

"Well…it's indecent."

"Eric Beau—" she began, then stopped.

She looked down at herself, at the rosy curves of the slender body he had always admired so much. Never before had she felt naked and embarrassed in his presence. Frantically, she looked for something to cover her. The curtains. Running to the window, she ripped the flowered cloth from the rods, wrapped it around herself, and returned miserably to the table.

The house is cleverer than I am, she thought despondently. *I've lost another round. Last night I was exhibited to my husband in the role of a dipsomaniac. This morning I seem to be cast as a bawd. But how did a Puritan widow of strict moral principles ever learn to fight so shrewdly? How can I fight back? Am I going to be thrown out in spite of anything I can do? Is that sanctimonious old vixen going to steal my husband completely, and turn him into a nasty-minded, puritanical, comfort-loving prig?*

What can I do about it?

There was always the hotel, of course, or she could go home to her parents. But without Eric?

She could not bear the thought. She began to cry, silently, deeply, tears rushing into her eyes and throat, choking her so that she could not even swallow the fresh coffee he had poured for her.

Presently she felt his hand on her shoulder. "I'm sorry, Iris. I didn't mean to hurt you. Let's be friends again."

She could only sob as he bent to touch her forehead.

"I didn't mean to make you feel bad," he said again. "Let's do something together. I'll tell you what—you haven't posed for me in a long while. Will you? The way you used to?"

"Are you serious?" she whispered incredulously.

"Yes, I'm serious. I don't know what gets into me, sometimes. But let's forget it now, and I'll get some painting done."

"But what about your landscape?"

"Not today," he said, grinning. "Today I'll do me a nude."

THE day went so well that Iris could hardly believe it was not a dream. Reclining on the couch in the big room under the skylight, her flesh round and rosy against the rich yellow brocade he had draped as a background, she made herself be unobtrusive as Eric set to work.

He whistled as he put canvas on easel and squeezed color from tubes onto palette. Eyeing her thoughtfully, he arranged her pose, smiled when she got it just right, and then began blocking in the areas of dark and light on the canvas.

"Comfortable?" he said once.

"Mmmmm."

"My favorite model. Can't think why I've neglected her for so long."

Is it going to be as easy as this? thought Iris. What had happened? This morning she had been practically beaten. All her attempts to neutralize the blandishments of the house had boomeranged...until an hour ago. And what had happened then? She had only begun to cry. And Eric had been concerned about her feelings for the first time in weeks. Did this mean that to conquer the woman that was the house, she had only to act—and be—the woman she herself was? Was that all?

The day passed in friendliness. Eric was obviously pleased with his painting as he set it aside to be resumed the following weekend, and before they left the room he took the innocuous "View of the Pines" of the day before and carelessly turned it to the wall.

There were no unpleasant incidents all that week, not even when Eric was away at work and she was alone in the house. She was still wary, however, and did not risk her luck too far. She stored her frivolous china dishes on the top shelf of the cupboard and replaced them with plain blue plastic, she planned meals that did not require the oven, and she took care never to turn on the radio or TV unless Eric was in the room. Dutifully she brushed her hair each morning before going down to breakfast, and even in the privacy of their bedroom she kept her body hidden in a dark blue long-sleeved robe whose neckline was decorously high.

It was a calm week, without a single quarrel, and she shut her eyes to the knowledge that it was rather dull. Without further discussion, both Beauchamps were now non-smokers and non-drinkers. Conversation at table was genteel, if not animated. Each evening they sat sedately in the living room and read until half-past nine, at which time Eric yawned, turned out the lights, and led the way to bed. As the week came to a close without aggressive action from any part of the house, Iris was elated, for she had thought of a plan—a plan to rescue Eric.

SUNDAY was another agreeable morning. They had toast and one cup of coffee each (more than one, Eric had announced recently, was bad for the health), and after breakfast they went up to the studio.

Modestly, Iris kept her robe on until the moment he was ready for her to pose, then resumed her position against the yellow brocade. It was difficult for her to keep her breath coming slowly and evenly, she was so excited. Eric had been so amiable all week, and the house so subdued that she felt quite certain of success. She wondered if her act of vandalism in tearing down the breakfast nook curtains had frightened the house into better behavior, for since that incident there had been no overt act. One of those women, she thought contemptuously, who valued her material possessions above any possible emotional consideration.

And Eric seemed to be content. Rather ponderous, even stodgy, but content. If he was not exactly affectionate, at least he no longer looked at her as though he despised her.

"Eric?" she began.

"Hmmm?"

"Is it all right for me to talk?"

"Talk away."

"All right, but if I distract you, let me know. I was wondering—Labor Day weekend is coming up soon. Have you made any plans for the holiday?"

"Nothing in particular. Though I might try to finish up my 'View of the Pine Woods,' if I can get your portrait finished by then."

Her heart skipped a beat. Landscapes again? She'd hoped they were through with those pretty, sterile pictures he'd been turning out.

She hid her dismay, and tried to keep her voice casual. "I thought you might enjoy a change of scene."

"Yes? Turn your head just half an inch. That's it."

"Yes. We've seen nothing but this village all summer, and I thought it would be nice to run up to Quebec for the weekend. They say it's still like a glimpse of Old France."

"Sounds possible."

"Well...shall we plan on it? I mean, I'll have packing, and so on. Can we?"

She held her breath as he slowly nodded his head.

"Promise?"

"You've gone all tense, Iris. Relax, or I won't get this line just right."

"Promise?" she begged again.

"Promise what?"

"That next weekend we'll go to Quebec for our holiday. No matter what happens, you solemnly promise that we'll go."

"Oh, all right," he said. "I promise." He threw down his brush, then. "And now let's break for a while. I'm tired."

Eric settled himself on the nearest chair.

AFTER that, nothing went quite right.

Eric suggested fish chowder for lunch. Iris searched the pantry shelves twice, and could not find the cans of fish chowder she could have sworn were there. Hoping he would not notice the difference, she got down her good china and served clam chowder instead. Once he wouldn't have cared—he would have grinned and remarked that after all chowder was chowder no matter how you sliced it, but now, he pushed his bowl aside, unfinished. The salad had been bruised too much, he pointed out; and he swore when he bit on a cherry pit in the ice cream.

Even then, Iris did not feel seriously alarmed...such things might happen in any household.

Eric shoved his saucer away and stood up. "It's getting late. I don't know how you manage to spend so much time preparing such an unsatisfactory lunch."

Hastily, she began to clear the table.

"And even the breakfast dishes aren't done," he observed. "If I don't want to waste the whole afternoon, I suppose I'll have to help you."

As he rinsed the dishes, she stacked them in the washer—plates, saucers, bowls, cutlery, cups, and glasses. She put in the detergent, closed the lid, and turned the switch.

Pandemonium broke loose. The water rushed in with a roar, the lid vibrated, the dishes rattled, the silverware banged, and crash followed crash.

"Call Mr. Braun," shouted Eric. "The damned thing's gone crazy."

Dazedly, she switched off the machine, and they surveyed the wreckage. Only the plastic dishes and the silverware were still intact. Every piece of glass and china was in fragments.

Iris felt cold. The lull was over. The house was attacking again. She must not let it wreck her plans.

"There's nothing to get so excited about," she told Eric laughingly. "You wouldn't want to bother Mr. Braun on a Sunday, when all that happened was that I stacked the dishes carelessly?"

Eric subsided, but Iris was very thoughtful as she cleaned up the pieces.

Back in the studio, the light had changed. Eric fussed over her pose for fully half an hour, and when he did begin to paint, he worked in silence, growing more and more tense.

"Damn," he said at last.

"What's wrong?"

"Take a break. Come and see for yourself."

He had been working on the yellow brocade, and had somehow smudged the yellow into the pink of the thigh.

"Don't worry," she said, returning to her place. "You can fix that easily."

"It only gets worse," he muttered. "It looks like hell. Well, I'll let it go and work on the face."

GLOWERING, he dabbed on pinheads of color, scraped them off, put on others, jabbed at the canvas with nervous, jerky strokes.

"Why can't you lie still?" he shouted finally. "How can a man paint when you keep fidgeting and shifting the shadows?"

Suddenly he dipped his brush into the Prussian blue, and slashed a giant X of paint across the figure. He slammed the palette to the floor and turned on her:

"No wonder a man takes to landscapes when he has to work with a model like you! You don't know even the rudiments of modeling—you fidget, you move, you jabber like a schoolgirl, and you haven't even got a decent figure to begin with. Look at it!"

Timidly she crept over to look at the canvas.

Staring out at her was a scrawny, raddled nude, one leg a sickly orange, the rest of the body a dirty pink against the gold of the drapery. Lank black hair clung to the face in strings, the mouth sagged at the corners, the chin slumped into the neck, and the eyes were those of a drunken old prostitute.

Iris backed away, shivering. "What have you done to me?" she whispered. Drawing her robe tightly around her to cover her shame, she huddled in the corner.

"Nudes," Eric cried. "I'll never paint another nude as long as I live. After this, I stick to landscapes."

Iris heard a woman sigh...herself, she wondered? For the first time she realized how terrible a revenge the house could take. A little matter of color values, of shadow and highlight, and it had turned her portrait into that—obscenity.

She felt sick. She had no real hope now of keeping Eric, but she clung fast to the only chance that remained to her.

"You won't let this make any difference, will you?" she whispered.

"Difference to what?"

"Your promise. That we could go away next weekend."

"I don't want a holiday. I want to stay home and paint."

"I know," she pleaded. "But you did promise. You said we'd go."

"You mean you're going to hold me to it?"

She nodded.

The contempt in his eyes was searing, but she would not look away until he answered.

"All right," he said at last. "I'll keep my promise. But I'll never forgive you for making me."

IN the week that followed, she kept out of his way as much as possible, anxious not to irritate him, terrified of angering the house. She gave up wearing lipstick and rouge; she slicked her hair back behind her ears; she wore her plainest dresses. She cooked Eric's favorite dishes, with great care, and when she walked through the living room she avoided even looking at the radio sitting there, voiceless. She spent hours in the haven of the garden, staring at the demure complacency of the house, fearing it, hugging her hope of defeating it.

She lived only for Saturday, the day they would leave the house for their trip to Quebec. Eric might be angry with her, he might refuse to speak to her, he might even despise her; but still she would rescue him from the wizening, stunting, crippling embrace of the house. Soon, she thought, it will be Saturday, and then— we'll never come back. Once he gets away, he'll change back to himself, and we'll never have to come back.

Quietly, almost furtively, she packed their clothes, and by Friday noon there was nothing left to do. All afternoon she sat in the garden, waiting apprehensively for Eric to come home. Only when he arrived did she have the courage to enter the shadowed living room.

"I'm tired," he said, slumping into his chair. "Dead tired."

She was shocked by the exhaustion in his face. His skin was drawn, his eyes were ringed with black, his voice high and unsteady. She realized guiltily that she had been too much absorbed in her own fears to give any thought to his feelings.

"You're probably hungry," she said. "Are you ready for dinner?"

"Let me rest a while first." Sighing, he dragged himself to his feet. "I'll go up and change clothes, and put on my slippers."

Huddled in her chair, she heard him clump up the stairs to the bedroom, then the noise of his shoes dropping.

"Get me some music, Iris," he called down. "Something to take this ache out of my bones."

She hated to approach the radio. It took all her nerve and all her determination to put her hand on the switch.

But Eric's here, she thought. It won't hurt me when Eric's here. It doesn't dare.

Still she hesitated, hand raised. She heard him at the head of the stairs, starting down.

"Didn't you hear me?" he shouted. "Music!"

Reluctantly, she forced herself to turn the knob.

A cacophonous wail, a frenzy of maniacal frequencies shrieked into the air. From the stairway came a cry of terror, a crash, a series of thuds. Iris silenced the machine and rushed to the door.

Eric lay at the foot of the stairs, his forehead covered with sweat, his face distorted.

"Damn music made me trip," he groaned. "I think I broke my leg."

THE house had beaten her at last.

Eric lay tranquilly in the guestroom bed, his leg pegged and braced, his hands idle, his conscience obviously clear. He *would* have kept his promise to go away for the holiday...but now, of course, it was impossible. He had broken his leg.

Like an automaton, Iris took care of him. She had no more fight left in her. Her only problem was to decide how soon she dared leave him and go back to her parents. The house gave her no trouble; even the oven behaved itself; but Iris hated every hour she stayed. She had no right there. She was the other woman. Physically, perhaps, Eric was still hers; but emotionally he now belonged to the house. She would leave just as soon as Eric was able to get about on crutches.

One morning he took his first hobbling steps, then collapsed into bed, trembling with the effort. This was the sign she had been waiting for, and after he was asleep she retired to her room and began to pack the pretty clothes she no longer wore, her jewelry, the rose red robe that she had had cleaned and never worn again.

That night, as she sat by his bed and watched him eat a fluffy yellow and white piece of lemon meringue pie, she told Eric.

He put down his fork, pushed away the tray, and fell back against his pillow.

"You mean you're going to leave me? But *why?*"

"You know why, Eric. This house and I—we don't get along. And you won't move away."

"No," he said slowly. "I can't do that. I like it here. I feel that, in a way, I belong here. But what will I do without you?"

When she did not answer, he turned his face to the wall.

His breakfast tray, next morning, returned to the kitchen scarcely lighter than when it went up. The golden brown rolls at lunchtime were ignored, and the lobster soufflé at dinner went back to the kitchen, a flabby, dispirited-looking mound.

Iris exerted herself to prepare the most delectable dishes she could think of, and the stove cooperated perfectly, but he was never hungry. He lost weight visibly from one day to the next; his skin grew pale and translucent. Lying on the bed, or crutching feebly to the window, he looked like a man who had been ill for months.

I can't help it, Iris reminded herself as she locked her trunk the afternoon of the day she planned to leave. *He's not my responsibility any longer. I'm too tired to struggle any more. The house has got him, and it's up to the house to make him eat, or let him die. Anybody cruel enough to break a man's leg in order to keep him probably wouldn't hesitate to starve him to death rather than give him up. But it's not my problem any longer.*

SHE was locking her jewel case when the front doorbell rang.

She went down to admit Mr. Braun, the repairman, who waited with his bag under his arm.

"Heard about your husband's accident, Mrs. Beauchamp. That's why I haven't been around sooner."

"What do you mean?" said Iris.

"Didn't think you'd want me underfoot the first few days after he'd just broke his leg, so I thought I'd wait a while longer for that repair job."

"I still don't understand, Mr. Braun...I didn't call you."

"I know you didn't, ma'am, but your husband reported a couple of weeks ago that the dishwasher was acting up. Something about the way he described it made me think I'd better check up on things again. Sometimes the equipment in these old houses does act temperamental. If you don't mind, I'll just have a look at the circuit box."

She followed him into the cellar, where he opened the box and inspected the array of controls, then jiggled a tester in his hand, speculatively.

"How's the TV set behaving these days?"

"I never play it any more."

"I heard it was going the night he broke his leg?"

"Yes...it was. He asked me to turn it on."

"Everything normal?"

"Now, look here, Mr. Braun," she said wearily. "What do you expect me to say? You know you don't consider me a reliable witness. Anyway, it's not my affair any more. I'm going home."

He peered into the box, shaking his head. "Can't take it? Well, some people can't. You never know. Well, now, this is funny..."

"What's funny?"

"This refrigerator control. Bet a nickel you've been having trouble with it, and yet you've never said a word about it."

"No. I never could remember. It defrosts itself every now and then, usually just when we want some ice."

"Shouldn't be surprised," he said, clicking his tongue. "The way these controls are set isn't at all what I like to see. Too much latitude. I'd better fix it."

"It doesn't matter now...my husband doesn't drink any more, and as I told you, I'm going away."

"Fix it anyway," he said, inserting a screwdriver. "I like to see things in tiptop shape. There. It ought to behave itself now."

HE closed the box and followed her up the stairs. "And now for that dishwasher. Been throwing her weight around, I shouldn't wonder. But I'll settle her, all right. How's your husband's painting going these days?"

She shrugged her shoulders.

"That takes care of the dishwasher," he said. "I'll just look in the refrigerator. Plenty of ice now, I see. Useful on a hot day like this one, when you're hot and tired."

Iris smiled. "Would you like a drink, Mr. Braun? Say, a dry Martini?"

Beaming, he sank down on a kitchen chair, while Iris broke out the ice cubes and mixed the drink. She was amused at his delusion that a few turns of a screwdriver could daunt this house; it could behave angelically when it wanted to. Also, it was evidently indifferent to the dissipation of strangers, since it hadn't bothered to defrost for Mr. Braun's drink.

"Have one with me?" he urged.

The ice was still unmelted, she saw with surprise; she made herself a drink and sat down facing Mr. Braun, who leaned back and put his fingertips together.

"Now look here, Mrs. Beauchamp. I'm only a repairman—an adjuster, you might say, but still, I think about things. I told you the last time I was here you'd have to learn to get along, or else move to the hotel. You have to learn to adjust. Have you honestly tried your best, before running off home? Don't you realize everybody has to adjust to something? Maybe this house was harder to deal with than I realized at first—if you'd only mentioned that defrosting business, I'd have been into the control box sooner. Not much I can do, of course. But why not think things over a little longer?" He put down his glass and stood up. "Remember, ma'am—in this world you got to give, and take."

WHEN he had gone, she sat on alone, wondering what life would be without Eric. But could she honestly regret losing a man who had altered as much as he had? What she longed for, she knew, was the old Eric, the one she had known before the house took him.

Restless, she got up and walked into the living room, pacing the floor. Impulsively, she turned on the radio as she passed it, wondering what the cacophony would sound like this time.

Immediately there issued from the cabinet a gentle, placating strain of symphonic music.

More tricks, she thought, and turned it off.

But the sound haunted her, and she switched it on again, to hear the exalted melancholy of the Berg Violin Concerto. The clarinet spoke pleadingly, the violin supplicated in sad arpeggios, the whole complex harmony cried: *Reconciliation.*

She heard it with complete skepticism. *Too late now, my friend,* she thought. *The struggle's over, and you've won. What have you got to be resigned to? You can quit your tricks now.*

Defiantly she went to the kitchen and mixed another Martini. Back in the living room, she stirred the ice, sipped the drink, and thought of Mr. Braun. Peculiar little man. Nice to be able to have a cocktail now and then. Adjust, the man had said.

Adjust... What was he trying to tell her?

What was the violin saying?

Adjust?

Suddenly she put down her glass and ran upstairs to her bedroom. Unlocking her trunk, she tossed clothes to the floor, hunting. She put on her most frivolous afternoon frock, the cherry-colored one with the frills at the low neck. She looked in the mirror. Why, she looked pretty! Prettier than she had been all summer.

So far so good, she thought.

Taking out her lip rouge, she rubbed some into her lips—but the image in the mirror grimaced at her with such a dark, misshapen mouth that she hastily wiped away the color.

All right, she thought, *I am allowed to wear pretty clothes, but no makeup. Right?*

She ran down to living room, where the radio still pleaded. At the window, she lifted her hands to the white curtains and began to take them down. Horns and violas grated in harsh dissonance. She lowered her hands, and the music resolved itself into a chord.

Laughing, she backed away from the curtains. *All right, all right. Furniture not to be meddled with. And now let's see if you really mean it...*

IN the studio, the lifeless landscapes stood about in stacks. She turned one to the wall, tentatively. Nothing happened. She turned another. Nothing happened. But when she turned the "View of the Pine Woods," a cloud cut off the sun from the skylight. Quickly, she turned them all back to a visible position.

Taking a deep breath, she approached her own portrait. A faded splash of blue still criss-crossed the body, but the skin tones were no longer the sickly color of decay, and the face of the portrait was her own.

She nodded her head. *I see,* she thought. *I let you play in my yard, you let me play in yours. He can do landscapes to please your tastes; but he can paint nudes too.*

And now—

She tiptoed into Eric's room. His wasted face was pale, but he grinned feebly when she waked him.

"Hi there, my pigeon."

Her heart nearly stopped beating. This was the first time he had spoken her pet name since—since the day the house found him.

She watched him carefully. "Eric, would you—would you like a cigarette before I go?"

"No, Iris," he said gently. "Have you forgotten? I've given up smoking."

"Oh. So we don't smoke. Hard on the curtains, I suppose. Well, would you like a drink? A nice, cool Martini?"

"A drink? Well…I don't know…heck, why not? After all, one little drink'll never do us any harm."

So the house wants to arbitrate, she thought jubilantly. *It's afraid. She's afraid he'll die and she'll lose him.*

"Try to rest, Eric. I'll bring your drink."

"But won't you be late? Won't you miss your train?"

"It doesn't matter," she said. "Perhaps I won't be going."

She stopped in her bedroom for a moment, and as an experiment took off her dress and stood before the mirror in only her slip. Dropping that to the floor, she stood there, nude. At once she began to shiver in the cold breeze from the window. Darting to the open trunk, she took out the rose red robe and wrapped it around her bare body. Yes, that was delightfully warm.

All right, she thought. *I'm to keep myself covered, but I may wear the most seductive frivols I can find.*

DOWNSTAIRS again, she mixed the drinks, and set them on the living room table while she approached the radio.

Let's get this clear, she thought.

You won't give up Eric; but you realize that if you want to keep him alive, you'll have to let him keep me, too. That means we'll have to adjust. I'll compromise if you will. I won't use makeup, at least in your house. I won't go around without any clothes on, and I'll leave the furniture as it is. But you'll have to stop tormenting me. And if you want me to stay, you'll have to quit trying to reform Eric. Let him alone. Let him be himself, paint what he likes, drink what he likes, and be fond of me when he likes. You'll have him living with you, but let him be himself. Understand?

The violin soared elegiacally.

Lifting the tray of drinks, Iris thought briefly of Mr. Braun, the repairman, who had always wanted to paint. What kind of a house had him, she wondered that he never managed to find the time?

As she started up the stairs, she giggled. She had just realized the meaning of the bargain they had made. The Iris Beauchamp of a month ago, the respectable, conventional housewife, would have refused indignantly. And the other housewife, the prudish, strait-laced personality, which prided itself on the austerity of its moral principles, would have died of shame if it had been suggested to her during her widowhood. Who could have imagined that either woman would ever have agreed to a ménage à trois?

But women are realists, Iris thought, opening the door to Eric's room.

So each of Eric's wives had agreed to accept the other.

THE END

RESURRECTION FROM HELL

By David Wright O'Brien

The madman of Europe came back from Hell in the flesh, but he came back minus his soul—and Rudolph Hess, rotting in an English prison, went mad when he saw what was in the eyes of this resurrected corpse!

IT WAS in the spring of 1935 that I cabled the yarn about the hidden munitions and plane plants scattered around the German countryside that resulted in the terse communication from the Press Office of the Third Reich saying, in effect, that I was to pack up my portable and get the hell out of the land of Strength Through Joy. And with alacrity too!

They were extremely gentle about it, those D.N.B. gentlemen who, with hurt feelings and sad firmness, assured me there was no other course open to them after I had displayed such marked "unfriendliness" toward their "aims."

My paper, on the other hand, found a spot for me in Paris, ordering me to hang my hat there no later than six days after I'd received my walking papers from Naziland. This cut down what was left of my stay in Berlin by four days. For the Gestapo had permitted me ten days in which to clear out.

None of which hurt my feelings in the slightest. For my usefulness in Berlin was officially at an end, and there would have been no point in my hanging around even ten days longer since I was unable to file any more dispatches. I'd have left the morning after the eruption if it hadn't been for the fact that there was to be a gigantic Nazi Party conclave in Berlin just two days later, and my curiosity concerning certain information about friction between two of its leaders just itched to be satisfied.

By staying on a few more days, I knew, I could pick up some hot stuff for a non-fiction book I'd promised to do for an American publishing house some day. So I took my time packing my portable, and pretended to ignore the two stolid gentlemen who had been standing watch across the street from my little apartment for the twenty-four hours since I'd had my clear-out notice from the Gestapo.

I was feeling very smart about taking literal advantage of the ten-day order, and exceptionally smug about what a hell of a news story I'd unearthed to cause all this trouble.

Feeling very smart and smug, that is, until Blake Pearson dropped in on me on the afternoon of the eve of the Nazi shindig. Blake was the Berlin man for International Press Features, and we'd been close friends during the three years we both covered the German capital.

BLAKE was big, raw-boned, tow-headed. His features were angular and he'd been born in the Arkansas hill country. He was plenty worried as I let him into my apartment.

He didn't waste any time getting to the point.

"Listen, chum," he told me, walking over to the window to look out at the two Gestapo shadows across the street, "you're on a spot—but hot."

I didn't get it, and I grinned, waving him to a chair.

"You mean those clucks out there?" I said. "They've been standing by ever since yesterday morning when—"

Blake didn't sit down. He cut me off.

"Hell no. I don't mean those guys. And I don't mean anything about your get-out-of-town instructions from Himmler. This is something worse than that. Something I picked up from Jessert just two hours ago."

"Jessert?" My eyebrows went up a notch. He was Blake's special stool. A German who hated the hell out of the Nazis. Every correspondent has several such grapevines.

Blake Pearson nodded. "Jessert got it from a cousin in the Gestapo. Your neck is on the block. They don't want you to get out of here alive."

I got very sober and felt suddenly chilly along the spinal column. Naturally. I fished for a cigarette with hands that just wouldn't stay steady, and sat down before my knees gave out.

"Well," I said weakly. "Well, well."

"What in the hell did Krommer tell you?" Blake demanded.

Krommer was my special stool. He was a young Austrian whose sister had died after an attack by a Storm Trooper. He'd never thought much of the swastika swine after that.

But I hadn't seen Krommer in over forty-eight hours. I'd cut connections with him and wiped out traces immediately after I'd gotten in hot water with my yarn about hidden plane and munitions plants. It had been the one break I could give him.

"Krommer hasn't seen me since I cabled that story," I said. "He hasn't told me anything."

Blake put his hands on my shoulders.

"Look, chum," he said, "I don't want your damned story. Whatever he told you is no concern of mine. But don't try to tell me he hasn't tipped you off to something plenty hot, and within the last twenty-four hours, too…"

This was getting damned involved.

"On the level, Blake," I told him. "I haven't seen Krommer in two days."

The insistence in my voice convinced him. But his expression was grimly worried. "Then he had something for you, some information, which he tried to get through," Blake said half to himself. "Whatever it was, it must have been dynamite."

"Why do you say that?" I demanded.

"Krommer died. This morning. An overdose of castor oil. Gestapo headquarters."

I sat there stunned. After a minute I was able to mutter, "Good God…"

"And the brownies evidently are sure that Krommer got to you with whatever he'd picked up," Blake said quietly. "For you're next on their list."

"They could never get away with it," I said desperately.

"Couldn't they?" Blake said acidly.

I didn't answer.

"They'd have a tough time putting you under arrest, officially," Blake went on after a moment. "That would cause a hell of a stink. You have a little too much push behind you to make framing you wise. But there are other ways in which a correspondent could be rubbed out."

"Such as?" But my question was just a formality. I knew them, lots of them.

"Accidents," Blake said. "Cars run over people. Men have been known to get dizzy and fall from tall buildings. Electric sockets can play hell if the current's jazzed up."

I held up my hand. "Don't bother about the sub-classifications," I implored him. "I'll admit them."

Blake lighted a cigarette, and I burned my fingers on the one I'd dragged down to a stub. But I didn't mind the burn. It reminded me that I wasn't dead. Yet.

There was a silence while Blake walked over to the window again and moved the curtains back slightly to have another look at the two splendid examples of Nordic brutality standing across the street.

He let the curtains fall back in place and put a hand in his pocket. His cigarette dangled loosely from the corner of his wide mouth and he squinted at me through the smoke.

"They sharp?" he asked.

I looked up.

"Those cauliflowers' across the street?" he amplified. "Have you tried shaking them yet? Have you been able to leave here without their catching on?"

I nodded. "For three hours last night," I said. "I slipped out just for the hell of it. Had a few drinks and came back. They never got wise. I got a big laugh out of it."

"Someday your sense of humor is going to kill you," Blake predicted dryly. "How'd you slip them?"

"At the end of the hall," I nodded toward the door, "there's a passage up to the roof. This building is jammed up against another just the same height. There are four roofs after that of the same height. The last one has a fire ladder running down from it to an alley. I went out and came back that way."

Blake made a discouraged face. "All for a beer," he said.

"I was thirsty."

Blake shrugged his shoulders helplessly. "You're so coy," he observed. He sighed, then. "Think you could make it that way again?"

"Don't know why not."

Blake looked at his watch.

"It'll be dark in another two hours," he said. "There'll be a car waiting for you in that alley. Motor'll be running. Keys'll be there. You can send it back to me when you get across the border."

I got a lump in my throat, choked it back.

"You're taking a big chance, Blake," I told him, "for me."

Blake made a smoke ring and punched one of his long, big knuckled fingers through it.

"You'll find papers, identification and all, in the glove compartment," he said. "I figured they've already taken your other papers away."

"They have," I admitted. "I was going to be personally escorted to the border as soon as I was ready to leave. They told me my Gestapo escorts would preclude any necessity for me to have papers."

Blake Pearson nodded. "And they weren't kidding, chum. You don't need a visa to hell."

I ignored the unflattering conception of the place from which I'd cable my last dispatch.

"I'll never forget this," I told him. He grinned suddenly, rubbing his jaw. "Maybe I won't either," he said.

I tried to reassure him. "If they pick me up before I can make the border, I'll tell 'em I stole the car and had the papers forged myself."

Blake really grinned this time.

"My, my," he drawled. "You're not only coy, you're naïve."

The limousine was a low-slung, rebuilt British job, with a Roll's motor and ninety miles an hour under its black hood. The alley was deserted, and the keys were in the ignition.

When I put my hand in the glove compartment, I felt the forged papers there and something else. A German Army pistol. It was in fine shape, and Blake had wrapped a note around the barrel of it.

"Chum: This thing is loaded for bear. Good luck."

Getting out of Berlin proper wasn't too easy. For, as I said before, it was the eve of the Nazi Party conclave, and the place was lousy with brownies, whooping it up and getting underfoot at every intersection you encountered. Those who weren't stinking drunk and chasing ten-year-old girls, were stationed at the important road crossings leading in and out of Berlin. They carried leaded clubs and scowled darkly at all passing vehicles, looking for any excuse to vent the spleen they felt at being left out of their comrades' none too clean fun.

But I knew the city, and managed to keep out of the way, and in something less than forty-five minutes, I was roaring out of the last suburbs of Berlin and onto some of Adolf's best country roadways.

Of course I kept off the main highways. They were too well patrolled, for it was along one of them that Der Fuehrer was expected to make his majestic journey into Berlin from his mountain retreat. And there had been rumors that he would arrive in Berlin that evening, for he was slated to open the Nazi convention with a speech on the morning of the first day.

I kept my eyes open and my fingers crossed during the next several hours. And finally, when I figured my luck had been holding out for just about as long as I could expect on those particular highway stretches, I found a fairly decent but lesser traveled route and turned off onto it gratefully.

It was a narrow roadway, not new, but still in good condition and just wide enough to permit two cars heading in opposite directions to pass one another without collision.

Checking on several of the road maps I'd brought along with me, I found that it would add from two to three hours time to my border destination. But that was all right with me. Plenty all right. Just as long as it kept me out of close contact with the brown-shirts.

An hour later I found the road skirting into thickly wooded sectors, hilly, winding and steep, and I was forced to slow down a bit. Thick forest preserves were more and more frequent until at last the route was continually banked on either side by trees, and the road itself was arched in an avenue of leafy, intertwining branches.

The sky was blotted from view, by now, and it wasn't until I heard the first rumblings of thunder that I realized bad weather was on the menu.

It wasn't long before the rain started. Lightly at first. Then with greater intensity, until at last it was a relentless downpour. I thought of the festive Nazis in Berlin, and smiled at the realization that this would make a wet mess of the ceremonies they'd planned for the next day.

And then I stopped smiling, as I realized that this was showing signs of making my own plans damply uncertain. Showing very definite signs of it, for already the road itself was some six inches under water, with the torrent continuing unabated and promising much, much more.

I cursed myself roundly for having taken this route that had at first seemed so clever. Any other roadway in less hilly and non-irrigated sectors would have been better than this.

Somewhere up ahead of me there would be a washout. There was scarcely any reason to hope otherwise. For by now the rain had reached deluge proportions, and I was already splashing through occasional sections lying as much as two feet under water.

I thought of turning back. But there was little sense in that, even if it wouldn't have been additionally hazardous. The roadway I'd already covered on this route was just as liable to be washed out as the sections that lay ahead.

"You're a bright boy," I told myself sickly. "A very bright boy."

My palms were damp, and I'd take first one then the other from the wheel to wipe them dry against the front of my trench coat. My forehead was beaded with sweat and I listened to the smooth hum of the motor with sick suspense. Waiting. Just waiting, for the awful splutter that would indicate those motor points had been drenched into uselessness and that the limousine had stalled.

I was navigating the more frequently occurring washed-under sections much more slowly, now. But there was little comfort in such caution. For they were getting deeper with every mile.

Once I stopped the car to get out those road maps in an effort to figure out where in the hell I was. But where they'd once seemed crystal clear in my scanning of them, I now found it utterly impossible to line up any of the landmarks I'd passed in the last hour with what I saw on the maps.

I remembered several forks in the road that had cropped up, and thought of the confident assurance with which I'd taken what—in each case—had seemed the obvious continuation of the route.

Now, I wondered if I'd been right. Maybe the other way had been the correct one. Maybe there were recent detours added. Maybe—

I didn't want to think about it. I didn't even want to recognize it as a possible factor. But finally I said it aloud.

"Judas—I'm lost."

Now, I began to wish frantically for signs of the one thing I'd prayed desperately to avoid up until now—cars. Any cars and all cars. Anything with four wheels and someone in it to get me straightened out and clear of this forest labyrinth. Hell, I'd have been glad to take the chance of brazening through any suspicion or demand for identification.

And then I came to the tree lying straight across the roadway.

It was a gigantic, massive trunked affair, one side stripped white of bark by the jagged flash of lightning that had felled it.

I had to stop. I couldn't get around, over, or under that tree. It blocked off the entire roadway. All out. End of the line.

Thunder crackled gutturally and the rain continued to drench down relentlessly. I sat there behind the wheel of the limousine, staring out through the waterfall cascading down my windshield like a half-witted mute.

What now? What to do? What in the *hell* to do?

I reached into the glove compartment, and without quite being aware of what I was doing, stuffed the papers from it into the inner pocket of my trench coat. I removed the German Army pistol also, placing it in the pocket of the coat.

Then I climbed out into the driving rain.

Slogging through the three inches of water that covered the road, I went around the car out in front of the white glare of the headlights. I tried to move the fallen tree.

In two minutes I was soaked outside by the rain, and drenched inside from the sweat of my futile exertions. I hadn't moved the massive trunk an inch.

I went back to the car, switched off the headlights, and removed the keys. Then I returned to the fallen tree, looked sickly at the grim, unyielding bulk of it, and stepped around it to the other side.

About twenty yards down there was a sharp bend in the road. I would have driven on past that bend if it hadn't been for the catastrophe of the tree across the road. Now I decided to walk on up to it, on the chance that there might be something of help to me—what, I had no earthly idea—beyond that bend.

A minute later and I'd climbed the ascension of that road bend. It formed a little hill perhaps twenty feet higher than the forest levels on either side of it, and there were crude railings on both sides to remind travelers of the roadway that the turn was none too safe.

One of the railings, the one on my right, was shattered.

It took perhaps half a minute for me to see the twisted wreckage of the once sleek, long, black limousine that lay overturned twenty feet down beneath the shattered guard railing.

Sliding on the slick clay of the embankment, and catching at bushes and branches to keep from falling headlong, I let myself down that drop until I stood beside the wreckage of the limousine.

A brief search of the car and the broken underbrush around it showed me that the occupants, whoever they had been, were no longer around.

There was nothing about the car itself that would serve for any identifying purposes. Except, of course, that it was new, expensive, and had had luxurious furnishings.

I climbed laboriously back up to the top of the bend and stood there looking around.

It was then that I caught first sight of the castle.

Perhaps half a mile back from the roadway, topping an enormous tree sheltered knoll, it stood gaunt and forbiddingly black against the white glare of the lightning flash that brought it to my attention.

And with the brief illumination of that lightning gone, I had to strain my eyes to find it a second time. But there it was. It hadn't been illusion. Dark, blackly majestic, a landmark of the ancient, feudal teuton era.

My eyes were accustoming themselves to the darkness of the night and the torrential veil of the ceaseless rain. And now I saw the four pinpoints of light glimmering from the upper turret towers of the castle.

FOR no longer than two or three minutes I debated my next move. And then, once I'd settled it in my mind, I started out toward that castle. There would be people there. Who they'd be, I had no way of knowing. But neither did I know where I was, or how I'd ever manage to make the border before being tracked down by the Gestapo.

With my forged credentials and a slightly plausible story—which I'd have to invent along the way—there'd be some chance, my only chance. Perhaps, if the castle was inhabited by some rich old peer, there'd be servants and landtillers to help me move the tree from the roadway, and directions that would help me find my way to the Polish border.

It was a risk I had to take.

I found a muddy lane leading off the roadway, up the huge knoll through the trees, to the grim old castle. It took me more than ten minutes to cover this. And when I finally emerged from this lane into the wide, lawned clearing around the castle, I caught my breath.

There were two sleek black limousines, similar to the wrecked machine I'd discovered below the shattered guardrail along the road bend, parked before the vast, flagstone entranceway to the ancient castle.

I stopped dead, staring breathlessly at them while my heart went through a series of somersaults. My hand had instinctively gone to the pistol in my pocket, and the touch of it was reassuring, reminding me of what had to be done.

It took me fully a minute to make certain that there were no occupants in those limousines, and all of another minute to decide that there was no one present in the open area around the castle grounds.

Cautiously, then, I crossed the clearing, carefully skirting the parked machines, and made my way up the flagstoned stretch to the huge front door of ancient timber.

I stood there then, less than three feet from the castle door, listening.

Save for the rumbling of thunder in the distance and the torrent of rain washing down from the blackened sky, there were no sounds.

I stepped back several paces and craned my neck upward, gazing at the pinpoints of light that still lanced forth from the four turret tower windows at the top of the castle.

Something prevented me from calling out. Something stranger than a sense of caution.

Silently, I moved back to the great old door. And now, for the first time, I became aware that it was slightly ajar.

I stepped up to it, pressing gently inward with my hand against its ancient iron reinforcements. It gave slowly, without betraying noise.

I stepped inside, into a long, stone, barren hallway. A hallway illuminated but faintly by an ancient wick lamp. There was no one in the hallway, and just to the right of the door I saw a narrow stone staircase leading upward...to where?

Again I paused, holding my breath and listening anxiously. There was no sound but the fury of the storm outside. I hesitated, eyeing that staircase, weighing the implications of the silence and the cars out front. The lights came from the tower windows. The occupants were up there.

Quietly I moved across the hallway and started up those stone steps. The staircase turned sharply with the tenth step, and I saw another ancient lamp on a landing just above it.

I moved up to the landing, hesitating as I looked up and down another dim hallway leading off of it on either side. The stairway continued on, and I decided to follow it.

And then I heard the footsteps and voices up above me. Hard, ringing, boot-clad steps.

A heavy door slammed shut somewhere up there, and the footsteps, growing louder, were coming down toward me.

I looked wildly right and left for refuge. There was an alcove in the center of the dim hallway. Quickly, I moved down to it. It proved to be the door to another room. I tried the door and it was locked. I pressed back hard against the door, taking full advantage of its scant concealment.

The footsteps rang heavily down toward me now, and I heard deep, worried, guttural voices speaking in the German tongue.

Then the steps were at the landing, and continuing down the first flight of stairs. I poked my head out quickly—and saw the backs and steel helmets of two Nazi soldiers.

They disappeared down the staircase, and I heard the sound of their hard-heeled boots ringing across the first floor hallway, moving obviously toward the door. Then they stopped.

The Nazi soldiers had obviously taken post at the door.

I was, quite obviously, trapped.

FOR fully a minute I had all I could do to calm the frantic efforts of my heart and stomach to switch places. Only then was I able to step softly out of the doorway alcove and move ever so cautiously down the dimly lighted hall to the staircase landing.

I didn't realize it then, but my instincts of caution and sanity were losing their ancient and bitter grudge feud with my instincts of newspaper curiosity. My heart was hammering now through excitement and a burning desire to find out what this was all about, rather than through fear.

The soldiers, the limousines outside, the lights and voices up in the tower, the wrecked limousine down at the road bend below the shattered guardrail.

All those things fitted together, even though I couldn't explain how or why, into something that my sixth sense told me was dynamite. My sixth sense—a flimsy thread of hunch. But it had never failed me before, and now it was screaming to be followed.

There was no going down. Not down those stairs. Nazi soldiers stood post there now. I'd have a hell of a lot of fun passing off forged papers on suspicious Nazi soldiers.

I started up the second flight of stone stairs. Another turn, another landing, another flight continuing onward. I didn't hesitate, I went on.

The stairway came to an abrupt ending at the fourth floor hallway. A hallway just as long, just as dimly illuminated as the other two below it. But there were three massive timbered doors immediately to the right of the last stone step. And from the cracks at the bottom of each of these streamed light.

I stood there scarcely breathing, as from behind those doors came mumbled conversation. German voices.

And then I heard the sound of the automobile motor coming up into the courtyard before the castle outside. It must have been heard by the occupants of the rooms just to the right of me. Their voices grew louder, and I heard one of them say in German:

"Thank God, he has come."

I didn't wait. Whoever had just arrived would be coming up here to this floor, would be coming to see whoever was in those rooms. I thought I heard footsteps from behind one of the doors moving toward it as if to open it.

Swiftly, as noiselessly as I could, I started off down the hallway to the left. There had been a doorway alcove two flights before. There had to be one now.

But there wasn't.

Not another door in the hallway, save those three back to the right of the staircase ending. I moved on desperately, I was coming to the end of the hallway. And then I saw it—a tiny alcove just to the right of the very end of the hall.

It was another staircase, leading upward. Cobwebbed and thick with dust. Long unused. Down below, I could hear voices and footsteps starting up the first flight of stairs.

I heard the nearest door at the end of the hallway squeak as someone inside started to open it. There was no hesitating now. I ducked up the narrow, dusty little staircase, pushing my way through the heavy tangle of cobwebs. There were some fifteen stone steps to the little stairway, and I covered them in less than many seconds.

They ended at an opening that revealed a dark, cold, vast sort of attic. It, too, was layered with dust and veiled by cobwebs. I pulled myself up through the aperture until I was standing there at last, cold with sweat and shaking with excitement.

Below I could hear the sound of voices and footsteps, muffled footsteps; muttering, guttural voices. I'd moved none too quickly.

Standing there, I heard the door on the floor below me close— at which instant the voices suddenly seemed much more distinct.

I frowned, getting snatches of germanic conversation, trying to figure this out while I adjusted my eyes to the darkness. And by the time I was able to see fairly well around me, I had figured out the reason for the new proximity in voices.

The place in which I was now standing was the castle's equivalent of a loft. It was the top story, and it extended over all the rooms on the floor just below it. Which meant there was an aperture of some sort in the floor of this loft, above one of the rooms from which the Nazi soldiers had come, and in which the other unknown occupants and the new arrival now were assembled. An aperture through which those voices now were coming.

And then I saw it. By "saw," I mean the pinpoint of light lancing up through a small slotted grating in the center of the loft quarters in which I now stood.

Very cautiously, fearing any echoes that might be set up in this empty, stone-floored loft, I moved over toward that tiny ribbon of light.

Standing just above it, and looking down through the small, slotted grating, I got an almost complete view of the well-lighted room below. An almost complete view that showed me that the three doors from which I'd heard voices coming all belonged to the same large room.

And, as far as I was able to discern at first, there were four people in that brightly illuminated room. Three of them wore uniforms, and the fourth wore civilian togs.

Of the uniformed three, two were dressed in the Nazi Party garb, and the third an extremely stout, scowling fellow, wore the uniform of an officer in the Luftwaffe.

Of the two men in Nazi Party uniform, one was well proportioned and of medium size. He was handsome in a rugged, rather brutal way. The other was small, thin, with a face full of rat-like cunning and twisted ferocity.

The man in civilian clothes was small, gaunt faced, and bald. He wore thick lensed glasses, and his high forehead above his thin nose was beaded with perspiration. His mouth twitched, and there was fear in his tortured eyes.

The officer in the Luftwaffe uniform was raging at the cowed little chap in civilian dress.

"You will do it, Ekhorn. You will do it, or else. Don't forget there is still your young son. Your wife remains at large, and your little daughter is also unharmed—for the present."

The little civilian spread his hands in a pathetic gesture of appeal.

"Gentlemen, please, my family—they have done nothing..."

The thin, rat-faced little man in the Nazi Party garb broke in.

"Doktor Ekhorn," he spat, "we guaranteed their safety, plus your own release from the concentration camp—*if* you succeed in this for us."

The little doctor seemed more shaken than before. His eyes were piteously pleading.

"But there is little assurance that such a thing could be done—" he began.

"Animals you have succeeded with," the Luftwaffe officer broke in, his huge jowls shaking angrily. "We know that. So why not with humans?"

The perspiration trickled down the little civilian's long forehead.

"But a human being," he protested hoarsely, "it is not the will of God that such a—"

The somewhat handsome fellow in the Nazi Party dress broke in for the first time, his face flushed, his eyes fanatic.

"It is the will of Destiny," he blazed. "You *must* do this thing."

The frightened little doctor opened his mouth to protest. The thin, rat-faced Nazi cut him off.

"Your wife, your son, your daughter, Doktor Ekhorn. For them, there will be sheer horror, if you refuse."

The trembling little doctor's last vestige of resistance crumbled.

"All right," he said thickly. "I shall attempt it. I can promise nothing. Nothing, you understand? But I shall try. You say all my old equipment was rushed here?"

"All that you will need," said the Luftwaffe officer.

"Your antiseptics, surgical gown and kit are in the next room," said the ruggedly handsome Nazi, running a shaking hand through his lank black hair.

The little doctor moved slowly out of my line of vision then, and I heard a door open and shut as he stepped into an adjoining room.

The ruggedly proportioned Nazi turned on the Luftwaffe officer then, his eyes blazing furious condemnation.

"Your mania for speed, speed, speed was the cause of this!" he blazed. "If this fails I will personally kill you."

The fat, scowling Luftwaffe officer glared back at him defensively.

"I could not foresee a washed-out road and such a breakneck turn," he said sullenly. I saw then, for the first time, that the big-bellied officer had a fresh bandage on the side of his head. It was tinted slightly red.

"If it had only been you who failed to emerge from the wreck," the rugged young Nazi snarled. "I would be overjoyed. But no... *He* had to pay for your madman's thirst for thrills."

Part of the pattern was fitting in. The smashed limousine down beneath the shattered guardrail on the roadway turn was now accounted for.

AND then, with the sound of a door opening and closing again, another cog fitted into place as the little man they had called Doctor Ekhorn reentered my area of vision. For seeing him suddenly in a white surgical gown, and instinctively breathing the name they'd called him by, brought back in a rushing flood the recollection of who and what he was.

Doctor Hans Ekhorn was one of Germany's most celebrated surgeons. For years he had been the president of one of Europe's greatest medical universities. And in 1934, little than a year before this moment, he had mysteriously "disappeared."

"Your own release from the concentration camp." The words spoken by the rat-faced little Nazi but moments ago came back to jolt me. So that, then, was the place to which the famed little Doctor Ekhorn had vanished...

And suddenly my brain was madly sorting and shifting this wild chain of circumstances, seeking a solution. The great Ekhorn released temporarily from the hell of a concentration camp, brought here to this desolate castle, for what?

Doctor Ekhorn moved out of my line of vision until I could see only his legs and the end of a wheeled operating table. I could see the eyes of the other three men in the room watching him tensely. Then I heard Ekhorn's voice.

"How long?" he asked simply.

"Four hours," the rugged young Nazi answered hoarsely.

"There are no scars, no mutilations," the Luftwaffe officer put in. For the first time his voice was shaky.

"An internal concussion was the cause of his death," I heard Ekhorn's voice say. "How did it occur?"

The Luftwaffe officer answered again, hoarsely.

"An automobile crash. I—I was at the wheel. We were doing close to a hundred. Through a rail guard on a steep turn."

I could see the eyes of the rugged young Nazi Party man boring hatefully into the face of the pot-bellied Luftwaffe officer as he spoke.

"Four hours makes it almost a certain impossibility," Ekhorn's voice declared. "Had I been able to attempt it sooner after the dea—"

I saw the rat-faced little Nazi draw forth a nasty looking German Army pistol and point it in the direction of Ekhorn as he cut him off.

"You will succeed," he grated.

"On animals you have succeeded in cases which have been over six hours gone," the Luftwaffe officer began.

"Shut up," the young Nazi blazed furiously, his rugged features twisted in agony of torment.

I saw Ekhorn's legs move, as he turned away from the operating table to face the Luftwaffe officer.

"The respiratory-surgery machine," he said quietly.

The Luftwaffe officer and the young Nazi moved out of vision to a corner of the room, while the rat-faced little Nazi still held his pistol on the doctor. I heard wheels squeaking, and suddenly the young Nazi and the Luftwaffe officer came back into my focus of vision, pushing a huge, cumbersome machine. T hey wheeled it around beside the operating table until it, too, was just in the edge of my vision area.

Then they returned to join the rat-faced little chap with the pistol. All three pairs of eyes fixed intently on the drama in that corner of the room then, as Doctor Ekhorn's legs moved out of vision and he began his preliminary routines.

Minutes passed. Endless minutes broken only by the faint sounds of activity coming from the corner of that room where the celebrated German surgeon was working with desperately incredible brilliance.

All three of the uniformed men were sweating profusely, their faces frozen in granite-like hypnosis as they stared at the corner of that room.

The time continued to crawl by, until every bone in my body was aching from the strain of the vigil, and my nerves were tautening to the breaking point.

It must have been twenty-five minutes after he had started that Doctor Ekhorn's utterly fatigued voice broke the terrible silence.

"It is accomplished," he declared. "He breathes. Life has returned."

Tears welled in the eyes of the ruggedly handsome young Nazi, rolling down his cheeks unashamed.

The rat-faced little Nazi looked evilly triumphant.

The Luftwaffe officer's face wore a curiously unfathomable expression. He licked his tongue across his dry, fat lips.

"The machine," Doctor Ekhorn's weary voice said, "remove it. It is no longer necessary."

He came into my line of vision, taking a surgical mask from his face. His eyes, beneath his thick lensed glasses, were utterly weary. And there was something else written in them. Something sickly terrified.

"He lives," he repeated dully. "But in what manner I cannot say. I can make no promises as to what will happen when the ether wears off. I can make no promises as to what will arise from that operating table."

The rat-faced Nazi grinned contemptuously at him.

"Fool talk," he spat. "You have brought him back from the dead, Ekhorn."

DOCTOR EKHORN nodded slowly. "He was dead four hours. Now he lives and breathes again. Shortly he will walk and talk once more. I have brought his *life* back into his body, but I do not know if it was too late to recapture the soul for that body."

"The soul?" There was scorn in the word as the rat-faced Nazi hurled it at the doctor. "Such rot from a man of science."

Doctor Ekhorn answered.

"I have tampered with things man was never meant to touch. I have resurrected. I have defied the law of creation and death. There is a penalty for such things. In animals, my experiments were but for purposes of scientific curiosity. In this, my first human resurrection," he shrugged, "I cannot predict the result."

"You are a fool," the rat-faced Nazi blazed. "He lives—and we will see that he never dies again. He is as before."

Doctor Ekhorn turned his back on the rat-faced Nazi at that instant, peeling off his surgical gloves.

I am never sure, in thinking back, whether or not the thin, rat-faced little Nazi pulled the trigger through a sudden mad impulse, or according to previous plan. But the shots, three of them, blasted forth nevertheless.

Little Doctor Ekhorn fell forward to the stone floor, his head pillowed in his own blood. He looked ironically peaceful and at rest.

The younger Nazi and the bloated Luftwaffe officer had wheeled at the sound of the first shot. They watched Ekhorn crumple to the floor impassively.

The rat-faced little Nazi returned the smoking gun to his pocket with a grin.

"Now we must destroy the machine," he said. "No one must ever know of this. After that, we can call Doctor Henzul. We must tell him only that there was the accident, and that he miraculously escaped with his life. Doctor Henzul can nurse him back to strength."

The pot-bellied Luftwaffe officer and the young Nazi moved out of sight toward the operating table and the weird machine. They moved the latter back to the opposite corner where it had originally been.

The rugged faced Nazi spoke then. His voice was tremulous.

"Let us look just once at his face," he said huskily. "At his face, alive and vital once more."

The rat-faced Nazi nodded.

"If you wish, Rudolph."

The Luftwaffe officer followed the rugged young Nazi to the operating table, with the rat-faced Nazi bringing up the rear. I could now only see their legs as they grouped around the person on that operating table.

"He breathes, oh God, I dared not hope for this…"

The exclamation was torn from the young Nazi, Rudolph.

"His eyes," said the voice of the rat-faced Nazi suddenly, "are fluttering. *They open!*"

I HEARD the simultaneous gasp from the throats of all three, then. Sharp, jagged, horrified.

It was the voice of the young Nazi, Rudolph that cried out.

"Mein Colt, his eyes, his eyes! What has happened?"

It was the voice of the Luftwaffe officer that said hoarsely, horrified, *"Gott in himmell, they are the eyes of the Devil!"*

It will always be a matter of undying regret to me that I never saw the body lying on the operating table in that mountain castle in Germany; the body that was brought back across the black gulf of Death itself, to live and breathe once more.

For I had a gun in my pocket, and I'm certain I'd have used it to send that creature back to the abyss of Hell into which his death from that automobile wreck had sent him.

But I had to use that gun rapidly and well, in the next thirty seconds when two German soldiers burst in on me in that castle loft. I had the advantage of darkness. Their flashlights gave them away. My aim was excellent. It had to be.

Finding the small door that led to the castle roof was sheer luck. But find it I did. And one of those incredibly huge trees provided the ladder by which I made my way to the ground.

I'm certain that those two soldiers were the only others in the castle save those I'd watched in that room. And it must have taken the Luftwaffe officer, the rat-faced Nazi, and the black-haired young Rudolph considerable time to locate the sound of the shots and find the bodies of their guards.

I was gone by then, in one of their limousines, leaving the other two with punctured gas tanks. Even today, I cannot reveal the names of the peasant farmers who helped me across the Polish border.

But I can reveal the names of the men in that room. And it is not too hard to speculate on what has happened among them thereafter. Much of it is recorded history.

The fat man in the Luftwaffe officer's uniform was Hermann Goering.

The young Nazi with the given name of Rudolph had the surname of Hess.

The thin, rat-faced little Nazi was Joseph Goebbels.

And I submit that the creature on the operating table, the thing called back from the black voids of Death to live again, was *Adolph Hitler*.

Check the newspaper files concerning that Spring Nazi Party gathering in Berlin, 1935. Der Feuhrer was "suffering from a cold" and put in no appearance.

Check, too, if you will, the sudden tremendous increase in Nazi atrocities and brutalities through Germany itself from that Spring of 1935 until the day the Terror flamed quite suddenly across the world with the invasion of Poland.

The man whose soul had fled the dead body lying on that table in the lonely mountain castle on the eve of that Nazi Party conclave in 1935, was a vicious, sadistic bully, an underhanded politician, a most cunning opportunist. That was the Hitler who had died.

The thing that was resurrected from the very pits of hell itself, on that same evening, was nothing human, nothing earthly. It was the incarnation of Evil, a hideous, slavering monster in human form. A monster that is at this moment grasping for the world.

I know not what thing it is that inhabits the shell of the petty beast who met his death that night. I only know that Adolf Hitler died in the spring of 1935. Died in the smashed and twisted wreckage of a car driven by the speed-crazy Goering, who somehow escaped alive.

I only know that Germany's most brilliant surgeon, a man who had brought animals back from death in "curiosity" experiments, made life pulse again that night in the body of a tyrant he despised. And I recall his words of warning before that monstrous resurrection:

"I can make no promises as to *what* will arise from that operating table if I succeed."

And I can still recall the shrill scream from the lips of Rudolph Hess as he looked into the eyes of the thing that had struggled back from slime of hell to breathe once more on that operating table.

A Rudolph Hess who is rumored to sit this very day in the black corners of an English cell—quite impossibly mad.

THE END

PLACE OF MEETING

By Charles Beaumont

They met in the night, in the shadow of a spire, for a purpose that can't be told...

IT SWEPT DOWN from the mountains, a loose crystal-smelling wind, an autumn chill of moving wetness. Down from the mountains and into the town where it set the dead trees hissing and the signboards creaking. And it even went into the church, because the bell was ringing and there was no one to ring the bell.

The people in the yard stopped their talk and listened to the rusty music.

Big Jim Kroner listened too. Then he cleared his throat and clapped his hands—thick hands, calloused and work-dirtied.

"All right," he said loudly. "All right, let's us settle down now." He walked out from the group and turned. "Who's got the list?"

"Got it right here, Jim," a woman said, coming forward with a loose-leaf folder.

"All present?"

"Everybody except that there German, Mr. Grunin—Grunger—"

Kroner smiled, he made a megaphone of his hands, "Grüninger—Barthold Grüninger?"

A small man with a mustache called out excitedly, "Ja, ja...! S'war schwer den Friedhof zu finden."

"All right. That's all we wanted to know, whether you was here or not." Kroner studied the pages carefully. Then he reached into the back pocket of his overalls and withdrew a stub of pencil and put the tip to his mouth.

"Now, before we start off," he said to the group, "I want to know is there anybody here that's got a question or anything to ask?" He looked over the crowd of silent faces. "Anybody don't know who I am? No? All right then."

135

It came another wind then, mountain-scattered and fast: it billowed dresses, set damp hair moving; it pushed over pewter vases and smashed dead roses and hydrangeas to swirling dust against the gritty tombstones. Its clean rain smell was gone now though, for it had passed over the fields, and so it was filled with the odors of rotting life.

Kroner made a check mark in the notebook. "Anderson," he shouted. "Edward L."

A man in overalls like Kroner's stepped forward.

"Andy, you covered Skagit valley, Snohomish and King counties, as well as Seattle and the rest?"

"Yes, sir."

"What you got to report?"

"They're all dead," Anderson said.

"You looked everywhere? You was real careful?"

"Yes, sir. Ain't nobody alive in the whole state."

Kroner nodded and made another check mark. "That's all, Andy. Next: Avakian, Karina."

A woman in a wool skirt and grey blouse walked up from the back, waving her arms. She started to speak.

Kroner tapped his stick. "Listen here for a second, folks," he said. "For those that don't know how to talk English, you know what this is all about—so when I ask my question, you just nod up-and-down for yes (like this) and sideways (like this) for no. Makes it a lot easier for those of us as don't remember too good. All right?"

There were murmurings and whispered consultations and for a little while the yard was full of noise. The woman called Avakian kept nodding.

"Fine," Kroner said. "Now, Miss Avakian. You covered what? Ah…Iran, Iraq, Turkey and Syria. Did you find anybody alive?"

The woman stopped nodding. "No," she said. "No, no."

Kroner checked the name. "Let's see here. Boleslavsky, Peter. You go on back, Miss Avakian."

A man in bright city clothes walked briskly to the tree clearing. "Yes, sir," he said.

"What have you got for us?"

The man shrugged. "Well, I tell you. I went over New York with a fine-tooth comb. Then I hit Brooklyn and Jersey. Nothin', man. Nothin' nowhere."

"He is right," a dark-faced woman said in a tremulous voice. "I was there too. Only the dead in the streets, all over, all over the city…in the cars I looked even, in the *offices*. Everywhere is people dead."

"Chavez, Pietro. Baja California."

"All dead, senor chief."

"Ciodo, Ruggiero, Capri."

The man from Capri shook his head violently.

"Denman, Charlotte, Southern United States."

"Dead as doornails…"

"Elgar, David S…

"Ferrazio, Ignatz…

"Goldfarb, Bernard…

"Halpern…

"Kranek…O'Brian…Ives…"

The names exploded in the pale evening air like deep gunshots; there was much head shaking, many people saying, "No. No."

At last Kroner stopped marking. He closed the notebook and spread his big workman's hands. He saw the round eyes, the trembling mouths, the young faces, he saw all the frightened people.

A girl began to cry. She sank to the damp ground and covered her face and made these crying sounds. An elderly man put his hand on her head. The elderly man looked sad. But not afraid. Only the young ones seemed afraid.

"Settle down now," Kroner said firmly. "Settle on down. Now, listen to me. I'm going to ask you all the same question one more time, because we got to be sure." He waited for them to grow quiet. "All right. This here is all of us, everyone. We've covered all the spots. Did anybody here find one single solitary sign of life?"

The people were silent. The wind had died again, so there was no sound at all. Across the corroded wire fence the grey meadows lay strewn with the carcasses of cows and horses and, in one of the fields, sheep. No flies buzzed near the dead animals, there were no maggots burrowing. No vultures, the sky was clean of birds. And in all the untended rolling hills of grass and weeds that had once sung and pulsed with a million hidden voices, in all the land there was only this immense stillness now, still as years, still as the unheard motion of the stars.

Kroner watched the people. The young woman in the gay print dress; the tall African with his bright paint and cultivated scars; the fierce-looking Swede looking not so fierce now in this greying twilight. He watched all the tall and short and old and young people from all over the world, pressed together now, a vast silent polyglot in this country meeting place, this always lonely and long-deserted spot—deserted even before the gas bombs and the disease and the flying pestilences that had covered the earth in three days and three nights. Deserted. Forgotten.

"Talk to us, Jim," the woman who had handed him the notebook said. She was new.

Kroner put the list inside his big overalls pocket.

"Tell us," someone else said. "How shall we be nourished? What will we do?"

"The world's all dead," a child moaned. "Dead as dead, the whole world…"

"Todo el mund—"

"Monsieur Kroner, Monsieur Kroner, what will we do?"

Kroner smiled. "Do?" He looked up through the still-hanging poison cloud, the dun blanket, up to where the moon was now risen in full coldness. His voice was steady, but it lacked life. "What some of us have done before," he said. "We'll go back and wait. It ain't the first time. It ain't the last."

A little fat bald man with old eyes sighed and began to waver in the October dusk. The outline of his form wavered and disappeared in the shadows under the trees where the moonlight did not reach. Others followed him as Kroner talked.

"Same thing we'll do again and likely keep on doing. We'll go back and—sleep. And we'll wait. Then it'll start all over again and folks'll build their cities—new folks with new blood—and then we'll wake up. Maybe a long time yet. But it ain't so bad; it's quiet, and time passes." He lifted a small girl of fifteen or sixteen with pale cheeks and red lips. "Come on, now. Why, just think of the appetite you'll have all built up!"

The girl smiled. Kroner faced the crowd and waved his hands, large hands, rough from the stone of midnight pyramids and the feel of muskets; boil-speckled from night-hours in packing plants and trucking lines; broken by the impact of a tomahawk and a machine-gun bullet; but white where the dirt was not caked, and bloodless. Old hands, old beyond years.

As he waved, the wind came limping back from the mountains. It blew the heavy iron bell high in the steepled white barn and set the signboards creaking and lifted ancient dusts and hissed again through the dead trees.

Kroner watched the air turn black. He listened to it fill with the flappings and the flutterings and the squeakings. He waited, then he stopped waving and sighed and began to walk.

He walked to a place of vines and heavy brush. Here he paused for a moment and looked out at the silent place of high dark grass, of hidden huddled tombs, of scrolls and stone-frozen children stained silver in the night's wet darkness; at the crosses he did not look. The people were gone; the place was empty.

Kroner kicked away the foliage. Then he got into the coffin and closed the lid.

Soon he was asleep.

THE END

THE CORPSE ON THE GRATING

By Hugh B. Cave

In the gloomy depths of the old warehouse Dale saw a thing that drew a scream of horror to his dry lips. It was a corpse—the mold of decay on its long-dead features—and yet it was alive!

It was ten o'clock on the morning of December 5 when M. S. and I left the study of Professor Daimler. You are perhaps acquainted with M. S. His name appears constantly in the pages of the Illustrated News, in conjunction with some very technical article on psychoanalysis or with some extensive study of the human brain and its functions. He is a psycho-fanatic, more or less, and has spent an entire lifetime of some seventy-odd years in pulling apart human skulls for the purpose of investigation. Lovely pursuit.

For some twenty years I have mocked him, in a friendly, half-hearted fashion. I am a medical man, and my own profession is one that does not sympathize with radicals.

As for Professor Daimler, the third member of our triangle—perhaps, if I take a moment to outline the events of that evening, the Professor's part in what follows will be less obscure. We had called on him, M. S. and I, at his urgent request. His rooms were in a narrow, unlighted street just off the square, and Daimler himself opened the door to us. A tall, loosely built chap he was, standing in the doorway like a motionless ape, arms half extended.

"I've summoned you, gentlemen," he said quietly, "because you two, of all London, are the only persons who know the nature of my recent experiments. I should like to acquaint you with the results."

He led the way to his study, then kicked the door shut with his foot, seizing my arm as he did so. Quietly he dragged me to the table that stood against the farther wall. In the same even, unemotional tone of a man completely sure of himself, he commanded me to inspect it.

For a moment, in the semi-gloom of the room, I saw nothing. At length, however, the contents of the table revealed themselves, and I distinguished a motley collection of test tubes, each filled with some fluid. The tubes were attached to each other by some ingenious arrangement of thistles, and at the end of the table, where a chance blow could not brush it aside, lay a tiny phial of the resulting serum. From the appearance of the table, Daimler had evidently drawn a certain amount of gas from each of the smaller tubes, distilling them through acid into the minute phial at the end. Yet even now, as I stared down at the fantastic paraphernalia before me, I could sense no conclusive reason for its existence.

I turned to the Professor with a quiet stare of bewilderment. He smiled.

"The experiment is over," he said. "As to its conclusion, you, Dale, as a medical man, will be skeptical. And you," turning to M. S., "as a scientist you will be amazed. I, being neither physician nor scientist, am merely filled with wonder!"

HE STEPPED to a long, square table-like structure in the center of the room. Standing over it, he glanced quizzically at M. S., then at me.

"For a period of two weeks," he went on, "I have kept, on the table here, the body of a man who has been dead more than a month. I have tried, gentlemen, with acid combinations of my own origination, to bring that body back to life. And…I have—failed.

"But," he added quickly, noting the smile that crept across my face, "that failure was in itself worth more than the average scientist's greatest achievement. You know, Dale, that heat, if a man is not truly dead, will sometimes resurrect him. In a case of epilepsy, for instance, victims have been pronounced dead only to return to life—sometimes in the grave.

"I say 'if a man be not truly dead.' But what if that man *is* truly dead? Does the cure alter itself in any manner? The motor of your car dies—do you bury it? You do not; you locate the faulty part, correct it, and infuse new life. And so, gentlemen, after remedying the ruptured heart of this dead man, by operation, I proceeded to bring him back to life.

"I used heat. Terrific heat will sometimes originate a spark of new life in something long dead. Gentlemen, on the fourth day of my tests, following a continued application of electric and acid heat, the patient—"

Daimler leaned over the table and took up a cigarette. Lighting it, he dropped the match and resumed his monologue.

"The patient turned suddenly over and drew his arm weakly across his eyes. I rushed to his side. When I reached him, the body was once again stiff and lifeless. And—it has remained so."

The Professor stared at us quietly, waiting for comment. I answered him, as carelessly as I could, with a shrug of my shoulders.

"Professor, have you ever played with the dead body of a frog?" I said softly.

HE SHOOK his head silently.

"You would find it interesting sport," I told him. "Take a common dry cell battery with enough voltage to render a sharp shock. Then apply your wires to various parts of the frog's anatomy. If you are lucky, and strike the right set of muscles, you will have the pleasure of seeing a dead frog leap suddenly forward. Understand, he will not regain life. You have merely released his dead muscles by shock, and sent him bolting."

The Professor did not reply. I could feel his eyes on me, and had I turned, I should probably had found M. S. glaring at me in honest hate. These men were students of mesmerism, of spiritualism, and my commonplace contradiction was not over welcome.

"You are cynical, Dale," said M. S. coldly, "because you do not understand."

"Understand? I am a doctor—not a ghost."

But M. S. had turned eagerly to the Professor.

"Where is this body—this experiment?" he demanded.

Daimler shook his head. Evidently he had acknowledged failure and did not intend to drag his dead man before our eyes, unless he could bring that man forth alive, upright, and ready to join our conversation.

"I've put it away," he said distantly. "There is nothing more to be done, now that our reverend doctor has insisted in making a matter of fact thing out of our experiment. You understand, I had not intended to go in for wholesale resurrection, even if I had met with success. It was my belief that a dead body, like a dead piece of mechanism, can be brought to life again, provided we are intelligent enough to discover the secret. And by God, it is *still* my belief."

THAT WAS the situation, then, when M. S. and I paced slowly back along the narrow street that contained the Professor's dwelling-place. My companion was strangely silent. More than once I felt his eyes upon me in an uncomfortable stare, yet he said nothing. Nothing, that is, until I had opened the conversation with some casual remark about the lunacy of the man we had just left.

"You are wrong in mocking him, Dale," M. S. replied bitterly. "Daimler is a man of science. He is no child, experimenting with a toy; he is a grown man who has the courage to believe in his powers. One of these days…"

He had intended to say that some day I should respect the Professor's efforts. One of these days! The interval of time was far shorter than anything so indefinite. The first event, with its succeeding series of horrors, came within the next three minutes.

WE HAD reached a more deserted section of the square, a black, uninhabited street extending like a shadowed band of darkness between gaunt, high walls. I had noticed for some time that the stone structure beside us seemed to be unbroken by door or window—that it appeared to be a single gigantic building, black and forbidding. I mentioned the fact to M. S.

"The warehouse," he said simply. "A lonely, God-forsaken place. We shall probably see the flicker of the watchman's light in one of the upper chinks."

At his words, I glanced up. True enough, the higher part of the grim structure was punctured by narrow, barred openings. Safety vaults, probably. But the light, unless its tiny gleam was somewhere in the inner recesses of the warehouse, was dead. The great building was like an immense burial vault, a tomb—silent and lifeless.

We had reached the most forbidding section of the narrow street, where a single arch-lamp overhead cast a halo of ghastly yellow light over the pavement. At the very rim of the circle of illumination, where the shadows were deeper and more silent, I could make out the black mouldings of a heavy iron grating. The bars of metal were designed, I believe, to seal the side entrance of the great warehouse from night marauders. It was bolted in place and secured with a set of immense chains, immovable.

This much I saw as my intent gaze swept the wall before me. This huge tomb of silence held for me a peculiar fascination, and as I paced along beside my gloomy companion, I stared directly ahead of me into the darkness of the street. I wish to God my eyes had been closed or blinded.

HE WAS hanging on the grating. Hanging there, with white, twisted hands clutching the rigid bars of iron, straining to force them apart. His whole distorted body was forced against the barrier, like the form of a madman struggling to escape from his cage. His face—the image of it still haunts me whenever I see iron bars in the darkness of a passage—was the face of a man who has died from utter, stark horror. It was frozen in a silent shriek of agony, staring out at me with fiendish maliciousness. Lips twisted apart. White teeth gleaming in the light. Bloody eyes, with a horrible glare of colorless pigment. And—*dead*.

I believe M. S. saw him at the very instant I recoiled. I felt a sudden grip on my arm; and then, as an exclamation came harshly from my companion's lips, I was pulled forward roughly. I found myself staring straight into the dead eyes of that fearful thing before me, found myself standing rigid, motionless, before the corpse that hung within reach of my arm.

And then, through that overwhelming sense of the horrible, came the quiet voice of my comrade—the voice of a man who looks upon death as nothing more than an opportunity for research.

"The fellow has been frightened to death, Dale. Frightened most horribly. Note the expression of his mouth, the evident struggle to force these bars apart and escape. Something has driven fear to his soul, killed him."

I REMEMBER the words vaguely. When M. S. had finished speaking, I did not reply. Not until he had stepped forward and bent over the distorted face of the thing before me, did I attempt to speak. When I did, my thoughts were a jargon.

"What, in God's name," I cried, "could have brought such horror to a strong man? What—"

"Loneliness, perhaps," suggested M. S. with a smile. "The fellow is evidently the watchman. He is alone, in a huge, deserted pit of darkness, for hours at a time. His light is merely a ghostly ray of illumination, hardly enough to do more than increase the darkness. I have heard of such cases before."

He shrugged his shoulders. Even as he spoke, I sensed the evasion in his words. When I replied, he hardly heard my answer, for he had suddenly stepped forward, where he could look directly into those fear twisted eyes.

"Dale," he said at length, turning slowly to face me, "you ask for an explanation of this horror? There *is* an explanation. It is written with an almost fearful clearness on this fellow's mind. Yet if I tell you, you will return to your old skepticism—your damnable habit of disbelief."

I looked at him quietly. I had heard M. S. claim, at other times, that he could read the thoughts of a dead man by the mental image that lay on that man's brain. I had laughed at him. Evidently, in the present moment, he recalled those laughs. Nevertheless, he faced me seriously.

"I can see two things, Dale," he said deliberately. "One of them is a dark, narrow room—a room piled with indistinct boxes and crates, and with an open door bearing the black number 4167. And in that open doorway, coming forward with slow steps—alive, with arms extended and a frightful face of passion—is a decayed human form. A corpse, Dale. A man who has been dead for many days, and is now—*alive*."

M. S. TURNED slowly and pointed with upraised hand to the corpse on the grating.

"That is why," he said simply, "this fellow died from horror."

His words died into emptiness. For a moment I stared at him. Then, in spite of our surroundings, in spite of the late hour, the loneliness of the street, the awful thing beside us, I laughed.

He turned upon me with a snarl. For the first time in my life I saw M. S. convulsed with rage. His old, lined face had suddenly become savage with intensity.

"You laugh at me, Dale," he thundered. "By God, you make a mockery out of a science that I have spent more than my life in studying. You call yourself a medical man—and you are not fit to carry the name. I will wager you, man, that your laughter is not backed by courage."

I fell away from him. Had I stood within reach, I am sure he would have struck me. Struck me! And I have been nearer to M. S. for the past ten years than any man in London. And as I retreated from his temper, he reached forward to seize my arm. I could not help but feel impressed at his grim intentness.

"Look here, Dale," he said bitterly, "I will wager you a hundred pounds that you will not spend the remainder of this night in the warehouse above you. I will wager a hundred pounds against your own courage that you will not back your laughter by going through what this fellow has gone through. That you will not prowl through the corridors of this great structure until you have found room 4167—*and remain in that room until dawn.*"

THERE WAS no choice. I glanced at the dead man, at the face of fear and the clutching, twisted hands, and a cold dread filled me. But to refuse my friend's wager would have been to brand myself an empty coward. I had mocked him. Now, whatever the cost, I must stand ready to pay for that mockery.

"Room 4167?" I replied quietly, in a voice, which I made every effort to control, lest he should discover the tremor in it. "Very well, I will do it."

It was nearly midnight when I found myself alone, climbing a musty, winding ramp between the first and second floors of the deserted building. Not a sound, except the sharp intake of my breath and the dismal creak of the wooden stairs, echoed through that tomb of death. There was no light, not even the usual dim glow that is left to illuminate an unused corridor. Moreover, I had brought no means of light with me—nothing but a half empty box of safety matches which, by some unholy premonition, I had forced myself to save for some future moment. The stairs were black and difficult, and I mounted them slowly, groping with both hands along the rough wall.

I had left M. S. some few moments before. In his usual decisive manner he had helped me to climb the iron grating and lower myself to the sealed alleyway on the farther side. Then, leaving him without a word, for I was bitter against the triumphant tone of his parting words, I proceeded into the darkness, fumbling forward until I had discovered the open door in the lower part of the warehouse.

And then the ramp, winding crazily upward—upward—upward, seemingly without end. I was seeking blindly for that particular room that was to be my destination. Room 4167, with its high number, could hardly be on the lower floors, and so I had stumbled upward…

IT WAS at the entrance of the second floor corridor that I struck the first of my desultory supply of matches, and by its light discovered a placard nailed to the wall. The thing was yellow with age and hardly legible. In the drab light of the match I had difficulty in reading it—but, as far as I can remember, the notice went something like this:

WAREHOUSE RULES:

1. No light shall be permitted in any room or corridor, as a prevention against fire.

2. No person shall be admitted to rooms or corridors unless accompanied by an employee.

3. A watchman shall be on the premises from 7 P.M. until 6 A.M. He shall make the round of the corridors every hour during that interval, at a quarter past the hour.

4. Rooms are located by their numbers: the first figure in the room number indicating its floor location.

I could read no further. The match in my fingers burned to a black thread and dropped. Then, with the burnt stump still in my hand, I groped through the darkness to the bottom of the second ramp.

Room 4167, then, was on the fourth floor—the topmost floor of the structure. I must confess that the knowledge did not bring any renewed burst of courage. The top floor. Three black stair-pits would lie between me and the safety of escape. There would be no escape. No human being in the throes of fear could hope to discover that tortured outlet, could hope to grope his way through Stygian gloom down a triple ramp of black stairs. And even though he succeeded in reaching the lower corridors, there was still a blind alley-way, sealed at the outer end by a high grating of iron bars...

ESCAPE. THE mockery of it caused me to stop suddenly in my ascent and stand rigid, my whole body trembling violently.

But outside, in the gloom of the street, M. S. was waiting, waiting with that fiendish glare of triumph that would brand me a man without courage. I could not return to face him, not though all the horrors of hell inhabited this gruesome place of mystery. And horrors must surely inhabit it, else how could one account for that fearful thing on the grating below? But I had been through horror before. I had seen a man, supposedly dead on the operating table, jerk suddenly to his feet and scream. I had seen a young girl, not long before, awake in the midst of an operation, with the knife already in her frail body. Surely, after those definite horrors, no *unknown* danger would send me cringing back to the man who was waiting so bitterly for me to return.

Those were the thoughts pregnant in my mind as I groped slowly, cautiously along the corridor of the upper floor, searching each closed door for the indistinct number 4167. The place was like the center of a huge labyrinth, a spider-web of black, repelling passages, leading into some central chamber of utter silence and blackness. I went forward with dragging steps, fighting back the dread that gripped me as I went farther and farther from the outlet of escape. And then, after losing myself completely in the gloom, I threw aside all thoughts of return and pushed on with a careless, surface bravado, and laughed aloud.

SO, AT length, I reached that room of horror, secreted high in the deeper recesses of the deserted warehouse. The number—God grant I never see it again—was scrawled in black chalk on the door—4167. I pushed the half-open barrier wide, and entered.

It was a small room, even as M. S. had forewarned me—or as the dead mind of that thing on the grate had forewarned M. S. The glow of my out-thrust match revealed a great stack of dusty boxes and crates, piled against the farther wall. Revealed, too, the black corridor beyond the entrance, and a small, upright table before me.

It was the table, and the stool beside it that drew my attention and brought a muffled exclamation from my lips. The thing had been thrust out of its usual place, pushed aside as if some frenzied shape had lunged against it. I could make out its former position by the marks on the dusty floor at my feet. Now it was nearer to the center of the room, and had been wrenched sidewise from its holdings. A shudder took hold of me as I looked at it. A living person, sitting on the stool before me, staring at the door, would have wrenched the table in just this manner in his frenzy to escape from the room...

THE LIGHT of the match died, plunging me into a pit of gloom. I struck another and stepped closer to the table. And there, on the floor, I found two more things that brought fear to my soul. One of them was a heavy flash-lamp—a watchman's lamp—where it had evidently been dropped. Been dropped in flight. But what awful terror must have gripped the fellow to make him forsake his only means of escape through those black passages? And the second thing—a worn copy of a leather-bound book, flung open on the boards below the stool.

The flash-lamp, thank God, had not been shattered. I switched it on, directing its white circle of light over the room. This time, in the vivid glare, the room became even more unreal. Black walls, clumsy, distorted shadows on the wall, thrown by those huge piles of wooden boxes. Shadows that were like crouching men, groping toward me. And beyond, where the single door opened into a passage of Stygian darkness, that yawning entrance was thrown into hideous detail. Had any upright figure been standing there, the light would have made an unholy phosphorescent specter out of it.

I summoned enough courage to cross the room and pull the door shut. There was no way of locking it. Had I been able to fasten it, I should surely have done so; but the room was evidently an unused chamber, filled with empty refuse. This was the reason, probably, why the watchman had made use of it as a retreat during the intervals between his rounds.

But I had no desire to ponder over the sordidness of my surroundings. I returned to my stool in silence, and stooping, picked up the fallen book from the floor. Carefully I placed the lamp on the table, where its light would shine on the open page. Then, turning the cover, I began to glance through the thing that the man before me had evidently been studying.

And before I had read two lines, the explanation of the whole horrible thing struck me. I stared dumbly down at the little book and laughed. Laughed harshly, so that the sound of my mad cackle echoed in a thousand ghastly reverberations through the dead corridors of the building.

IT WAS a book of horror, of fantasy. A collection of weird, terrifying, supernatural tales with grotesque illustrations in funereal black and white. And the very line I had turned to, the line that had probably struck terror to that unlucky devil's soul, explained M. S.'s "decayed human form, standing in the doorway with arms extended and a frightful face of passion!" The description—the same description—lay before me, almost in my friend's words. Little wonder that the fellow on the grating below, after reading this orgy of horror, had suddenly gone mad with fright. Little wonder that the picture engraved on his dead mind was a picture of a corpse standing in the doorway of room 4167!

I glanced at that doorway and laughed. No doubt of it, it was that awful description in M. S.'s untempered language that had made me dread my surroundings, not the loneliness and silence of the corridors about me. Now, as I stared at the room, the closed door, the shadows on the wall, I could not repress a grin.

But the grin was not long in duration. A six-hour siege awaited me before I could hear the sound of human voice again—six hours of silence and gloom. I did not relish it. Thank God the fellow before me had had foresight enough to leave his book of fantasy for my amusement.

I TURNED to the beginning of the story. A lovely beginning it was, outlining in some detail how a certain Jack Fulton, English adventurer, had suddenly found himself imprisoned (by a mysterious black gang of monks, or something of the sort) in a forgotten cell at the monastery of El Toro. The cell, according to the pages before me, was located in the "empty, haunted pits below the stone floors of the structure…" Lovely setting. And the brave Fulton had been secured firmly to a huge metal ring set in the farther wall, opposite the entrance.

I read the description twice. At the end of it I could not help but lift my head to stare at my own surroundings. Except for the location of the cell, I might have been in the same setting. The same darkness, same silence, same loneliness. Peculiar similarity…

And then: "Fulton lay quietly, without attempt to struggle. In the dark, the stillness of the vaults became unbearable, terrifying. Not a suggestion of sound, except the scraping of unseen rats—"

I dropped the book with a start. From the opposite end of the room in which I sat came a half inaudible scuffling noise—the sound of hidden rodents scrambling through the great pile of boxes. Imagination? I am not sure. At the moment, I would have sworn that the sound was a definite one that I had heard it distinctly. Now, as I recount this tale of horror, I am not sure.

But I am sure of this: There was no smile on my lips as I picked up the book again with trembling fingers and continued.

"The sound died into silence. For an eternity, the prisoner lay rigid, staring at the open door of his cell. The opening was black, deserted, like the mouth of a deep tunnel, leading to hell. And then, suddenly, from the gloom beyond that opening, came an almost noiseless, padded footfall."

THIS TIME there was no doubt of it. The book fell from my fingers, dropped to the floor with a clatter. Yet even through the sound of its falling, I heard that fearful sound—the shuffle of a living foot. I sat motionless, staring with bloodless face at the door of room 4167. And as I stared, the sound came again, and again— *the slow tread of dragging footsteps, approaching along the black corridor without.*

I got to my feet like an automaton, swaying heavily. Every drop of courage ebbed from my soul as I stood there, one hand clutching the table, waiting…

And then, with an effort, I moved forward. My hand was outstretched to grasp the wooden handle of the door. And—I did not have the courage. Like a cowed beast I crept back to my place and slumped down on the stool, my eyes still transfixed in a mute stare of terror.

I waited. For more than half an hour I waited, motionless. Not a sound stirred in the passage beyond that closed barrier. Not a suggestion of any living presence came to me. Then, leaning back against the wall with a harsh laugh, I wiped away the cold moisture that had trickled over my forehead into my eyes.

It was another five minutes before I picked up the book again. You call me a fool for continuing it? A fool? I tell you, even a story of horror is more comfort than a room of grotesque shadows and silence. Even a printed page is better than grim reality.

AND SO I read on. The story was one of suspense, madness. For the next two pages I read a cunning description of the prisoner's mental reaction. Strangely enough, it conformed precisely with my own.

"Fulton's head had fallen to his chest," the script read. "For an endless while he did not stir, did not dare to lift his eyes. And then, after more than an hour of silent agony and suspense, the boy's head came up mechanically. Came up—and suddenly jerked rigid. A horrible scream burst from his dry lips as he stared—stared like a dead man—at the black entrance to his cell. There, standing without motion in the opening, stood a shrouded figure of death. Empty eyes, glaring with awful hate, bored into his own. Great arms, bony and rotten, extended toward him. Decayed flesh—"

I read no more. Even as I lunged to my feet, with that mad book still gripped in my hand, I heard the door of my room grind open. I screamed, screamed in utter horror at the thing I saw there. Dead? Good God, I do not know. It was a corpse, a dead human body, standing before me like some propped-up thing from the grave. A face half eaten away, terrible in its leering grin. Twisted mouth, with only a suggestion of lips, curled back over broken teeth. Hair—writhing, distorted—like a mass of moving, bloody coils. And its arms, ghastly white, bloodless, were extended toward me, with open, clutching hands.

IT WAS alive! Alive! Even while I stood there, crouching against the wall, it stepped forward toward me. I saw a heavy shudder pass over it, and the sound of its scraping feet burned its way into my soul. And then, with its second step, the fearful thing stumbled to its knees. The white, gleaming arms, thrown into streaks of living fire by the light of my lamp, flung violently upwards, twisting toward the ceiling. I saw the grin change to an expression of agony, of torment. And then the thing crashed upon me—dead.

With a great cry of fear I stumbled to the door. I groped out of that room of horror, stumbled along the corridor. No light. I left it behind, on the table, to throw a circle of white glare over the decayed, living-dead intruder who had driven me mad.

My return down those winding ramps to the lower floor was a nightmare of fear. I remember that I stumbled—that I plunged through the darkness like a man gone mad. I had no thought of caution, no thought of anything except escape.

And then the lower door, and the alley of gloom. I reached the grating, flung myself upon it and pressed my face against the bars in a futile effort to escape. The same—as the fear-tortured man— who had—come before—me.

I felt strong hands lifting me up. A dash of cool air, and then the refreshing patter of falling rain.

IT WAS the afternoon of the following day, December 6, when M. S. sat across the table from me in my own study. I had made a rather hesitant attempt to tell him, without dramatics and without dwelling on my own lack of courage, of the events of the previous night.

"You deserved it, Dale," he said quietly. "You are a medical man, nothing more, and yet you mock the beliefs of a scientist as great as Daimler. I wonder—do you still mock the Professor's beliefs?"

"That he can bring a dead man to life?" I smiled, a bit doubtfully.

"I will tell you something, Dale," said M. S. deliberately. He was leaning across the table, staring at me. "The Professor made only one mistake in his great experiment. He did not wait long enough for the effect of his strange acids to work. He acknowledged failure too soon, and got rid of the body." He paused.

"When the Professor stored his patient away, Dale," he said quietly, "he stored it in room 4170, at the great warehouse. If you are acquainted with the place, you will know that room 4170 is directly across the corridor from 4167."

THE END

VACATION IN SHASTA

By Rog Phillips

Over a cliff on Shasta he fell—and into a world of unearthly terror and death.

THE path went steeply downward, numerous small rocks making walking a precarious occupation. Marg—that's my wife—was a few steps ahead of me. Her thirty-five-dollar hairdo looked really worth it with the sun reflecting from it in blonde cascades of light. And her seventy-five-dollar hiking outfit made her million-dollar figure look like a billion.

I'm a business man. Strictly business. When I start up a business it's got to have class. A million-dollar front. It's the same way with Marg. I've got to let people know that my business is good. So she dresses well. All the time. I don't look so bad myself. Jack Sloan's my name. Sloan's Neighborhood Markets. I own a pretty good slice of the government, too. Stockholder. Only forty-one a month ago, and made it all myself except the first thirty thousand. Never mind how I got that.

This path wound down the side of the cliff, a narrow ledge, I guess, and the drop to the valley floor must have been at least three hundred feet. On Mt. Shasta. Maybe you have been over it yourself. I never get tired of looking at Marg. She enjoys that. Anyway, the next thing I had stepped on a round rock and my feet shot out from under me—and the path too.

I dived off that path into space in the most perfect back flip I ever made. Not straight out or I would have missed the outcropping just below, but sort of back the way we came. So that I was almost sliding down the face of the cliff head first, if you see what I mean. I was trying to yell and climb back up and see where I was headed all at the same time.

Anyway, I saw, the ledge just before I hit. It was like a small balcony in front of a second story window like some houses have, only of course, it was just like a natural stone foundation and no

155

railing. I was lucky to fall where I did because the rest of the cliff below the path was smooth as a concrete highway. I put out my hands to break my fall, but was going too fast. I might have been able to have changed my landing into a harmless roll like I used to in high school if there had been any room to roll. There wasn't, though. I went out like a light. One minute I saw the ledge and struck out my hands like you do when you're going to hit the water. All these thoughts went through my mind in nothing flat. The next second I was in here just waking up. At least it seemed like the next second. And don't ask me where "in here" is because I don't know.

There must have been a tunnel opening where I lit and someone must have dragged me quite a way because there's not the slightest bit of light. It bothers me because I'm never sure whether my eyes are open or shut. I've been in here a long time now and it still bothers me.

To get on with the story, I guess I wasn't hurt much in the fall. I didn't even get a headache. I tried a few cautious moves with my arms and legs. Nothing seemed to be wrong so I stood up. I felt a little nauseated and was dizzy for a second. That passed, though.

Stretching out my arms in all directions around me I couldn't touch a wall anywhere. It scared me. Suddenly I thought I had it. The fall had blinded me and I was still on that ledge. The thought of being there, hundreds of feet up the cliff on a small ledge made me so dizzy I sat down again. My hands felt of the floor. I moved along slowly feeling my way over the floor until I reached the wall. Then I stood up, leaning against it and reached upward. Almost out of my reach the wall curved inward. I wasn't blind. At least maybe not. It was a cave. Believe me it was a relief to find I wasn't blind.

I SAT down to do a little thinking. Someone obviously had brought me here and had gone to get help. Maybe it was Marg. The thing to do was stay right where I was put until they came back. So I stayed there.

For perhaps an hour absolutely nothing happened. And I mean absolutely nothing. There wasn't the slightest sound. Not even the drip of water. Nor was there even the faintest trace of light. It was comfortably warm, and there was no breeze.

I felt in my pockets for a match and discovered I didn't have any. Since I don't smoke I very often forget to carry matches. So I just sat there in the darkness and quiet on the floor of the cave, alone in the universe with my thoughts.

Suddenly my thoughts were brushed aside by the forceful odor of a sweating body. The smell you get when you are wrestling with a guy and have your nose next to his sweaty skin. Only this odor was about ten times as strong. And just as suddenly the smell vanished. Then it came back faintly, and the queerest thoughts coursed through my mind. "I must be very quiet. I must move cautiously. Maybe I could suddenly bite a mouthful of this man sitting ahead of me and run away before he could hurt me."

Believe me, I never had such thoughts in my life. I had heard of cannibals, of course. Who hasn't? But to smell a man and enjoy the odor like you do that of a sizzling steak—ugh. I was certainly disgusted with myself.

There came suddenly the first sound I had heard. A pattering sound along the floor. I felt a sharp pain in the calf of my right leg. Instinctively I swatted and connected with a furry body the size of a rat. I could hear it scamper away in the darkness, and I could feel the pain in my leg. But at the same time I could smell that odor again and I felt a tremendous disappointment that I had not been able to get a mouthful of that delicious flesh... Sure, the truth forced itself on me. I was getting those thoughts from the mind of the rat. Either the fall had made me able to read minds or the rat was able to project thoughts as no creature I had ever heard of before could do.

The rat was getting ready to make another attack. His hunger was so acute that it made me hungry. But my excitement and fascination in the exercise of my new faculty of reading a mind engrossed my attention. I analyzed the thoughts I was receiving from him. They certainly weren't words, although my own thoughts had been associated with words so much that it seemed that the rat's thoughts were in the form of words. But careful attention to the thoughts I was receiving enabled me to separate the received thought from the association in my mind quite easily.

Rising to my feet, senses alert, I prepared for the second attack. The rat's anger and fear and hunger were strong in my mind. My odor was a delectable thing in his mind. He darted toward me. I raised my right foot and brought it down with crushing force. I felt the soft yielding body under my foot, the emotion of alarm and panic hit my mind like a sledgehammer blow. Then suddenly my thoughts were entirely my own again.

MY FIRST reaction was one of regret that I had killed the creature. Then loneliness surged through my mind as I realized that I was again alone with my thoughts. I kicked the rat's body to one side in the dark and sat down again to reflect on my amazing experience. Was I actually able to read the rat's mind or was he gifted with the ability to project thoughts so that anyone could have read them? I instantly rejected the thought that I might be crazy and the whole incident a product of my imagination. It had been too vivid and too real. I decided to try an experiment.

Making my mind as nearly blank as I could, I thought loudly, slowly, and clearly, "Help! Help! Can anyone hear my thoughts?" Then I listened with my ears and mind keyed up, but skeptical of results, for it was madness to even think that I would get an answer. So I was really startled when my mind began to hear a voice as slow and distinct as my own mental voice.

"Yes. I can hear you." Amusement, the self-assuredness of one long practiced in the thing he is doing, and friendliness seemed to come with the words as a subdued overtone. "I have been getting a great deal of enjoyment out of listening to your thoughts while you were awakening to your new ability to hear them."

"Who are you and where am I? How do I get out of here?" I asked in a rush of thought.

"I think you are in the passage from the cliff," came the answer. "You will have to guess which way is down and start out. You needn't be afraid. There are no pitfalls in your way. Feel along the wall and you will be all right. My name is Max. I live in here. Have lived here for hundreds of years."

Naturally I thought I hadn't heard him right on that hundreds of years. Later I found that was correct. He had lived in here that long. Anyway, I did as he said and started out down the cave passage. Slowly and cautiously. As I went I talked with Max some more. I explained what had happened to me and who I was.

"How does it happen I can receive and project thoughts?" I finally asked him.

"Everybody down here can do that," he replied. "Your nature was changed by your fall so that you not only can read and talk to other minds down here by telepathy, but also with those outside the cave. The next time you run into a rat you don't need to kill him. Just think fear and the desire to run away. He will think these are his own thoughts and follow them by avoiding you."

"Can I contact Marg, my wife?" I asked eagerly.

"Not yet. But you will be able to after your mind gets stronger," came the reply. Just then the wall started to curve away from me. Max sensed the turning. "Stop just a minute," he said. I stopped and waited for a few minutes.

"What's the matter?" I thought out.

"I'm just contacting the minds of the rats near you who are aware of your proximity in an effort to place your position," Max answered. "There. Now, put your back to the wall and take three steps forward. That should bring you to the opposite side of the branch passage. Ah. That's it. Now go back the way you came a few steps. That's right. A sharp turn. Uh huh. Now you're back on the main passage again. Just keep on."

"How can you hear the rats around me when I can't?" I asked.

"Oh, but you can," came the reply. "Just listen for them."

I listened with my mind and sure enough there was a faint cacophony of little thoughts and sensations impinging on my mind. Thoughts that had the same "feel" as those of the rat I had killed. I was silent for a while, walking along with a reasonable degree of caution. I had been doing a lot of thinking in the back of my mind. I knew I had fallen down that cliff far enough to hurt myself pretty badly. A horrible theory was forcing itself on my consciousness.

"Am I dead?" I asked Max, dreading the reply.

"Oh, no," came back instantly. "You are alive all right. It's just that this place makes you feel so strange. You are having the natural reaction everyone gets when they first come here."

"Everyone?" I echoed. "Don't they get out once they are here?"

"Those that want to can leave," Max answered. "But most of them don't want to by the time they can. You'll know all about that shortly."

SUDDENLY fingers clutched my shoulder and clamped tight. Uncontrolled panic engulfed me. But Max's mental voice broke in to my panic and arrested it. "Here we are," it said. "It's only me."

"*Whew,*" I exploded in relief. "Don't scare me so." I reached out and clutched his arm. Believe me, it was a comfort to touch a fellow man. He chuckled with amusement.

"Let's go where we can see," I demanded. "Or if you've got a match on you, light it. I've got to see if I can see. This darkness is getting me down."

Max chuckled again. Suddenly the cave lit up, and I could see everything. Max was standing just in front of me, his arm still on my shoulder, a smile on his handsome face. He was very tall. About six feet eight, and well built. His black hair went back in a messy pompadour, like he had been combing it back with his fingers instead of a comb. His face was as smooth as a woman's, without a hair on it. His clothes were a sort of cross between a yogi outfit and pair of coveralls. They were made out of a heavy sort of gray material like monk's cloth. And he was barefooted. His eyes were large and round, and a deep blue with a shade of gray in them. A wisdom and understanding seemed to come from them that made me recall his statement that he was hundreds of years old, and I almost could believe that, looking into those eyes.

I stepped back and looked around curiously. The cave walls were white like the surface of a salt lick and very smooth. I looked for the source of the light and couldn't find any. "Where did the light come from?" I asked.

"I made it," came the amazing reply. And Max's lips did not move. They had moved when he chuckled, but not now. He answered my wordless question, "My chuckle has a universal meaning, but I cannot speak your English language. So when I speak, it must be by telepathy and in mental and auditory concepts so that it seems like your language to you."

"How did you make the light?" I asked.

"There really isn't any light, Jack," he replied. "I just know how everything looks and project that knowledge into your consciousness. For example, if you look down at yourself now, you will seem to have no body. If you feel of the wall you will find it is rougher than it looks. The darkness is still here, but to give you comfort I will continue to make it seem like there is light. And since I know these caves very well you will hardly be aware of the difference. In fact, if you think of how you look, slowly, I will give you substance. Then you can see yourself."

Amazed and speechless, I nevertheless managed to think of my clothes, the way my hands look, and everything else about me. And slowly my fingers became solid and real. I looked at it critically and could find nothing wrong with it. I felt of different parts of me and they felt just as they looked.

"Well, I'll—be—darned," I exclaimed. "Now I've seen everything!"

"Oh, no you haven't," said Max, laughing. And now his lips moved so that I would have sworn he was talking. I marveled more and more.

Every part of his features was clear in detail. It seemed impossible that it was really dark, and that I was really seeing only a mental image in the mind of my new friend.

"Soon you will not need me to see," he said, reading my thoughts. "When you become stronger you will be able to 'see' objects in reality by sensing the feeble insect thoughts around you, paying attention only to their strength and direction, and fill in the gaps. You will be able to explore the caves and the surrounding country at will by reading what the various life forms are sensing around them. But, come. I can see that you are tired and hungry after your long hike up above, your fall, and subsequent adventures. I have taken the liberty to contact your wife and tell her of your whereabouts, since you are at present not sufficiently strong to do so yourself."

HOW right he was. I suddenly became aware that I was so tired and hungry that I would have laid down right there if I had been alone. Max turned and started down the passageway and I walked along beside him. After about a mile of this we emerged into a large open cave. The roof was not high. No more than twenty feet at the highest point. The floor was level. In the center of the cave there was a group of people of about the same appearance as Max. Most of them were lying on the floor in various stages of repose. A few were standing in a small group and seemed to be talking.

Max called out to them and they turned toward him. There followed an exchange of thought so rapid that I could get very little of it, and that little did not make any sense. The emotions that accompanied the exchange were plain, however, and they were mostly fear and puzzlement and worry. I gathered there was some sort of danger threatening them.

They became aware of my presence and asked Max about me. "He is the newcomer from the cliff," replied Max. "He has had enough for one day so we will feed him and let him sleep for awhile. Then he can meet all of us." They all smiled at me and nodded their heads in greeting. A table of food was brought to me and I was really pleased, for it might have come from the hotel down in the valley. Hot coffee, a standard salmon steak dinner with hot rolls, topped off with a piece of perfect apple pie.

I went to sleep shortly after, with a vague feeling that something was screwy somewhere, but I couldn't quite put my finger on it.

I AWOKE to complete darkness. For a second it made me panicky, then the memory of yesterday's events came back with a rush and I calmed down. Without moving, I probed the darkness. At first nothing came to me. Then, little by little, thoughts entered my consciousness that were like those of the rats. Little feeding thoughts, and odor thoughts with alien pleasure and fear associations accompanying them. For a while I amused myself by studying them and trying to identify the creatures that were thinking them. But soon I wanted to greet my new friend, Max, so I called out verbally, "Max, how about some light on the subject?" There was no answer, either verbal or mental.

I listened with all my senses alert, trying to get one thought that was human. I found that by imagining my mind was going out farther and farther, the insect and rat thoughts changed the same way they would have done if they were actual sounds and I was walking along, overtaking and then passing them. After a little practice I was able to point my thought receiving sense in one direction and cause it to travel forward or backward at any speed, or suddenly jump forward an unknown distance. But I had no way of knowing how far away any particular mind was, because the darkness made it impossible to coordinate my actual focusing with real distances.

I tried to remember how far it was across the cavern. As nearly as I could remember it was about two hundred feet. And I had lain down almost in the center. So it should be about a hundred feet to the wall in any direction. I directed my mental perception slowly forward in an attempt to contact insect thoughts on the wall of the cavern. It worked. At what I thought should be a hundred feet the faint conglomeration of feelings, thoughts suddenly became strong. I held my attention there and willed it to gradually focus on one insect. Soon it had done so so completely that consciously I was almost that insect. I was aware of its every thought—the sensory impressions it was receiving, the feeling of six legs moving in rhythm, the busy but contented mood of the thing as it found an occasional particle of food, and the taste of the morsel in its mouth. The taste, however, although it was pleasant to the insect was quite nauseating to me. The nausea upset my effort at concentration and I lost the contact I had with the bug.

My mind drew in on itself and I began to wonder what had become of my companions. That feeling that something was screwy, which I had had when I went to sleep, returned. It was the meal I had eaten, of course. Hypnosis. There had been no meal. But I had received some sort of nourishment because even now I felt full, and I must have been asleep several hours.

I grew restless and felt that I must get up and move around. Rising to my feet I sent my mind along the floor ahead of me and walked slowly toward the wall. It worked smoothly. I became aware of the wall as I neared it, and when I thought it must be only a foot in front of me I reached out and touched it. It really was a foot in front of me! Confidence surged through me. I turned and walked across the cavern again and again, exercising my new powers. It wasn't long before I felt that I could go anyplace in the caverns without bumping into a thing.

I HAD to laugh in sheer exultation. Here I was, Jack Sloan, owner and operator of a chain of grocery stores. My whole life had been wrapped up in price lists, bank balances, and paying my wife's bills. I had never gone to church nor read a serious book in my adult life, and now look at me…In twenty-four hours I had become a master telepathist. I didn't need any eyes. I could use the senses of the living creatures around me to tell me where I was. I felt a comradeship with nature come over me that was so overwhelming that a tear actually squeezed out of my eye and slid down onto my nose.

Where had Max and his friends gone? I tried to contact him again with nothing but silence for an answer. So I decided to start out looking for him. There were several tunnels leading off from the cavern. I picked one at random and decided to explore it for perhaps a mile. If I found nothing I would come back and try another one.

The one I had chosen led downward at a steep slant and was fairly straight. I went about a mile without finding anything other than the insects. So I returned and retraced my steps. I had come back about half way when the tunnel started to slope downward again. That was wrong… It should go uphill right back to the cavern. I must have taken a branch tunnel. I about-faced and retraced my steps a short way, slowly exploring for the juncture of the two tunnels. I soon came to it and followed the one that went uphill.

Now I went more cautiously, watching for branches. There were several, but I kept on the main one and went slowly, sending my new sense ahead to explore.

I had gone much more than the distance back to the cavern, and finally was forced to conclude that I was lost. One of those branches back there was the one to the cavern. But which one? Finding my way back now seemed out of the question. If I continued onward I would soon be completely lost. I might starve to death before Max could find me. My prospects seemed utterly hopeless. I sank to the floor in despair and self reproach. I should have stayed in the cavern until Max returned.

Now if I continued upward I would get hopelessly lost. If I went downward my chances of picking the right branch were pretty slim. And if I stayed here I would never get any place. Of the three choices, going back down seemed the most promising. Eventually I might stumble on a tunnel that would lead to the outside. I wondered if these caves in the heart of Mt. Shasta had ever been explored. Certainly the mountain must be honeycombed with them. I puzzled over the mystery of Max. Who was he and where did he fit? And greatest puzzle of all—how did it happen that I was sudden-gifted with the ability to read minds vividly? Had the fall on my head brought that about? Or was there some property of these caverns that made it possible? I was in a strange and utterly fantastic world. There was no doubt about that. If I ever got back into my own world and kept my ability to read minds—

I had to chuckle.

I went back down the way I had come, taking it easy and occasionally probing ahead of me as far as I could by reading the thoughts of insects, rats, and even an occasional snake that had wandered into the caves and became lost or, perhaps, had found food more plentiful and stayed. It was fascinating to exercise my new faculty of mind reading on all these creatures. I had by now become so adept at it that I could almost become a part of the creature, causing it to do things at my command.

The tunnel I was in wound downward at a slope of about thirty degrees, sometimes leveling off for a hundred feet or so. There were many branches, and sometimes no indication as to which branch to take. Several times I bumped my head when the ceiling dropped lower than my five-feet-ten.

I HAD been traveling in this fashion for what seemed like several hours, although I had no way of telling the passage of time and it might have been only a half hour, when I heard the vague murmur of human voices. They were so faint that at first I thought they were the sound of a waterfall, but as I went forward they became stronger and I could make out an occasional word. For some reason I became cautious, cloaking my thoughts or at least hoping I was doing that, while at the same time I tried to read the thoughts of those ahead of me. The sounds were traveling farther than my mind reading ability could reach, however, so I continued on downward. When I came to a branch I would go down the passage from which the sounds seemed to come. If they grew fainter, I would retrace my steps and try the other branch.

Needless to say, the going was very slow. I had to stop quite often and probe ahead, always being careful that my own thoughts were as quiet as I could make them. I remembered that Max had said that everyone here could read thoughts, and that Max's companions had been worried about something.

Suddenly a weight landed on my back. I turned in an attempt to throw it off and other bodies engulfed me so that in a matter of seconds I was completely overpowered. New thoughts beat against my mind. Evil exultation, glee, anticipation of some terrible thing that was to be done to me. They had been doing what I had thought I was doing—cloaking their thoughts so that I could not read them. And now that they were no longer doing so their evil minds delighted in letting me see what I was in for.

With at least two holding each of my arms and legs I was carried along, struggling, until we reached a cavern considerably larger than the one Max's friends had been in. In the center was a roaring fire, the smoke escaping through an opening in the roof. The flames lit up the cavern and my captors. Actually seeing them only served to increase my alarm. Where Max had been human, intelligent, and friendly in appearance, my captors were utterly beastly.

They were short. No taller than five feet at the most. Very wide and husky looking. Their bodies were naked except for loincloths, and covered with a scanty, fuzzy growth of downy white hair. Their legs were stocky and bowed like those of some Japs I had seen, their arms reaching to the knees like an ape's. Their faces, although entirely human in structure, were beastly in expression, with large lips and teeth. A sloping forehead retreated into a thatch of matted white hair that fell down over their shoulders in back. I saw with absolute certainty that I could expect no mercy whatever from them. They were depraved beasts—human only in form.

But even in my hopelessness I marveled that a race of such creatures could live in the heart of the Shasta Mountain without being discovered. Surely they would have to make forays into the surrounding country for food. Obviously they had been cave people for many generations to develop their present appearance. I had very little inclination to wonder about their history though, because they were crowded around me and pinching and poking me unmercifully as a few of them concentrated on tying my arms and legs together in such a way that I would be unable to move. They seemed completely insane and without any human characteristics.

I sent a desperate mental plea for Max to come to my aid. Instantly one of the brutes struck me in the mouth, crushing my lips against my teeth. "Do that again and you'll wish you hadn't," he telepathed. I sagged to the ground and gave up even the desire to live. But they were not through with me.

ONE of them crowded through around me and came back with a saw and a large knife. The others shrieked with delight. Evidently this was something they were going to especially enjoy, so I looked for the worst. The worst was beyond my ability to conceive.

"Ears first! Ears first!" clamored the crowd. Grinning, the devil bent over, grabbed an ear, and to my unspeakable horror, sliced. He stood up and swung my amputated ear in front of my eyes, grinning, his fat lips open and exposing his oversize teeth. My vision blurred and I fainted.

Not for long was I blessed with oblivion. I opened my eyes to see the circle of faces still around me. There was something in my mouth. I wondered what it could be and instantly the thought message, "Your ear, your ear, your ear!" beat on my staggering mind.

I spit it out, nausea and horror pouring over me in wave after wave.

The devil with the knife bent over me again. Soon I seemed to live in a stupor. As these unholy fiends progressed in their torture I became numb. No longer did they seem to know nor care how I reacted. They were too engrossed in their torture.

When they used the saw on my bones in their many and progressive amputations of my feet, legs, fingers, hands, and arms the rasping pain of the saw teeth cutting soon receded into a dull, inexpressible torture. The rest I was beyond feeling. I knew I had been cut up too much to live long. I waited only for death to deliver me.

My mind wandered. I tried to talk, but my lips were gone and my tongue was a bloody mass in my mouth. A few times my mind cleared enough for me to see my surroundings. Finally I was alone. I sank into oblivion.

I AWOKE at last. Opening my eyes I saw that the fire still burned. But, of my captors there was no trace. My ropes were gone. I rolled over onto my stomach and feebly raised up until I was swaying on my feet. Then, the memory of my torture came back. *But...I was standing...and my legs had been cut off inch by inch...* My arms? My hands? They were still on! I reached up and felt of my ears and they were intact. *But...I had seen one and had spit it out of my mouth...?*

My mind reeled. For a time I was completely insane. Laughing and crying I tried to run. My legs would fail me and cause me to sprawl forward.

Rising, I would frantically run on. Soon I stumbled into a tunnel. Whimpering and shivering I felt my way along the walls of the passage, stumbling from one wall to the other, no longer able to concentrate enough to progress as I had done before my nightmarish dream. I was gradually coming to believe it must have been a dream, for it would have been an utter impossibility to have actually lost my limbs and then regained them, not to mention my ears, lips, and tongue.

At first I feared pursuit, but as I traveled further and further downward this fear wore off. Soon I felt safe enough to sit down and rest and collect my thoughts. I tried not to think of my horrible experience, but instead, to concentrate on regaining my ability to read thoughts. After a time I was able to hear the little thought murmurs of the insects along the tunnel, so I arose and proceeded on my downward journey. My one paramount desire was to escape the darkness and horror of these caves and be once again in the heavenly sunlight of the outside.

How long I traveled downward I have no way of knowing. Sometimes I slept. I vaguely began to wonder if I had not gone so far down that I was underneath the valley at the base of the mountain. I had no desire to eat for some reason. My naps seemed not only to refresh me but to nourish me as well.

Soon I began to feel a mysterious presence. I could sense a mind observing me from time to time, but though I questioned it I received no reply. Most of the time it wasn't there. Then I would sense it just as I had about decided it must be imagination.

"Hello," I would telepath. But there was no answer. I studied my feelings toward this unknown mind. It did not seem to be evil. Yet it didn't seem to be friendly, either.

I came to a branch in the tunnel and decided to take the right fork. A powerful feeling pressed on me and against my will I turned to the left. It recalled to my mind the fact that I had done the same thing to a snake before I was captured by the cave devils. Fearful, I tried to turn back. I couldn't. Then the voice came.

It is impossible to describe that voice. Mental though it was, it had the qualities of sound. Deep and resonant. Calm and unhurried as though the mind in back of it were immeasurably ponderous and wise. Utterly clear and concise in detail came the voice.

"You do not need to be afraid. Come. Come to me and I will help you leave the caves."

With a new confidence I stepped forward. Hope was like a refreshing liquid coursing through my veins. But at the same time a suspicion was forming in the back of my mind. As if in answer to my thought the voice came again.

"Yes. I am a woman. My name is Ee."

I hurried, almost at a trot. No longer did I have to grope my way through the tunnel. My steps were firm and sure. At each branch I took the correct fork unhesitatingly.

And soon the darkness began to grow less. I could make out the walls of the passage and see ahead a way. The light grew until it was as bright as day. Yet I knew it was not light. It was the same as the brightness of Max's light. So it was mental. The darkness was still there but I could see.

Ee must have a metal power much greater than that of Max, I thought, to be able to do all this.

I ENTERED a long, straight tunnel that ran level for a hundred yards. At the far end the light was blinding. Suddenly, I knew that it was partly real light. Not the mentally induced illusion of lighted surroundings. I hurried ahead and in a moment was emerging from the tunnel into an underground world of such titanic proportions that I was stunned with amazement.

The cavern was so vast that it seemed almost to be an open valley under a noonday sun. Perhaps a mile away across a valley covered with yellowish grass the far wall loomed as a gigantic barrier, extending to the right and to the left almost as far as the eye could reach before curving inward to eventually join the cliff at my back. The roof was an immense dome whose curves were lost in a floating white mist, far overhead. Through this mist, or from it, came the light that gave life to this underground world.

Here and there on the grassy plain creatures something like deer grazed peacefully, and several small hills, on which grew stunted trees whose tortuously twisting branches were sparsely covered with yellow leaves, rose slightly to hide part of the landscape from view. It was a study in yellow and gray that would have challenged the world's greatest artists.

Coming toward me from the nearest wooded hill were several figures. Leading the group were Max and Ee. I ran toward them, an immense relief surging over me. In answer to my rush of questions Max told me that they had been surprised by a group of the cave barbarians and had barely escaped with their lives. Due to the fact that I had been asleep and they had drawn the barbarians off in their flight, I had escaped capture at that time.

I thought of my torture and my waking up to find my limbs were intact and decided to keep still on that so they wouldn't think me insane. Max, reading my thoughts, looked grim. "That is their way," he replied. "Physical torture is as nothing compared to that induced by hypnosis. They are masters at it."

But now I was close to the group. Getting a good look at Ee, I stopped, breathless. If I thought before that I knew what beauty was I knew now that I was wrong. She was about five-feet-six, slender, but well built. That part was more or less standard. Her face and eyes and hair were what took my breath. They had a beauty impossible to describe. It was a thing in itself that seemed to envelop her features, rather than be a part of them. Suddenly I remembered that they could read my thoughts and I blushed. Ee blushed too.

Max smoothed over our embarrassment by saying, "We had better get back to the temple. We are too exposed out here."

So with Max on one side of me and Ee on the other we hastened toward the wooded hillock they called their temple. The rest of the group were the same ones that I had met with Max what seemed ages ago. They all seemed to be of the same race. Whether it was any race found on the surface I don't know. But I am sure it wasn't any white European race.

Many things were puzzling me and I lost no time in asking about them. "How soon can I get out of here to the outside?" I asked anxiously.

"We will discuss that later," replied Max. "There are many things you must learn and many more you must do before you could possibly make it to the surface."

"The surface?" I queried. "Then we are actually under the surface of the valley?"

"No. We are under the mountain," Ee chipped in. "But our level is almost a mile under that of the valley."

I WHISTLED in amazement. We were now near one of the creatures grazing on the plain. I examined it in curiosity. Shaped something like a deer, it was nevertheless smaller and chunkier. Its horns were more like those of a moose, but lighter in build and longer and more branched, the branches having a bony web-like growth connecting them. They were completely unconcerned about our approach, not even lifting their heads at our passing.

"They must be pretty good eating," I remarked, nodding my head toward the one we were passing.

"I wouldn't know," replied Max, smiling. "You see, we are a vegetarian people down here. Not exactly vegetarian either. We take most of our nourishment in the form of pills. Their manufacture process has been handed down for generations and we have lived on nothing else for many generations also. Some vegetable substances go into their makeup, but for the most part they are chemical."

But now we were entering the wooded area. A few steps through the outer fringe of trees brought us to a stone entryway. I now perceived that what I had mistakenly thought to be a hill was in reality a building whose sides were sloping, and covered with soil. In this soil the trees found root. In fact, as I found later, they were planted and cultivated because the leaves were the vegetable source used in the manufacture of the food tablets.

The entryway gave access to a long narrow hall whose walls were made of large blocks of marble-like stone. On either wall along its length doorways could be seen. The doors were made of wood and slid into the wall, as I found when Max opened the third one we came to. The room we entered was a large oblong one with a high ceiling, dotted with lights. These, as I soon found upon inquiry, were globes of the same radioactive stuff that coated the dome outside, and were mainly chunks that had broken loose from time to time and fallen to the plain.

We were soon seated in large stone chairs that were cushioned with soft pillows covered with the same monk's cloth material as the clothes these people wore. There were perhaps a hundred people of both sexes in the room. I noticed that they all seemed to be about the same age—the men about forty and the women about twenty-five. It surprised me to find, after I had been there some time that the youngest of them was several centuries old. I could never quite bring myself to believe that we had looked the same when our pilgrim fathers were founding the new nation.

It seemed to be some sort of an assembly held to discuss my entry into their midst. While I was looking and taking in everything, Max was talking in a strange language to the assembly.

I tried to tune into what was being said and found to my amazement that I couldn't read thoughts in here. Maybe there was some sort of a blanketing device or maybe they were just cloaking their thoughts from me. Anyway, it was so much like my old life not to be able to hear thoughts that a feeling of loneliness crept over me. I started to think of Marg and the stores. I wondered if she thought I was dead. Then I remembered that Max had contacted her and told her I was all right. I chuckled. If he had done that the disembodied voice proclaiming my safety had more than likely convinced Marg that I was dead, rather than the opposite… Wouldn't she be surprised?

A slight tap on my shoulder brought me back to the present. Max had been saying something to me. He repeated it.

"Jack, we have been talking over your chances of making it to the surface. They are very slim. Impossible, the way you are now.

The droogas, those people, if you care to call them that, that tortured you, are a very numerous race. And they occupy all the avenues of escape from this underground world. We have never bothered to secure an avenue of access to the outside because we had no need of one. We are able, as you know, to contact the outside without going there, and are too contented with our life here to want a change. Here we have our libraries, which contain the history of our people, their science and culture, the history and development of your own people as we have observed it through their own eyes, together with our comments on it, and many other things."

Ans now, Ee interrupted him. "Jack, if you choose to stay with us I am sure you will be happy. You can learn and grow powerful in mind so that you can sit back like a god and read the hearts of mortal men. You will not become immortal, but you can live several centuries. And believe me, you will not regret it ever. I realize you love your wife very much, and that your past life was fascinating. That you enjoyed your business and your associates. But if you go back that joy cannot last more than another ten or twenty years. Your wife will grow old before your eyes. You will eventually have to relegate your business activities to the younger generation. And almost tomorrow, so to speak, you will die an old man. Here you will just have started to live." And there was a promise in her eyes that could not be mistaken.

"If you choose to go," Max broke in, "there is the very great risk of being captured again by the droogas. You will know that their torture is hypnosis, but that won't make it any less. In two years' time you can make your mind so strong that it will be possible for you to cloak your thoughts completely. Then you will stand a real chance of getting through. But then your wife will believe you dead, will have sold your stores and may be married again."

"What is wrong with several of you going along with me?" I asked. "Couldn't some of you help me get out? If that is impossible, why couldn't I write Marg a note? Something she could understand? And one of you who are so strong mentally take it to her or mail it to her?"

"Unfortunately," Max's voice was very sad, "the one of us who did that would die. You surface people have a virus, which only gives you a cold, but which causes us to die in great agony and fever. Here in the caves that virus dies in a week. But before that week could pass your messenger would be dead. That is why I could not bring you straight here when I first found you. I had to risk infection in order to give you enough food tablets to keep you nourished for a week. But it was necessary for you to wander around for a week until your cold virus had been killed by the sterilizing rays of the metals in the cave walls."

"You see," one of the others added, "we cannot permit anyone of us to take the risk for what we must consider a relatively unimportant thing. And it would be utterly impossible for you to reach the surface yourself without being captured and tortured many times. You would probably reach the surface an imbecile, your mind destroyed by the strain of dying a thousand horrible deaths."

I looked from one to the other of the assembly. "You are offering me a choice, but in reality there is no choice. Is that it?" I asked. And solemnly one after another nodded his head.

"There is no choice," Ee voiced their unspoken sympathy. "But we had to let you see it for yourself. If we had just said you had to stay you would have thought yourself our prisoner. Really, we would be very happy if we could restore you to your former life but we cannot."

"Well, I guess I'll have to make the best of it then," I concluded aloud, trying to sound cheerful.

"For the time being, at any rate," smiled Ee. Taking my hand she led me toward the doorway. "Come with me. I'll show you around. We have many beautiful works of art. And there is the library where you will have to spend a large part of your time studying."

THE library was a large, very long room with stacks crowding the whole floor, leaving narrow corridors between each stack of shelves, which went all the way to the ceiling. Off the library proper, and entered by a long row of doorways that stretched along one whole wall, there were small study rooms.

I picked a book off the shelves and looked at it. "Ha. You have overlooked something, Ee," I said. "These books are written in your own language and I was never any good at learning foreign languages."

"Look at it again," she answered with a peculiar smile on her face.

I looked, and the meaningless symbols that covered its pages suddenly became intelligible. Startled, I asked "How did that happen?"

"Oh, it's very simple. I just caused you to be able to understand the writing," she said. Wasn't that just like a woman? Later, after we had looked around some more she added, like an afterthought, "I will only have to cause you to understand the writing for a few days. Then you will have sufficiently strong memory tracts of the language to continue by yourself."

From the library we entered the art museum. There I saw the statues and paintings of things long ago lost to the world. People and animals in stone, and so lifelike in detail that I had to ask Ee if they were really stone or if they had been petrified by some chemical process. Paintings of strange landscapes and cities with buildings reaching thousands of feet into the sky. My mind was full of questions, but I left them unspoken. I had sensed a certain feeling of reverence and reserve come over Ee when we had entered this room and had the strange feeling that we should remain silent in here—like it was a church. So without a word we passed through this museum into the next room.

Here there were machines in orderly rows. They were strange. Some seemed to be nothing but boxes with a knob or two sticking out on the top. Some had a dome top that seemed to be separated from the base so that it might be turned about and aimed, and had a spiral coil of copper pipe attached on opposite sides, coiled in the shape of a flat, slightly concave disk. Like a cal-rod unit. These went into a ball joint in the dome. There were also large, transparent cylinders with complicated looking tubing and gloves of glass and copper attached to them in various places.

Ee broke the silence. "This is the storeroom for our machinery. We have had no use for it for a long time. We are now able to do most of the things these machines were designed for without them. For example, this machine was designed to renew the body so that it would last almost indefinitely. We can now do that by an effort of will—until it comes our turn to advance to the next world." She was pointing to one of the cylinders. Turning to one of the boxes with knobs she said, "This machine was designed to solve problems in logic and mathematics. We have no further use for it because it has long ago completed its work."

We left this room of wonders. Max was waiting for us in the hall. "Well, now that you have seen the sights, it is time to show you the room you are to live in while you are here. It will be yours to do with as you please," he said.

And so my first day ended in the city of my new friends. I call it day, though there was no night here. I was tired and completely exhausted. The reaction had set in from my nightmarish period in the dark of the tunnels and my capture by the Droogas. Here I thought I was safe. If I had known what was in store for me in the near future I wouldn't have felt quite so secure, though.

THE next few days went swiftly and were fascinating in the extreme. I learned to project my mind at will, sending it into the caves farther and farther each day. Finally I could reach as far as the outside. Then, for some reason, my schooling switched to history and other subjects. I resolved secretly to send my mind to the surface without the knowledge of my teachers but found that my room had been shielded to prevent my doing so.

The next morning I hunted up Max, and I was mad and determined to have it out. "Max!" I said when I ran into him in one of the workrooms. "What the hell is the matter with my sending my mind to the outside? My life is out there. My business, my wife, and all my friends. If you think for one minute that you can maneuver me into being in love with Ee and be content to stay down here you're crazy. And I don't want any of your superior airs, either. Even if you are hundreds of years old and so much smarter than me that you class me as an idiot."

"Just a minute, Jack," Max interrupted my mad outburst. "We thought you understood. You don't have the slightest conception of the nature of telepathy, do you?"

"Sure I do," I replied. "You just send out your mind, so to speak. It's a sort of organ like the eye or the ear, only it doesn't get developed in surface people. That is, the part you read minds with."

"Hmm. I see." Max looked serious and grave. "Did you ever entertain the possibility that it might be something—ah, radically different than that?" He gave me a piercing, studious look. "No, I see you haven't, Jack."

He was silent for so long I thought he had forgotten me or intended to ignore me. Just as I had thought up something to say that would really stir him up, he spoke.

"This calls for a meeting of better minds than mine. Skip your studies today, Jack, and go for a walk. Visit one of the other temples if you like. I'll send for you when we have discussed this."

"O.K." I said and turned to go.

"Don't do anything rash, Jack, and take the underground passages. Don't go out on the plain," called Max after me as I left the workroom.

"Nuts to you," I thought to myself and hoped he wasn't listening. I was still mad and intended to do as I pleased. Just to spite him I decided to go out on the plain, although I really wanted to take one of the underground passages. They were really interesting with their mural paintings of all kinds of historical scenes. I never tired of looking at them. When you looked at one intently for awhile it seemed to become real, with people moving, the wind blowing, or the waves moving, depending on what the picture was about. And after looking awhile longer you could almost get right into the painting and travel around and be there.

I left the temple by the same door I had first entered it. No one was in sight. Staying just within the outer fringe of trees I circled around to the side of the woods facing the nearest neighboring temple that was about two hundred yards away and about the same distance from the gigantic wall of the cavern as the one I had been in. As I circled I examined the plain, searching for signs of life other than the ever-present, grazing, deer-like animals. I could see the black opening I had come from when I entered the cavern. Also there were several others, widely separated, along the base of the cavern wall. Far up the face of the cliff several other openings could also be seen. But there was no sign of any human being.

I did not dare to probe outward with my mind, for, as yet, I was not too expert at cloaking my thoughts so that no one could be aware of them, and I did not want Max to know that I was disobeying him.

I struck out through the knee-high yellow grass in a fast, nervous stride, keeping my eyes peeled toward the many tunnel openings so that I would not be surprised by a sudden rush of the drooga people if they were hiding there.

To my right and perhaps fifty feet ahead a deer was grazing. Suddenly it started to run toward me, then veered off toward the wooded area I was headed for. I stopped in my tracks and peered intently toward where it had been. There was an almost imperceptible movement of the grass, as though someone or something were slowly creeping toward me.

I broke into a trot. In the next instant there arose from the grass dozens of the ape-like droogas in a circle about me. I was surrounded by them. My only hope lay in reaching one side of the ring before they could close in, and overpowering the one or two that blocked my way of escape, so I changed my trot to a frantic burst of speed. But they, sensing my purpose, headed me off.

Suddenly I was knocked flat by some inexplicable force. And in the air around me several glowing, golden balls of fire appeared, hovering motionless. The droogas came to a quick halt and above the head of each a small, black globe appeared, slowly enlarging until it was almost as large as the golden balls. The blackness of each seemed alive. It seemed to flow and undulate, recede and recede into the infinite distance and yet remain stationary. The golden ones about me seemed to have that same quality but with the additional appearance of angry, and unlimited power.

A bolt of raw force lashed out from one of the golden balls and struck a black one. The black one bounced backward, seemed to hesitate for an instant as though it were tied to the drooga by a string, and then, as if the string had suddenly broken, it darted upward toward the glowing mist in the top of the cavern, growing smaller as it receded, until it vanished. At the same time the drooga over which it had been hovering seemed to go lax. His eyes took on a vacant stare and he slowly dropped to his knees, then sprawled forward on his face into the tall grass.

There was a sudden silence that seemed to last for hours. The gold and the black balls hung motionless as if waiting, or gathering forces. Suddenly a flash of intense black lashed out toward a golden globe. A few feet away from it it seemed to strike an invisible wall, hesitate, and then vanish.

The droogas slowly began to step backward, their eyes toward the golden balls of fire around me, the black globes above them retreating with them, poised like boxers in the ring, ready to attack or defend themselves on an instant's notice.

One moment the golden balls were hovering around me, pulsing, cold fury radiating from them in surging waves. The next moment it was as if they had never been there. At almost the same moment the black balls vanished and the droogas turned and ran toward the nearest exit to the cavern.

The one who had fallen remained motionless. I got up out of the grass and approached him. He was dead all right, and as I watched his body seemed to melt and run into the soil. A vapor arose from his slowly vanishing form and drifted aimlessly toward the cliff. In a few moments there was no trace of him left.

Then, crystal-clear, came the mental voice of Max. "Return to the temple, Jack. We are ready to talk to you." Slowly I turned and retraced my steps to the temple. I felt like a child who was about to be reprimanded, and I was angry at Max and his friends for being so superior and making me feel so inferior, and angry at myself for the feeling. And I was full of wonder and puzzlement at what had just transpired. By the time I reached the entrance to the temple I was in a very humble and contrite mood.

Hesitatingly I walked down the corridor and slid back the door to the council chamber where I had first gone that day, so long ago it seemed, when I arrived. In it there were six men, including Max. They wore grave looks, and when they asked me to sit down I did so without a word. The six moved stools in front of me and sat on them, facing me. No word was spoken for a while. They seemed to be waiting. And I was too subdued to feel like doing more than wait and meet whatever was to happen when it happened.

Finally Max spoke, "Jack, we have decided the time has come for you to go on a journey." He turned his eyes toward the ceiling and they took on a faraway look. In that position he continued,

"You aren't ready yet. You should wait longer. But you aren't content. So we will have to accompany you on this journey to the surface. It will have to be a trip of the mind only. The droogas know that you are here and that you wish to return to the surface. They will keep a constant watch, and our power to defeat them does not extend beyond this cavern."

"Those gold and black balls…?" I queried.

Ignoring my interruption he continued, while the other five sat silent and poker-faced, watching me. "You may wonder how we can accompany you on a mental journey. Well, we won't go into any explanations now. You will be in constant mental contact with the six of us. We will be by your side, so to speak, and as aware of everything you see and think as you are yourself.

"We cannot be gone long," he went on, "because your mind is not yet able to take sustained journeys. So we will guide you to save time. You want to contact your wife, see her, and tell her you are all right? We will not have time for much more than that. In order for you to be guided you will have to enter a state of willing hypnosis. Tlon Atlee," and he nodded toward one of the silent five, "will put you in that state as soon as you feel up to the strain."

"I feel up to it right now," I put in hastily.

"Sorry," Max said. And his voice carried a tone of dismissal. "You must have a good night's sleep and be thoroughly at ease before we start. We will meet you here in the morning." He rose and the others also stood up.

"Okay," I said, also rising. "That's a date."

Smiling wryly, Max added a parting admonition as I turned toward the door, "Keep out of trouble meanwhile, will you, Jack?"

LIFE in the temple had a definite rhythm similar to that on the surface. Although there was continual light from the globes of radioactive stuff it could be covered by the sliding covers that each had so that darkness could be obtained for the period of sleep. There was no set time for sleeping, yet everyone slept at about the same time, the community interests more or less imposing a definite time for rest on the individual. I spent the rest of the day in the library, studying the history of Max's people before they had lived in the cavern.

They had been a powerful and numerous race of people, living in great cities and plying the oceans in motor ships thousands of years before the dawn of history as we knew it on the surface. Their science was much further advanced than ours of today. They had space ships, which were propelled by what they called the "light principle," and were a very superstitious race—although science and superstition shouldn't go together. Most of their history concerned itself with the development of the powers of the spirit and contained a lot of hocus-pocus about soul power. Also they seemed to put great store in ancestor worship, like the Japs, who claimed to talk regularly with departed spirits, and everyone seemed to believe them—or so the books said. However, there must have been a few sane people among them or they couldn't have built space ships and developed other scientific things we don't have yet on the present day world.

I am not mathematically inclined and not even Ee could "cause" me to become interested in the mathematical symbols that covered the pages in their books of science, so I learned nothing about their scientific theories.

The day finally wore to a close and I retired to my room. Eventually I slept. There must have been a mickey in the pills I had for my dinner. I noticed a peculiar gleam in the eye of the girl who brought them to me. At any rate I slept soundly and awoke in the morning refreshed and anxious to get going.

When I arrived at the council chamber the same six men were waiting for me. Tlon cast a professional eye on me, in the same way a trainer eyes a boxer who is about to go into the ring. "How do you feel?" he asked me.

"Oh, fine," I replied. "When do we start?" And I felt the same stage fright that I used to feel before I went in the ring when I used to box in college.

"Right now," Tlon answered. "Sit down over here where you can be comfortable and just let your mind relax. Put yourself in a receptive mood. You will have to be guided every minute, so don't try to think for yourself."

While he was talking I was being seated, and as he finished I laid my head back on the cushion placed on the chair back to accommodate it and looked into his eyes. He began to talk in a slow, melodious voice. And as he talked I let my mind follow his words passively...

There were seven of us speeding along at incredible velocity. I looked at them amazed, for they were balls of golden fire, and yet I knew they were my companions, Max, Tlon, and the other four, and could recognize them. Max was the ball of fire in the lead. Tlon was speeding along beside me. The six formed a ring about me. We were in one of the tunnels and travelling so swiftly that we bounced from one wall to the other in our forward flight so fast that I could hardly keep track. I seemed to travel through no volition of my own and keep to the center of the ring.

Suddenly we emerged into the light of day, but it was strange in some way. Without hesitation we sped across the valley floor to the slope of the mountain. We had emerged several miles from it and I saw it again as I had seen it with Marg when we first arrived for our vacation. A thousand years ago? It seemed that long.

We were a thousand feet above the surface. Below, climbing the mountain slope was a party of several men and one woman. As we drew nearer I saw that the woman was Marg. I started to speak and the voice of Tlon whispered, "Not yet."

So I watched. Devouring every line of her figure, every shade of expression on her lovely face, I watched. There were lines of fatigue and sorrow on her face, and her eyes were sad and red looking as if she had been crying a lot.

We hovered over the climbing figures, keeping pace with them. I wondered if one of them might look up and see us. The voice of Max whispered, "We are invisible to them."

They reached the path on the ledge that led up the cliff side where Marg had climbed that day. Slowly they toiled upward. One of the men had a rope coiled over his shoulder. "To let them down to the shelf where I entered the caves," I thought.

"Yes," came the tense, excited voice of Max.

"Now may I talk to her?" I asked.

"Not yet, Jack. Soon," came the voice of Tlon.

Time seemed to stretch out interminably as the slow march continued up the face of the cliff. Soon the valley stretched out below, the farms and farm buildings beginning to look like miniature drawings in color.

One of the men put out his hand to take Marg's arm and assist her. She shook her head in refusal and continued her weary plodding, the others trailing behind. Suddenly she quickened her pace, rounding a slight curve that hid the path ahead from view. We rounded the bend hugging the cliff wall.

Marg bent over, going to her knees and leaning precariously over the edge of the ledge. The man who offered to assist her took her shoulders and drew her back. The man with the coil of rope took one end and tossed the rest over the edge. Two of the others also took hold, and another took hold of the rope and slid over the edge of the ledge.

Slowly we drifted out from the face of the cliff to watch his descent. The shelf below came into view. On the shelf lay an object. I looked at the face of the cliff for the opening into which I had been dragged. The face of the cliff was bare and without any opening. In panic, not daring to think, I transferred my gaze back to the inert object.

My hiking jacket. My boots. Horror welled up in me from the depths of my being. That head…the skull was crushed flat! But the face—oh—that face… It was MINE!

"Marg!" I screamed. "Marg, Marg, Marg!" and blackness engulfed me…

"That's funny," said one of the men of the party who had accompanied Margie Sloan to get the body of her husband who had been killed in the fall from the path to the ledge just below several days before. Bending down he picked up a sparrow. It had been flying with five or six others in a group, following them for an hour. The sparrow was gasping for breath, its wings quivering. It seemed paralyzed. Slowly it recovered, and after a moment or two it had struggled free of his grasp and flew away. "Acted like it had heart trouble," he added in a puzzled tone of voice. "Never knew birds to have heart trouble before."

"Yes, Jack. I hear you," Marg was whispering inaudibly, a faraway look in her grief-stricken eyes.

There was no answer.

THE END

A CRYSTAL AND A SPELL

By Chester S. Geier

The crystal had the power to cause a spell—but in looking into the crystal there was danger, for it sapped the strength…

AFTERNOON sunlight, filtering like golden liquid through the leaves and branches of bordering trees, lay in bright puddles along the asphalt path. Amos Burrick hurried on rheumatic legs down the path, toward the small plaza at its end. He had unbuttoned his worn blue jacket, and his shapeless greenish black hat was pushed to the back of his untidy gray head.

In the somnolent quiet of the park came the many-toned twittering of birds, with an occasional nearby flutter of wings. Somewhere in the distance, a power-driven lawn mower buzzed, and the voices of playing children rang with muted stridence. A cool breeze, tangy with the mingled scents of grass and flowers, stirred fretfully on the warm air. The surrounding foliage rustled with a note of protest in the breeze, as if resentful of being disturbed.

Burrick squinted his fading brown eyes near-sightedly as he approached the plaza. In the center of it a granite Lincoln slumped broodingly in a granite chair. The statue was mounted upon a concrete pedestal, and around the sides of this wooden benches had been placed. Nobody was seated on the two benches visible to Burrick. He wondered anxiously if Jon Ten Eyck had come to the park this day.

Burrick felt a pang of apprehension that had in it all the poignancy of a child about to be deprived of its favorite toy. For a moment that old feeling of unutterable loneliness returned overwhelmingly. He had spent many pleasant hours in Jon Ten Eyck's company, and he had looked forward to this afternoon with especially keen anticipation.

Burrick hurried forward to get a view of the other two sides of the pedestal. He knew that if Jon Ten Eyck had come to the park at all, he was certain to be here, for like Burrick, he had found this portion of the park most to his liking. Though Ten Eyck was a newcomer to the park, Burrick had already learned this much.

It was on one of the benches around the pedestal a few days before that Burrick had met Ten Eyck. Burrick himself was a frequent visitor to the park, for the simple reason that he had nowhere else to go. He was just in the way at home, as his son's wife loudly and all too often informed him. A widower, he had come to live with his son several years previously, board payments from a skimpy savings account making him welcome enough. But now the money was gone, and he lived on charity and borrowed time.

The matter of charity did not bother him, for he felt that his son owed him that much. The matter of borrowed time was a worry, but he had learned not to think about it too often. What really hurt was the fact that he had nobody to talk to. His son was too busy for companionship, his son's wife too annoyed by his profitless presence to be amiable at any time, and the children had reached that age where they possessed little if any patience with the old. An elderly man is usually garrulous and loves company, and Amos Burrick was more typical than most.

BURRICK slowed his eager pace as he neared the statue. Rounding one corner of the pedestal, he saw an old man seated on a bench, reading a newspaper through gold-rimmed spectacles perched low on his round red nose.

Burrick sauntered up casually. "Hello, Mr. Ten Eyck," he said.

Ten Eyck peered over the top of his spectacles and smiled. "Ah, it is *Mynheer* Burrick." He gestured in invitation at his bench.

Still casually, Burrick seated himself beside the other. He removed his hat, and as if it were new and quite expensive, placed it carefully on the bench at his side. He crossed his legs in their shiny threadbare trousers and leaned back comfortably. He said:

"A nice day, Mr. Ten Eyck, a nice day."

Ten Eyck took off his spectacles and gazed about him as though for the first time. "It is that," he agreed. "Almost it is like a day in my native Pennsylvania." White hair grew in a thick fringe around the lower half of his head. His bald crown, like his cherubic face, had a ruddy scrubbed look. His short body was dumpling-like with good living. Well-dressed, his appearance made a strong contrast beside the seedy scrawniness of Amos Burrick.

Burrick, however, was unaware of the difference. Only one thing made any impression upon him. That was having someone to talk to.

"You find that relative of yours yet?" Burrick asked conversationally.

"My cousin Wilhelm?" Ten Eyck gave a somber shake of his head. "No, and the whole morning I have spent making inquiries. They told me it was here to this city that Wilhelm had come."

"The city's a big place," Burrick reminded.

"That, yes. But it has been a long time, and Wilhelm since may have left." Ten Eyck's rosy features became worried. "I know not what I shall do if I do not find Wilhelm. He was of the family the last. I have not much longer, and the crystal must to the next be passed on."

"The crystal," Burrick echoed significantly. He glanced at Ten Eyck with sudden slyness. "I still don't believe it can do all those things like you said the other day."

Ten Eyck gave a cherubic smile of confidence. "You do not believe it will cause spells in which you live again the past? But I promised to show it to you, did I not? To see is to believe."

"I sure would like to see it," Burrick said eagerly. He had been leading up to this, and now he reached quickly for his hat before Ten Eyck could change his mind.

"Come, then. It is but a short walk to my hotel." Ten Eyck placed his glasses carefully in a leather case and rose. Burrick followed, stifling a gasp as his rheumatic legs responded with a painful twinge.

Ten Eyck lived on a business street just across the park, in a small third-rate hotel that reflected his characteristic Dutch sense of thrift. The desk clerk payed little notice to either Burrick or Ten Eyck as he handed the latter his key.

There was no elevator, Burrick and Ten Eyck mounted a flight of stairs to the second floor. Ten Eyck's room was at the end of a narrow dark hall. He gestured Burrick inside and carefully locked the door.

"It is a risk I take, to live here," he told Burrick. "But they charge too much, the other places." He shrugged plump shoulders, and led Burrick to a chair beside a battered writing table. Then he pulled a bulging suitcase from under the bed, and went quickly through its contents. Finally he straightened, holding a small wooden box some three inches square. He stood quietly for a moment, regarding the box with a frown of deep thought.

"In my family this has been for many generations," he said at last. "Always it was passed on, from father to son—until now. I had no children, and Wilhelm was of my family the only one left." His reflective tone lowered, "How old is the crystal, I do not know. It was brought from India by one of my ancestors, a sea captain, at a time when Dutch ships sailed all the trade routes of the world. And already then it was very old."

As Burrick watched intently, Ten Eyck opened the box. From its padded interior he withdrew a blazing crystal octagon, which he placed before Burrick on the writing table.

Burrick stared at the octagon in sudden awe. It glowed in rainbow splendor like some great jewel. Its light did not seem to be reflected, but rather a part of itself, as though its interior was filled with prismatic radiance. Gazing into it, Burrick abruptly discovered that its internal light did not glow steadily as did light from an electric bulb. It waned and brightened rhythmically like the quick pulsing of an excited heart. And with each beat its multitude of glorious colors flashed and changed in a never-ending play of vivid hues. The throbbing flame with its endless chromatic transformation held the eyes hypnotically.

To Burrick, the room seemed to dim and fade away as he peered with breathless absorption into the depths of the octagon. He heard Ten Eyck speak again, but the other's voice came as though from a great distance.

"When one gazes at the crystal, into a spell he falls, and the events of his past life he lives again. If it is just a dream by the strange power of the crystal caused, or if one actually does in the past live again, I don't know. But it seems as real as the present."

Burrick was motionless in his chair, frozen. The room was gone. There was only the light in the octagon, pulsing, ever changing, numbing in its sheer kaleidoscopic splendor. Through the last thin crack in the closing door of his awareness, a voice spoke—a thin ghost of sound that might have come from some far end of the universe.

"But in looking at the crystal, there is a danger. It drinks at the strength. It is as if the energy of the body and mind it uses to cause the dreams. One careful must be not to…"

The door had closed. The voice was silenced. Burrick floated in a warm pulsing sea of rainbow color. He had a sense of weightlessness, of infinite peace. Time had stopped. Life itself seemed suspended.

Then the throbbing world of color paled and faded. A grayness came. Through the grayness, far away but coming nearer, sounds stirred. Inchoate and confused at first, but after a moment Burrick was able to make out the crash of rifles and the roar of artillery.

The sounds seemed poignantly familiar. He strove to place them in memory. All at once recollection came.

Abruptly the grayness was gone. He crouched, one of a long line of men in battle-stained uniforms, behind the scanty underbrush at the slope of a long hill. His bayoneted rifle was hot in his hands from constant firing. A spot on his shoulder burned where a bullet had grazed him.

They were waiting he knew, just giving the enemy entrenched on the hill something to think about, and waiting… Then the long-awaited signal came. A sudden thundering of horses hooves, and from off to his left a detachment of cavalry pounded into view, a flag fluttering at their head.

Even at this distance he recognized the Stars and Stripes. He forgot his burning thirst and the ache of his tired muscles. A fierce vibrant joy shot through him. He gripped his rifle tighter and looked up at the crest of the hill with eager eyes.

The thunder of the approaching horses shook the earth. A short chunky rider in the lead pounded for the slope, the sun glinting on his pince-nez glasses, his sword upraised. Burrick felt a surging thrill. It was Teddy, right out in front where he always was.

"*Charge!*"

The command rose above the tumult of battle. The shouted roar of exultant voices answered.

LIKE a shattering wave, the cavalry dashed itself against the hill and boiled upwards to the crest. Burrick followed through the choking dust, slipping, sliding, yelling like a demon. Then he was on the crest, panting, vibrant with the knowledge that a decisive victory had been won.

The battle of San Juan hill, and Burrick a teenaged private in the Spanish-American War.

He lived it all over again. It was so vivid and real that it was like something happening here and now, instead of something that had taken place in a dim and vanished yesterday.

One by one, the incidents of that golden era of his youth were recreated. The march into Manila...the return to the States...the parades and music... All was very sharp and clear. It was as though time had never passed beyond the scenes occurring.

And then the grayness returned. Color and pulsing movement came into it. He was back in the rainbow sea—but it was fading.

Burrick opened his eyes. For a long moment he gazed about him uncomprehendingly. Then awareness of his surroundings washed over him in a cold wave of understanding. He was once more just a shabby old man in a shabby hotel room. Just a shabby old man without purpose or hope. Realization of this struck into him with bitter sharpness.

He sat up in his chair. It took quite an effort to accomplish the movement, for he felt strangely listless and weak. His strength seemed to have ebbed during the interval under the crystal's spell.

The room brimmed with the shadows of evening. Ten Eyck stood patiently at the window, puffing at a large curve stemmed pipe. He turned as the sounds of Burrick's awakening broke the quiet of the room.

"Well, *Mynheer* Burrick, are you now convinced?"

Burrick nodded with feeble vehemence. "That crystal thing is the Devil's own contraption."

"But was it not real?"

"A mite too real, maybe." Burrick surveyed wryly his scrawny wrinkled hands and threadbare garments. "Compared to the spell, this is like a bad dream."

Ten Eyck chuckled softly, then sobered. He watched Burrick intently for some seconds. He asked, "You feel all right?"

"Kind of worn out," Burrick answered.

"The crystal, it has that effect," Ten Eyck said. "As I have explained, one's own strength it uses to cause the spells."

Burrick nodded vaguely and glanced at the window. He felt a wrench of apprehension as he noticed suddenly that it was evening. He rose on unsteady legs and reached for his hat.

"I'll have to be going, Mr. Ten Eyck. It's past suppertime, and Alma—that's my son's wife—is going to give me hell for being late. You'll be in the park tomorrow?"

Ten Eyck nodded. "I shall be in the city a few more days yet. The search for Wilhelm I cannot give up until convinced I am that he is not here."

BURRICK hurried home anxiously. As he had expected, Alma was shrill with anger over his tardiness.

"You're just an old bum," she accused. "All you're good for is eating and sleeping and gadding about. If you can't make yourself useful around the house, Lord knows the least you can do is come home to supper on time."

To make matters worse, Tom was not there to intercede for him as he usually did. Of course, Tom's help was rather half-hearted at best, but at least it was better than weathering the storm of Alma's tirades alone.

Alma, however, was not without a vestigial sympathy. After a while she calmed down enough to warm up for Burrick the supper leftovers, grumbling throughout the process about having to act as nursemaid to a worthless old man. In a hurry to escape from Alma's ill-tempered presence, Burrick gulped his food down quickly. He knew why his son, Tom, was absent from home so much. Tom claimed it was business, but the excuse was as good as any.

Finishing shortly, Burrick went up to his room in the attic. He undressed, donned a patched nightshirt and lay down on the hard cot that served him as a bed. He would have liked to listen to the radio a while, but that would have sent Alma into another fury. He knew only too well what she had to say on the subject of shiftless old men who listened to radios.

In the darkness, Burrick moved his bony shoulders in a shrug. He decided he could do without the radio if he had to. Slyly, he wondered if he could wheedle out of Tom in the morning the admission price to a movie. All Tom had from his pay was what Alma allowed him, but occasionally he managed to slip Burrick a few pieces of change.

Burrick felt a surge of self-pity. Fine life for an old man! Nobody to talk to, can't listen to the radio, no money for shows. He wished he were young again. Then he could work and do what he wanted.

Abruptly, he thought of Ten Eyck's crystal. Now there was something! Better than the radio, better than the movies. Better, even, than having someone to talk to. Almost as good, in fact, as being young again. He clutched at the thought of the crystal eagerly.

In the afternoon of the next day, Burrick hurried to the park. But it was not until almost evening that Ten Eyck appeared at the statue in the plaza.

They talked for a time. Ten Eyck admitted having had no success as yet in finding Wilhelm. Burrick cunningly led the conversation around to the crystal.

"I sure would like to see it again," he told Ten Eyck. "There's a lot in my younger days that I'd like to go over."

"You are sure you feel well?" Ten Eyck asked. "So soon after last night might not be good."

"I feel fine," Burrick insisted. "Never felt better, in fact."

Ten Eyck nodded reluctantly. "All right, then, I shall show the crystal to you once more."

"Tonight?" Burrick said. "I have to go home to supper now, but I'll sneak out afterwards."

"Tonight," Ten Eyck said. "I shall be at my hotel, waiting."

THAT evening, Burrick sat again at the writing table in Ten Eyck's room, gazing raptly into the blazing depths of the crystal. This time he went back to the days when he courted Marta, who subsequently became his wife. He'd had a good job, then, sporty clothes, and a horse and buggy that was the envy of his friend. Of all Burrick's memories, those of this period of his youth were the best. Good old days, lost along the road of years, but reborn under the crystal's spell. Once more, with Marta, he went for long rides under the summer moon, and attended the many well-remembered dances, picnics, and parties. It was all so real that when consciousness finally returned, Burrick felt more than ever that it was like falling into a bad dream than actually awakening.

Though exhausted by his sojourn under the spell, one thought was prominent in Burrick's mind—he had to see the crystal again. Within him the desire was as overpowering as an addict's hunger for drugs.

"I've got to see the crystal again," he told Ten Eyck. "Can I come back tomorrow?"

"But the danger..." Ten Eyck objected. "I have told you that looking at the crystal drains the strength. The body, fortunately, a sixth sense has, like an alarm clock that breaks the spell when the drain too great becomes. But with too much of the crystal, this warning sense dulls, and one into a spell falls from which he never awakens."

"I've just *got* to see the crystal again," Burrick insisted. "I'll feel all right by tomorrow."

Ten Eyck looked doubtful. "It is a risk. But if you are willing—" Abruptly he shrugged. "Tomorrow—so be it."

Exhausted but triumphant, Burrick returned home. It was late, and Alma reminded him of that fact scathingly.

But now with something eagerly to look forward to, Burrick scarcely felt the acid of her rebukes. He mumbled a vague excuse and went up to his cot in the attic, where he fell into a heavy slumber.

Under the spell of the crystal, the next day, Burrick lived over incidents from his life as a boy. Once more he took forbidden swims in the abandoned stone quarry outside of town, went on weekend camping trips in the hills, and stole apples from the trees on Sim Crockett's farm. Like everything else he had experienced while under the spell, all was very vivid and real. He could actually taste the apples, feel the water against his skin, smell the burning pine branches, pungent on the crisp air of evening.

When he regained consciousness—feeling more fatigued this time than before—Burrick was now so strongly gripped by the fascinations of the crystal that he pleaded again with Ten Eyck to be allowed to return the next day. But Ten Eyck proved adamant. It was only after almost tearful urgings that Burrick managed to win Ten Eyck's consent to return the day after the next.

"And that the last time will be," Ten Eyck said. "Convinced I am that Wilhelm is in this city no longer. But two days more will I try, and then to Pennsylvania I shall return."

Burrick went rigid with dismay. "You mean you're taking the crystal with you—that I won't be able to see it any more?"

"But naturally," Ten Eyck said.

"You can't—you mustn't!" Burrick wailed, with an anguished feeling of loss. The crystal had come to mean everything to him— the companionship he didn't have, the radio he couldn't listen to, the movies he couldn't afford. It was a key that unlocked the golden door of the past to give life new brightness and meaning. And now it was going to be taken away from him.

Burrick did not realize that his emotions were based on psychological principles. The old live in the past. In the present there is only ill health and loneliness, the gray drabness of existence without living. In the future there is only death. The past, with its glorious memories of youth, has enchantment and glamour.

The crystal had provided Burrick with a means of recreating the past with all the vivid semblance of actuality. In a way, it had been like possessing the ability to go back and live one's past life all over again. This had been one of Burrick's fondest dreams—as it all too often is among the old. And once having been able very nearly to do so, Burrick quailed in horror at the mere thought of being forced to stop.

Burrick grasped Ten Eyck's arms imploringly. "Please, Mr. Ten Eyck, don't go so soon. Stay a few days more. The crystal—I've got to see the crystal again."

Ten Eyck shook his head firmly. "To leave, my mind is made up. An inconvenience it would be to stay in the city longer."

"Then...then why not leave the crystal with me?" Burrick suggested in sudden cunning. "I could send it back to you later on."

Ten Eyck shook his head again, and with more vigor than before. "I am sorry, *Mynheer* Burrick, that I cannot do. The crystal in the family must stay, there are certain old stories—" Ten Eyck broke off with an abrupt gesture. A shadow crept into his blue eyes, and his ruddy features tightened. "What you ask is impossible. I must return home—and the crystal with me goes. The day after tomorrow, you shall see it the last time."

Gazing at the other's set expression, Burrick knew that further pleading was useless. Filled with an empty coldness at the thought of having to resume his former cheerless existence, he left.

As he weakly plodded home, Burrick revolted more and more at being deprived of the crystal. Within him a burning resentment arose that Ten Eyck should be so unsympathetic. And quite suddenly he found himself hating Ten Eyck with a bitter virulent hatred. Ten Eyck had money, freedom—*everything*. Why did he have to be so stingy where the crystal was concerned? Couldn't he understand that it made up for all the things Burrick didn't and could never hope to have?

Burrick brooded constantly on the impending loss of the crystal, and by the following day his hatred of Ten Eyck coalesced into a plan for murder. By killing Ten Eyck, he would come into possession of the crystal. It would be his—his with which to delve into the golden past any time he wanted to. The unhappy tedium of the present would forever be broken.

Burrick's plan was quite simple. When he visited Ten Eyck again, he would wait until an opportunity presented itself and dispatch the other in some way that would not raise an alarm. Then he would take the crystal and leave. The desk clerk paid little or no attention to him, being familiar with seedy people, and at best could give the police only a vague description. He was not known in that part of the city, and thus did not have to fear that some chance acquaintance would witness his departure from the hotel. This was just an affair between Ten Eyck and himself, and with Ten Eyck out of the way, he would have nothing to worry about.

As to how the deed itself was going to be done, Burrick was already decided on that point. A gun would have made too much noise—even if he did have one. A knife, if he were to take one from home, would have been missed. He settled on a length of rusty lead pipe that he found in a trash-heaped corner of the basement at home. The pipe had an elbow joint on one end, and made an excellent hammer-like bludgeon.

Burrick was quite determined. Yet when he presented himself for the last time at Ten Eyck's shabby hotel room, his heart pounded suffocatingly and his stomach was a hard knot of tension. He thought that Ten Eyck must surely notice his nervous manner and be warned.

But Ten Eyck did not notice. His mind was obviously taken up with the details of leaving. He nodded abstractedly at Burrick, gestured at the chair before the writing table, and turned to pull from under the bed the suitcase in which he kept the crystal.

This was the exact moment upon which Burrick had decided for going into action. From the right sleeve of his threadbare jacket where he had been hiding it, the elbow joint resting in his palm, Burrick shook the length of lead pipe. It looked like some barbarian's grotesque war club as he gripped it tightly in his sweating hand. His breath came with difficulty, as though he breathed through many layers of cloth. Excitement made the blood roar in his ears.

From the suitcase, Ten Eyck removed the familiar small wooden box. He started to straighten up. Behind him, Burrick crept up on unsteady legs, the length of lead pipe raised high. The utter horror of what he was going to do pulled Burrick forward as though in a trance. Wide and staring, his eyes were fixed on Ten Eyck's head.

As if having sensed Burrick behind him, Ten Eyck abruptly turned while still in the act of straightening up. His cherubic features twisted into a mask of terror as he saw the up-raised club.

Burrick acted out of the sheer fright of having been discovered. The muscles in his arm contracted spasmodically, and the pipe swept down in a clumsy chopping stroke. Ten Eyck managed frantically to jerk aside at just the right moment, and the elbow joint merely grazed the side of his head.

Pulled out of balance by the instinctive swing of his arm, Burrick collided with Ten Eyck's kneeling form and fell over his shoulders onto the bed. Ten Eyck grasped Burrick's legs in a terrified clutch and struggled to rise to his feet. In panic, Burrick sought to kick free, but he succeeded only in pulling Ten Eyck back to his knees. Moaning with dread, Ten Eyck clung desperately to Burrick's legs.

Twisting around on the bed, Burrick clawed himself into a sitting position. Once again, Ten Eyck was trying to rise. Suddenly mad with fear at the thought of failure, Burrick clubbed repeatedly at Ten Eyck's head. It seemed unreal, fantastic, like something out of a horrible nightmare. The sobbing gibbering thing that clutched insensately at his legs…raising the pipe up, bringing it down, up and down, over and over, again and again…the breath jammed in his throat, the blood thundering and pounding in his ears.

Burrick went almost crazy with despair. How much longer did he have to keep hitting? Wouldn't Ten Eyck ever die?

It was only after a long moment that he finally realized that the frenzied grip on his legs had loosened. Ten Eyck was dead.

Burrick rose weakly. Noticing that his trousers were spotted with blood, he brushed them quickly with a corner of the disarranged bed blanket. Then, seizing the wooden box from where it had fallen on the worn rug, Burrick left the room.

Apparently, the struggle had drawn no attention. The hotel was quiet. Moving slowly through a supreme effort of will, Burrick walked down the stairs and across the lobby. The desk clerk was reading a magazine. He did not raise his head as Burrick went out the door.

NO ONE was home when Burrick reached there. Alma and the children had gone to a movie. He went up to his cot in the attic and lay down. He felt almost sick with nervous exhaustion.

After a while, Burrick quieted. The business was over with—and he had successfully got away with it. The crystal was now his. Triumphant elation surged through him at the thought. Strength and Purpose rushed back to him.

Burrick turned on a light, and eagerly took the crystal from its box. It blazed gloriously in his hands. Pulling up a trunk that served him as a table, he placed the crystal upon it, then sat down on the bed. He stared into the depths of the crystal hungrily, anxious to escape in its spell the livid memory of what he had just done.

The pulsing sea of rainbow color crept up around him. He sank gratefully into its warm embrace. The grayness came…dissolved. He was sitting on a lumpy bed in a shabby hotel room. A mewling thing had his legs in a desperate vise-like clutch, and he was clubbing at it, again and again, over and over, and it refused to die. Up and down with the pipe, up and down, over and over, and it sobbed and moaned, and wouldn't die. His lungs bursting for breath, the blood shrieking and clanging in his head. Unutterable terror giving an insane strength to his flailing arm. Over and over, again and again. Wouldn't it ever end? Wouldn't the thing ever die?

Over and over, again and again, up and down, and up and down...

And then he was brushing at his trousers, forcing himself to walk slowly from the hotel. Climbing up to his cot in the attic, waiting for energy and calmness to return. Pulling up the trunk, looking into the crystal...

Burrick awoke, weak, numbed with horror. He stared at the crystal as though it were the embodiment of every fear he had ever known. A great cold hand seemed to close around him. What had happened? Why did the crystal no longer bring to life the happy memories of his youth?

Abruptly, Burrick recalled Ten Eyck's insistence that the crystal had to stay in his family, and the fearful shadow that had crept into Ten Eyck's face at his unfinished reference to "certain old stories." Was it that ownership of the crystal by others than those of the Ten Eyck family resulted in a frightful perversion of its powers? From what Burrick had just experienced while under its spell, this seemed to be the answer.

Burrick gazed at the crystal with sudden loathing. If he would undergo a repetition of his murder of Ten Eyck each time he looked at it, then it would have to be destroyed.

And now. Before Alma and Tom came home.

CAREFUL not to look at it directly, Burrick picked up the crystal and hurried down to the basement. He placed it upon a wooden chopping block, then obtained a large heavy hammer from the tool chest. He pounded the crystal into powdery fragments. With a broom, he carefully swept the dust onto a shovel and dumped it in the ash barrel.

Burrick sighed in relief. That was that. Nobody could ever connect him with Ten Eyck's death now. He returned to the attic. As he sat down on the cot preparatory to removing his shoes, a brightness caught his eye. He sought for it puzzledly. He found it. His heart seemed to turn over inside him.

On the trunk, pulsing, glowing with prismatic splendor, was the crystal!

Burrick stared at it. Before he could resist, he was sinking into the throbbing rainbow sea. And then he was back in that shabby hotel zoom, sitting on the bed, while a mewling thing held his legs in a desperate vise-like clutch. He was clubbing at it, again and again, over and over, and it refused to die. Up and down with the pipe, up and down, over and over...

Burrick opened his eyes. He was covered with perspiration. A tight band seemed to have closed over his chest, making it hard to breathe. His heart had a strange fluttery beat. The outlines of his attic room shimmered crazily.

A deluge of sudden fright impelled him into motion. The crystal. He had to get rid of it. He reached for it, avoiding its treacherous splendor. He stood up, swayed, fell back on the cot. He was appalled to find how weak he had become.

He had to get rid of the crystal. The thought beat at him. But he was too weak to go back down to the basement. What could he do?

Burrick glanced hopelessly around the room. His eyes settled upon the windows at the rear of the attic. That was it. The windows were open. He could hurl the crystal out into the night.

Burrick forced himself to his feet. Tottering, staggering, as though drunk, he made his uncertain way over to the windows. Summoning his last dregs of strength, he threw the crystal outside. Then he crept back slowly and painfully to the cot.

With weary listlessness, Burrick began to remove his jacket. Something bright caught his eye. He looked—and the world spun in chaos around him.

On the trunk, pulsing, glowing with prismatic splendor, was...the crystal.

He fought its spell, fought it frantically—but he was too weak to resist. The throbbing rainbow sea claimed him. And then he was back in that shabby hotel room, sitting on the bed while a mewling thing held his legs in a desperate vise-like clutch. And he was beating at it, again and again, over and over, and it refused to die. Up and down with the pipe, up and down, over and over...

And this time, with his last reserves of life force drained from him, there was no awakening. There was just a great cold blackness that came and never went away.

THE END

If you've enjoyed this book, you will not want to miss these terrific titles…

ARMCHAIR SCI-FI & HORROR DOUBLE NOVELS, $12.95 each

D-21   **EMPIRE OF EVIL** by Robert Arnette
THE SIGN OF THE TIGER by Alan E. Nourse & J. A. Meyer

D-22   **OPERATION SQUARE PEG** by Frank Belknap Long
ENCHANTRESS OF VENUS by Leigh Brackett

D-23   **THE LIFE WATCH** by Lester del Rey
CREATURES OF THE ABYSS by Murray Leinster

D-24   **LEGION OF LAZARUS** by Edmond Hamilton
STAR HUNTER by Andre Norton

D-25   **EMPIRE OF WOMEN** by John Fletcher
ONE OF OUR CITIES IS MISSING by Irving Cox

D-26   **THE WRONG SIDE OF PARADISE** by Raymond F. Jones
THE INVOLUNTARY IMMORTALS by Rog Phillips

D-27   **EARTH QUARTER** by Damon Knight
ENVOY TO NEW WORLDS by Keith Laumer

D-28   **SLAVES TO THE METAL HORDE** by Milton Lesser
HUNTERS OUT OF TIME by Joseph E. Kelleam

D-29   **RX JUPITER SAVE US** by Ward Moore
BEWARE THE USURPERS by Geoff St. Reynard

D-30   **SECRET OF THE SERPENT** by Don Wilcox
CRUSADE ACROSS THE VOID by Dwight V. Swain

ARMCHAIR SCIENCE FICTION CLASSICS, $12.95 each

C-7   **THE SHAVER MYSTERY, Book One**
by Richard S. Shaver

C-8   **THE SHAVER MYSTERY, Book Two**
by Richard S. Shaver

C-9   **MURDER IN SPACE**
by David V. Reed

ARMCHAIR MASTERS OF SCIENCE FICTION SERIES, $16.95 each

M-3   **MASTERS OF SCIENCE FICTION, Vol. Three**
Robert Sheckley, "The Perfect Woman" and other tales

M-4   **MASTERS OF SCIENCE FICTION, Vol. Four**
Mack Reynolds, Part One, "Stowaway" and other tales

If you've enjoyed this book, you will not want to miss these terrific titles...

ARMCHAIR SCI-FI & HORROR DOUBLE NOVELS, $12.95 each

D-121   **THE GENIUS BEASTS** by Frederik Pohl
   THIS WORLD IS TABOO by Murray Leinster

D-122   **THE COSMIC LOOTERS** by Edmond Hamilton
   WANDL THE INVADER by Ray Cummings

D-123   **ROBOT MEN OF BUBBLE CITY** by Rog Phillips
   DRAGON ARMY by William Morrison

D-124   **LAND BEYOND THE LENS** by S. J. Byrne
   DIPLOMAT-AT-ARMS by Keith Laumer

D-125   **VOYAGE OF THE ASTEROID, THE** by Laurence Manning
   REVOLT OF THE OUTWORLDS by Milton Lesser

D-126   **OUTLAW IN THE SKY** by Chester S. Geier
   LEGACY FROM MARS by Raymond Z. Gallun

D-127   **THE GREAT FLYING SAUCER INVASION** by Geoff St. Reynard
   THE BIG TIME by Fritz Leiber

D-128   **MIRAGE FOR PLANET X** by Stanley Mullen
   POLICE YOUR PLANET by Lester del Rey

D-129   **THE BRAIN SINNERS** by Alan E. Nourse
   DEATH FROM THE SKIES by A. Hyatt Verrill

D-139   **CRY CHAOS** by Dwight V. Swain
   THE DOOR THROUGH SPACE By Marion Zimmer Bradley

ARMCHAIR SCIENCE FICTION CLASSICS, $12.95 each

C-55   **UNDER THE TRIPLE SUNS**
   by Stanton A. Coblentz

C-56   **STONE FROM THE GREEN STAR**
   by Jack Williamson

C-57   **ALIEN MINDS**
   by E. Everett Evans

ARMCHAIR MASTERS OF SCIENCE FICTION SERIES, $16.95 each

G-13   **SCIENCE FICTION GEMS, Vol. Seven**
   Jack Vance and others

G-14   **HORROR GEMS, Vol. Seven**
   Robert Bloch and others

.